À ma plus fidèle lectrice —

Stephan Cooper

Book Two of The Chronicles of Ancient Earth

The Covenant

STEPHAN COOPER

Copyright © 2024 Stephan Cooper

All rights reserved.

ISBN: 9798301685835

This is a work of fiction. Unless otherwise indicated, all the names, characters, businesses, places, events, and incidents in this book are either the product of the author's imagination or used in a fictitious manner. Any resemblance to actual persons, living or dead, or actual events is purely coincidental.

"But then I sigh, with a piece of Scripture
Tell them that God bids us to do evil for good.
And thus, I clothe my naked villainy
With odd old ends stolen out of Holy Writ;
And seem a saint, when most I play the devil."

— **William Shakespeare, Richard III** —

PROLOGUE

Year 2069

1

Pierre-Antoine Lascombes' slender fingers paused mid-turn, the crisp paper of the report rustling in the still air of his office. Perched at the edge of a desk that bore the sheen of dark mahogany, his gaze was anchored to the stark images laid out before him. Jerusalem, once a city reverberating with the confluence of prayers and history, now lay desolate—a tableau of ruin wrought by his own hand[1]. The silence in the room was not empty; it resonated with the urgency of decisions that awaited the President of the Federation of Europe. His office, a testament to modern power dressed in fashionably austere lines, seemed to shrink under the weight of significance each document held. With an almost liturgical solemnity, Pierre-Antoine turned over another page, revealing yet another photograph: a haunting panorama of crumbled stones and ashen skies. The very air around him seemed thickened by the dust of those fallen buildings, the spectres of the ancient city rising

---

[1] Read *The Servant of the Light* - ©Stephan Cooper 2021.

like incense from the altar of devastation. The light streaming through the window painted shadows over his features, casting dark hollows in the valleys of his contemplative face. His gaze fell upon the charred remains of ancient walls standing like broken teeth amidst the ash, while shattered domes and minarets lay buried beneath rubble. Pierre-Antoine traced a finger over the images, feeling the sharp sting of guilt gnawing at his conscience. The destruction was his doing; it was his command that had unleashed the nuclear hellfire upon the holy city. He had championed peace, yet delivered apocalypse; sought unity, but sowed division. Jerusalem's nuking, a gambit of last resort, now lay upon his conscience, its heavy mantle a Sisyphean burden that no absolution could ease. He lifted one of the photos closer, tracing the edge with a nail kept immaculately manicured despite the current state of geopolitical disarray. The image captured a street he knew well, transformed into a canyon of debris. A lone olive tree, seared and leafless, stood sentinel amid the wreckage, blackened branches reaching skyward in supplication or accusation. *Mon Dieu*[2]*,* he thought, the words echoing like an unintended prayer. Here, within these four walls, away from the scrutinizing eyes of allies and adversaries, he allowed himself the luxury of remorse. Yet, Pierre-Antoine Lascombes was not a man easily conquered by sentiment. Clenching his jaw, he set the photo back onto the desk with a decisive motion. The echo of his actions, both past and present, would not deter the path he had carved for the future. Jerusalem's ashes bore the promise of rebirth—a phoenix yet

---

[2] My God

to rise from the throes of purifying flames—and he, with hands both scorched and sanctified, would shape its resurrection. His fingers lingered on the pages that bore witness to the discord unravelling at Jerusalem's heart, where faith and fervour collided with relentless intensity. The Jewish fundamentalists, their zeal unquenchable, demanded Solomon's Temple be resurrected from the annals of antiquity, its hallowed stones to kiss the sky once again. In opposition, the Muslim fundamentalists, equally resolute, yearned for the Al-Aqsa Mosque to reclaim its sacred silhouette upon the city's horizon. The ancient quarrel, as old as the scriptures themselves, now unfurled in ink and outrage upon the documents Pierre-Antoine scrutinized. His eyes, a steely reflection of resolve, absorbed the schism that divided brother from brother, each claim sanctified by bloodline and belief.

"Is it not enough that the city lies in ruins?" Pierre-Antoine muttered to himself, his brow furrowing in frustration. "Must they continue to tear at the fabric of peace with their unyielding demands?" As he read further, he could almost hear the cacophony of voices raised in anger and zealotry, a discordant chorus echoing through the shattered streets of Jerusalem. He pictured the furious faces of the fundamentalists, their eyes burning with righteous indignation, their hands gripping stones and banners as they faced off in bitter confrontation. "Solomon's legacy pitted against Muhammad's—a tale of two temples," he murmured, the words dissolving into the silence of the room. Such was the weight of history, bending the backs of men who sought solace in their gods, yet found only the endless echo of their obstinance. A bitter taste of irony tinged

Pierre-Antoine's palate as he contemplated the immutable divide. Had it not been for this very schism, perhaps the calamitous decision that incinerated Jerusalem might have never come to pass. But as the reports detailed the continued bickering, entrenched and intransigent, a cold clarity crystallized within him. "Fractious children squabbling over a sandbox," he concluded with a scoff that was both dismissive and defensive. The guilt that had momentarily gnawed at his insides receded like the tide, replaced by a resurgence of vindication. If they could not share the holy land, then perhaps they did not deserve it. "Unity forged through devastation," he whispered, the notion coalescing into a dark mantra. It was a bitter medicine, laced with the poison of necessity, but one he had administered in the belief that from the ashes of Jerusalem, a more harmonious edifice might arise. One where the prayers of all her children could ascend in concert rather than cacophony. "Let them see the futility of their ceaseless contention," he uttered. "If this is all they have to offer – strife and division in the face of tragedy – then perhaps the destruction of Jerusalem was justified after all." The words hung heavy in the air, a dark cloud of rationalisation that threatened to choke out any lingering remorse.

The door to Pierre-Antoine's office suddenly burst open, admitting a figure whose arrival was as unexpected as it was silent. Pierre-Antoine's heart raced with a mixture of disbelief and indignation at the sudden intrusion, but he could not tear his eyes away from the man who now stood before him. *"Par tous les diables*,³" he muttered under his breath, suddenly recognising the individual standing before him. Lief, his ever-vigilant secretary, appeared momentarily in the doorway, his face flushed with the embarrassment of failure and exertion.

"Mr. President, I tried to stop—"

"It's alright, Lief, leave us," Pierre-Antoine commanded, silencing Lief mid-protest. Lief hesitated for a moment before reluctantly closing the door, leaving the European president alone with the uninvited visitor.

The mysterious man stood before him; an enigma wrapped in the guise of a gentleman. His presence seemed to stretch beyond the physical dimensions of the room, enveloping the space with an aura that spoke of authority and ancient wisdom. Tall and imposing, his posture bore the rigidity of military discipline, yet there was something undeniably regal about him. Cloaked in a tailored suit that whispered of bespoke craftsmanship, the colour was a deep blue that rivalled the twilight sky over Strasbourg. His silver hair, cropped close to the scalp, shone like a halo under the muted lighting of the office, casting a stark contrast against his pale, faintly lined skin. The man's eyes, piercing and sharp, were the grey of storm clouds ready to burst forth with torrential revelations.

"I'll be damned," Pierre-Antoine began, his tone measured as he regarded the man who emerged from his past, "Robert William Kay. What wicked wind has brought you from your nefarious den across my threshold today?"

---

³ By all the devils.

"Let us dispense with the circumlocutions," the man continued, each syllable measured, a metronome ticking away the seconds. "Time, as we both know, is a river that flows relentlessly onward, heedless of the desires of men."

Pierre-Antoine leaned forward, his fingers steepled in thought. Before him stood a shade from another age, a herald of omens yet to unfold.

"Pierre-Antoine," Kay said, his voice carrying the resonance of a prophet's call, "I come bearing a portentous message, wrought in the crucible of divine reckoning."

"Speak, then," the president urged with a hint of sarcasm.

"Yea, I say unto thee," the man continued, his words unfurling with the solemnity of scripture, "the path thou hast chosen is fraught with peril, for it leads not to the Promised Land but to the Valley of Hinnom, where the worm dieth not, and the fire is not quenched." The gravity of his pronouncement hung in the air, heavy with foreboding. "Thou hast set thy hand to the plough and looked back, sowing salt in the fields of Jerusalem," Mr Kay went on, his indictment sharp as flint. "Repent and turn back, lest the judgments reserved for the days of wrath be visited upon thee."

Pierre-Antoine felt a chill creep up the spine of his resolve, the biblical cadence of Mr. Kay's warning echoing against the walls like the distant tolling of a bell. Yet, he erupted into a cynical laugh, mocking the sinister augur.

"Your command of the scriptures will never cease to amaze me, Bob. However, your words are as empty vessels," he retorted coolly, the timbre of his voice betraying a controlled ire. "Jerusalem lies in ruin by necessity, not whimsy. The path I tread is set in stone, immutable as the laws of the Medes and Persians."

"Stone may shatter, Pierre-Antoine," Kay countered, his grey eyes alight with fervour. "The idolatry of your certainty shall be your undoing. Like Nebuchadnezzar, you exalt yourself above all, but you will be humbled in due course."

"Save your sermons for those with ears to hear them," Pierre-Antoine sneered, his arrogance rising like a shield against the onslaught of Kay's forewarning. "I am the architect of the new Jerusalem, not some Ozymandias blinded by hubris."

"Yet even the great Pharaoh Ramses could not halt the exodus ordained by the Almighty," Robert Kay's voice thundered, echoing through the office with the solemnity of a death knell. "Heed the signs, lest plagues yet unseen visit themselves upon you, shall you not repent for the abominable sin you have committed."

"Enough!" Pierre-Antoine's fist collided with the desk, an explosive punctuation to the tension that crackled between them. If you have something worthwhile to say, then speak plainly – or leave my office at once!"

"Very well," Kay said, his expression grave. "Your actions have angered the heavens, Pierre-Antoine. You walk in the shadows of Sodom and Gomorrah, blinded by pride and ambition. Should you continue down this path, destruction will follow in your wake, and the weight of your transgressions shall crush you beneath its heel."

"Are you threatening me, Robert?" he managed to answer, his voice shaking despite his best efforts to keep it steady.

"You, more than anyone else, know I don't answer well to threats." He stared murderously at the man before declaring: "you've seen what I am capable of. Make no mistake: I'll do it again if you force me to, Bob."

Kay's lips pressed into a thin line; disappointment etched across his worn features. He opened his mouth to speak again but was interrupted by the sudden burst of the door.

"Robert William Kay!" Monika Richter stormed into the room, her light blond hair framing her face like a halo gone askew, her blue eyes blazing with righteous indignation. "What devilry brings you here?"

"Monika—" Pierre-Antoine started, taken aback by her unexpected presence and the tempestuous aura that seemed to swirl around her.

"Silence, Pierre-Antoine," she commanded, her gaze locked on the American evangelist. "Whatever business brought you here, Mr Kay, you are not welcome. Keep your evil tricks for those gullible enough to believe them. And now, get out!" she spat, pointing to the door. "Leave this place, and never darken our doorstep again!"

Robert Kay gazed at her with a cool, impassive gaze, then inclined his head ever so slightly. "As you wish, Commissioner Richter." And with that, he slipped through the doorway like a wraith, leaving behind a palpable residue of unease.

Monika faced Pierre-Antoine with a wrath that seemed to blaze from her very core, igniting the staid air of the office. "Have you lost your mind?" she demanded, her words lashing out like whips. "Consorting with that… that fiend? Do you not recall the havoc he wrought upon your career, the calamities that befell your reputation?"

Pierre-Antoine stood motionless before her; his hands clasped behind his back as if to steady himself against the onslaught. The memories of those tumultuous times cascaded through his thoughts, each one a scorching reminder of his past follies. "Monika," he began, his voice low and steady, "I assure you, my faculties remain intact. I have no design to tread upon those pernicious paths again."

His friend's blue eyes bore into him, searching for the conviction in his words. "You were ensnared once by his serpentine whispers, seduced by the siren call of power veiled in piety. It took years to untangle the web he spun around your ambitions. And here you are, receiving him quietly as if nothing had happened. If Lief hadn't warned me, God knows what maleficence he would have convinced you to join again.

"Monika, you know better than anyone that I cannot forget the damage he has done," Pierre-Antoine replied, his words measured and deliberate. "But I assure you, I am no longer the same man who once fell prey to his seductive promises. The lessons of my past have been carved into my very soul."

"Then why entertain him at all?" she pressed, her tone softening yet still edged with concern.

"Consider it an audience with a spectre from the annals of my history—a momentary haunting that I had to exorcise." Pierre-Antoine turned away from Monika, looking out the tall window where the sun's rays graced the horizon with molten gold. "My only wish was to hear his warning, to understand the extent of the threat he represents. Knowledge is power, Monika, and we must arm ourselves against him."

"Knowledge can be a double-edged sword," Monika warned, an air of solemnity settling around her like a shroud. "I pray that you wield it wisely."

"Trust me, Monika," Pierre-Antoine implored, his gaze locked onto hers as he spoke from the depths of his heart. "I have learned from the bitter fruit of our past mistakes, and I will not allow history to repeat itself."

"See that you don't," Monika said quietly, her voice softening as she turned towards the door. "Because if you do, the consequences may be more dire than we can imagine. Remember, Pierre-Antoine," Monika murmured, her voice suffused with a gravity that belied her calm exterior. "Robert William Kay is not merely a man; he is the embodiment of Machiavellian guile, cloaked in the vestments of faith. His touch corrupts, and his whispers wither the soul."

With a final searching glance, she stepped through the door, allowing it to close with a soft but definitive click, sealing Pierre-Antoine within the tomb-like silence of his office. His fingers tapped restlessly on the edge of his desk as his thoughts churned, unease gnawing at the edges of his consciousness. He recalled the events of thirty-one years past when he had first encountered the enigmatic Mr Kay — a meeting that had set in motion a chain of events as catastrophic as they were irreversible. That summer 2034, he had been a younger, more naïve man, eager to grasp at the promise of power and influence that Robert Kay had so tantalizingly dangled before him. But in his hubris, he paid a dire price for his lack of wisdom. Now, as the twilight deepened outside his window, Pierre-Antoine felt the spectre of history looming over him once more, its icy fingers reaching out to ensnare him in its relentless grip. The air seemed to grow colder, as if the very atmosphere bore witness to the malevolence that permeated Mr Kay's presence. He rose from his desk, pacing the room as the echoes of shattered dreams reverberated through the chambers of his soul, a solemn reminder of the consequences of his past transgressions. *Never again,* he vowed, a steely resolve taking root in the depths of his being. *I will not be swayed by the siren call of heavenly grand design, nor will I allow that man to wield his dark influence over me or those I hold dear again.* As night descended in earnest, the shadows from his past gathered around him, vindictive harpies shrieking in a nefarious choir, R*emember! Remember!* ...

PART ONE

Expectations

Year 2037

2

Under the vast, vaulted ceilings of Dulles International Airport, Pierre-Antoine Lascombes strode forward with purpose, his polished shoes echoing against the gleaming floor. At twenty-four, he was a rising star of the French conservative party, his keen intellect and unyielding ambition propelling him ever upwards, eager to make his mark on the world stage. He had crossed the Atlantic, invited by the Covenant Foundation, to steep himself in the doctrines of American conservatism—a six-month tutelage designed to mould the sinews of his political ideology with a transatlantic vigour. Pierre-Antoine regarded this invitation as nothing less than a sacred summons, an opportunity to forge alliances and expand his intellectual expertise under the auspices of a brotherhood revered for its unwavering adherence to tradition. As he navigated the terminal, his eyes alighted upon a figure holding a sign with his name, standing apart from the crowd. Tall, with hair like strands of spun gold and eyes that mirrored the cerulean depths of the Mediterranean, stood John Frederick Heider, the resident of the Covenant's house assigned to pick him up. In his mid-twenties, his physique bore the hallmarks of disciplined athleticism, and his presence seemed to command the space around him with an effortless gravitas. John extended a hand, his grip firm, as a fraternal smile played upon his lips.

"Monsieur. Lascombes? I'm John Heider," he began, his accent tinged with the cadence of American confidence. "Welcome to the United States. I trust your flight was agreeable?"

"Most agreeable, thank you, John" Pierre-Antoine replied, his formal articulation betraying none of the fatigue from his transatlantic voyage. "But please, call me Pierre-Antoine."

As they walked toward John's car, the air was thick with the scent of kerosene and the distant rumble of jet engines, it quickly became apparent that they shared a great deal in common. They spoke of politics and religion, exchanging ideas and concepts with ease, their conversation filled with biblical and historical allusions. Their shared interests and beliefs immediately ignited a spark between the two men, as if they had known each other for a long time. The car journey to the Covenant's house was filled with lively debate, as each man sought to learn from the other.

"Tell me, Pierre-Antoine," John said, his voice tinged with curiosity, "what are your thoughts on the current state of our nations? How do you envision us moving forward together?"

Pierre-Antoine paused for a moment, gathering his thoughts before responding. "In times of turmoil and uncertainty, it is crucial that we remain steadfast in our beliefs, drawing strength from our shared values and traditions. We must be the beacons of light in this dark world, guiding others toward a brighter future."

"Ah, well said!" John exclaimed, his eyes shining with admiration. "I believe that together, France and America can lead the Western world towards a new age of prosperity and stability, built upon the foundations of our Judeo-Christian heritage."

"Indeed! What about you, John, how did you first become involved with the Covenant?" Pierre-Antoine inquired, genuinely curious about the path that had led his newfound companion to this moment.

"Ah, well," John began, his eyes momentarily distant as he recalled his journey. "America's conservative lineage is a beacon unto the nations," John declared, his gaze fixed on the horizon as if envisioning a promised land yet unseen. "One that we must preserve against the encroaching sands of time and change. I was drawn to the Covenant's emphasis on preserving that heritage, and their dedication to instilling our values in the next generation of world leaders. My father was also a member of the Covenant. At thirty, he was the youngest elected governor of Virginia since the American Civil War. He was intended for the highest functions if not for the tragic car accident that took him from us at thirty-five…"

"I'm sorry to hear that," replied Pierre-Antoine with genuine sorrow. "It must have been a very difficult time for you."

"It would have been if not for my father's best friend, Robert Kay. Bob took my mum and me under his wing, providing for my education in the best school and college. You can say I was nurtured in the Covenant's hands, a pure product of their ambitions as Bob's protégé. Some members would even have the audacity to see in me their future "messiah", John suddenly whispered, as if revealing a worthy secret. "But shush, keep this only between you and me as it could be considered as a blasphemy…" He stared at Pierre-Antoine with the intensity of a man invested with a sacred duty before exploding into contagious laughter. "Oh Man! You should have seen your face just a second ago. I swear I took a picture to show the others.

Pierre-Antoine blushed from awkwardness, feeling embarrassed by the captivation he felt a moment ago from the young man's aura.

"My apologies if I made you uncomfortable, friend," John continued with a cheerful bonhomie. "You'll have to get used to it for the next six months" he concluded jovially before gently slapping the young Frenchman, left thigh.

As their conversation continued, Pierre-Antoine found himself drawn to John in a way he had never experienced before. There was an undeniable connection between them, both intellectually and emotionally. The young man could not help but wonder if fate had brought them together, allowing him to forge a bond that would shape his political career and reveal the depths of his own heart.

As the car turned a final bend in the winding road, Pierre-Antoine caught his first glimpse of Arcturus Lodge. He could not help but gasp at the sight before him: an imposing, magnificent mansion nestled within 16.5 acres of lush forest and meticulously manicured gardens. The shining white walls of the residence stood proudly against a backdrop of verdant greenery, its black roofs adding a touch of elegance to the stately façade.

"Here we are, Arcturus Lodge, 7979 East Boulevard Drive, Alexandria," John announced with a knowing smile as if he had anticipated Pierre-Antoine's awe.

"Mon Dieu," the Frenchman breathed, unable to tear his eyes away from the architectural marvel. "It is... it is breathtaking."

"Wait until you see the inside," John said as they approached the grand entrance, flanked by towering pillars that seemed to reach towards the heavens. Together, they crossed the wide arched doorway and entered the opulent realm within.

Pierre-Antoine's breath hitched as he took in the splendour of the interior, the sumptuous furnishings and ornate mouldings adorning every surface. An exquisite spiral staircase rose majestically from the centre of the foyer, beckoning them to explore the upper floors. They ascended slowly, each step accompanied by the soft creak of polished wooden treads beneath their feet.

"Your room is on the top floor," John said, guiding Pierre-Antoine down a long, luxurious hallway illuminated by warm, golden sconces. At last, they reached the door to his new living quarters.

"Et voilà," John announced, pushing open the heavy door.

Before the Frenchman lay a bedroom of colonial elegance – spacious and adorned with antique furnishings that whispered tales of a bygone era. He walked towards the window and stood in silent awe. The view was resplendent, French-style gardens stretched out before him, their geometric precision a stark contrast to the natural curves of the Potomac River beyond.

"This is... too much," Pierre-Antoine uttered in chock. "You are spoiling me."

"Anything for our friends," John replied jovially. Welcome to America! Your fellow residents will be eager to meet you," he then said, gesturing towards the door. "Shall we?"

Pierre-Antoine nodded, his heart pounding with anticipation as they descended the staircase and entered a grand parlour where he was introduced to eight young men, each a mirror of his ambitions, five forged in the crucible of American idealism, and three, like himself, hailing from distant shores. Their introductions were brief, cordial exchanges that hinted at the rigorous discipline that would define the next six months of their shared existence.

After a moment, Pierre-Antoine went aside and took his smartphone to make a call.

"Tsk tsk," said a voice behind him. "Rule number one: no phone calls allowed during your stay, except once a month or in case of an emergency." John was staring at him with a suspicious eye.

"Consider this as my first monthly call, then," Pierre-Antoine replied with a wink. "I really need to call a friend to reassure her that I arrived safe."

"Her? Ooh, our little Frenchie has a sweetheart!"

Pierre-Antoine's face turned purple before prattling: "No..., no, just my best friend."

"Yeah, yeah, of course," John mocked. "I leave you alone."

Pierre-Antoine headed to the veranda dominating the stylish gardens and offering an astounding view of the Potomac River flowing majestically through lush green landscapes. His call was answered almost instantly.

"Pierre-Antoine?"

"Yes, Monika, it's me."

"Oh my God, I was getting worried. Is everything alright?"

"Yes, Monika, everything is fine, just relax," he replied with a reassuring voice. "I was just a bit busy and couldn't call you before."

"So, how is it?" she asked, excited.

"Mon Dieu, if you could see this. It's just incredible. The house, my room, the people. It goes beyond anything I expected."

"I'm so happy to hear this. Don't forget to send me some pictures."

"And what news from Germany?"

"Well," she answered, a bit embarrassed, "the Christian Democratic Union has asked me to become the leader of their youth movement. I'm not quite sure—"

"That's fantastic news, Monika," Pierre-Antoine interrupted. "Go for it! Why are you hesitating?"

"I don't know about this. It's a lot of involvement ... and I still need to complete my degree..."

"Oh, come on! It's a once-in-a-lifetime political opportunity. And we'll be able to see each other more often. You, as the youngest leader of the Junge Union, and me, of the Mouvement de la Jeunesse Républicaine. Remember our goal, Monika," Pierre-Antoine's voice crescendoed enthusiastically, "our vision to reform Europe as a community of nations and get rid of that maze of out-of-touch technocrats. Again, go for it. You know you have my full support. And organised as you are, I have no doubt you will easily manage those new responsibilities with your studies."

"Alright, alright," she finally said, surrendering to her best friend's fervour. "I'll accept the nomination."

"Bravo! This is the Monika I know, the fighting woman. If I could just convince Jorge, now, we would become the incredible three—"

"Ahem…" John interrupted Pierre-Antoine with an insisting look.

"One more minute, please," the Frenchman whispered back. "Listen, Monika, I must go. But before that, there's something I need to tell you. But please, don't stress."

"Why? What's happening?"

"Nothing. I said don't stress. It's just…," he hesitated a couple of seconds, "they have this weird rule, here. No phone use and only one phone call a month. So… I won't be able to talk to you until next month…"

"What!" she erupted. "What is this place? A monastery? How can they forbid you from calling anyone?"

"Well, it's their rules, and if I want to fully integrate, I need to follow them."

"Still, that's not—"

"Come on, Monika," he reprimanded her, "it's only for six months. It's an experience I don't want to miss and, I guess, we can still write to each other…" Pierre-Antoine looked hesitantly to John, who nodded in approbation.

27

"Very well," yielded Monika. "But be weary of those American evangelists. If they suddenly realise…"

"I promise I'll be careful. Bye now." Pierre-Antoine hung up before giving his phone to the young American. "My apologies, John, he carried on a bit embarrassed, "Monika is my closest friend and can be overprotective of me. I really needed to talk to her."

"It's okay, Pierre-Antoine. It's a wonderful thing to be able to count on real friends. A blessing from God. I'll make sure to take good care of it until next month," he then concluded, exhibiting the phone before locking it inside a nearby cabinet. "Come on, let me show you the rest of Arcturus Lodge."

3

Two days later, in the last rays of the setting sun, Pierre-Antoine gathered with his fellow residents in the opulent parlour for a welcome party. The large fireplace at its centre was blazing with rapidly dancing flames casting a show of light and shadows across the wooden panels. Despite the idyllic atmosphere, Pierre-Antoine could feel the weight of expectation hanging heavy in the air.

"Before we proceed further," John began, "I must acquaint you with the living rules here at Arcturus Lodge." He proceeded to enumerate the strict guidelines that governed their daily lives: no swearing, no drinking, no sex, no individualism, watch out for magazines, don't waste time on newspapers and never watch TV, one phone call per month, eat meat, and, most importantly, study the Gospel. "

"Understood," Pierre-Antoine affirmed, accepting these restrictions with solemn determination, despite their stark harshness. He knew that these rules were meant to maintain discipline and focus within the Covenant.

"Come on, let me introduce you to Bob," John said, placing a firm hand on Pierre-Antoine's shoulder.

As they approached, Pierre-Antoine couldn't help but be struck by the man's presence. Robert "Bob" William Kay stood tall and broad, exuding authority and power, while his sharp dark eyes seemed to pierce through everything they landed upon.

"Bob, this is Pierre-Antoine, our newest member," John said, stepping aside to allow their handshake.

"Ah, Mr. Lascombes," Robert Kay greeted him warmly, extending a firm hand. "It's a pleasure to finally meet you in the flesh."

"Thank you, sir," Pierre-Antoine replied, shaking his hand with equal vigour. "The honour is mine."

"Please, call me Bob, like everyone. John has told me much about you," he continued, his eyes appraising Pierre-Antoine with an intensity that belied his cordial demeanour. "He believes you have great potential, and I am inclined to agree after all the praises I've heard from your fellow conservatives in France."

"Exaggerated statements, for sure," replied the Frenchman, blushing with embarrassment.

"And modest, too," the older man praised. "However, don't be ashamed by your achievements, Pierre-Antoine. Here, at the Covenant, we take pride of them and see them as an undeniable sign of Jesus' favour. As a future leader among the masses, you should always show pride in your realisations.

Modesty, as admirable as it is, will always be seen as a sign of weakness and cast doubt on your abilities to lead. Especially when you carry the torch of conservatism."

"I understand, Bob," Pierre-Antoine replied, listening to his elder with intense interest and passion.

"Conservative values," Robert Kay continued, his voice warm yet authoritative, "are the backbone of our society. They provide structure, tradition, and guidance in an otherwise chaotic world. Conservatism isn't just about politics," he continued, his voice low and measured, eyes locking onto Pierre-Antoine's with an intensity that belied his calm demeanour. "It's a way of preserving what is sacred, of upholding the natural order as God designed it."

The young man listened intently, eager to absorb every word. "I've always believed in conservative values, sir. But, if I may, what do they have to do with Jesus' message?"

"Ah," Bob said with a benevolent smile, "that's where things become truly interesting. You see, Jesus himself upheld many conservative principles – family, obedience, hard work, and personal responsibility. By following His example, we can bring order to the world and allow His divine will to lead us."

"Order," Pierre-Antoine echoed, the concept resonating within him. He had always been drawn to the idea of an ordered existence, one free from the commotion of his youth.

"Precisely," Bob asserted. "By embracing conservative values and Jesus' teachings, we are better equipped to guide the fate of the world. This is why I've dedicated my life to spreading His word and creating a global community of Followers."

"Followers?" Pierre-Antoine asked, his curiosity invigorated.

"Indeed," Bob answered with a nod. "The members of the Covenant are not mere joiners; we are Followers of Christ. We believe in obedience above all else. Faith and kindness, while important, are secondary to our mission."

"So, we are primarily Christians…"

"No," Robert Kay answered assertively, "we are not simply Christians. That term has been diluted, lost amidst the cries for tolerance and acceptance.

"Then what are we?" Pierre-Antoine asked, his voice barely above a whisper, captivated by the gravity of the moment.

"Followers of Christ," Bob stated, his eyes alight with fervour. "We adhere to the true essence of His teachings, not swayed by emotion or contemporary mores. Our path is one of obedience—obedience to the divine law above all else."

"Obedience, not faith?"

"Faith is the bedrock, yes, but without obedience, it is nothing but empty belief," Robert Kay lectured, his fingers steepled together. "Compassion has its place, but we are soldiers, Pierre-Antoine. Soldiers in the army of God, fighters for Jesus. How do you feel about this?"

Pierre-Antoine realised abruptly that the room had become silent and that all eyes were keenly watching the two men engaged in their debate.

"Sir," Pierre-Antoine went on, his voice full of conviction. "I believe that Christian politicians are meant to be a beacon in the night, providing spiritual light to a lost and dying world.

It is our duty to guide those who have strayed from the path back into the loving embrace of Jesus."

Robert Kay paused and looked at the Frenchman, his eyes reflecting the determination he saw in the young man's face. "You speak with such passion and wisdom, Pierre-Antoine. It is rare to find someone so devoted to this cause."

"Thank you, Bob," Pierre-Antoine replied, feeling a sudden warmth in his chest.

"Tell me, what do you think about America?" Bob asked, watching the young man closely.

"I see a nation filled with potential, but one that has lost its way," Pierre-Antoine answered. "However, after spending two days here, I also see the seeds of a future where those blessed with Jesus' wisdom help those who need it most to regain their faith and hope." The Frenchman's candour sparked enormous fervour and appreciation throughout the assembly. "It should be an inspiration to the coming generations, both in America and Europe!"

While the surrounding crowd erupted in a clamour of approbation, Robert Kay could not stop scrutinising the young man, startled by his zeal. *Could he be the one we've been waiting for so long?* He thought. *With John at his side, they would represent a powerful force for our cause, like a double-headed eagle soaring above America and Europe. This is our opportunity to rectify the errors from a decade ago and chart the course to the Covenant's ultimate goal.* He nodded thoughtfully, considering the Frenchman's words. "I am impressed by your insight, Pierre-Antoine. You remind me of a young man here named John. He, too, has a fire burning within him, driving him to serve the Lord with all his heart."

"Then John and I should cultivate those similarities," Pierre-Antoine said, intrigued by the possibility of forming a connection with another like-minded individual.

"Indeed," Bob agreed, a glimmer of excitement in his eyes. "I can envision the two of you channelling the aspirations of our two nations, forging steady ties across the Atlantic. The two heads of a same body solely dedicated to the achievements of the Covenant's final objective."

"Sir," Pierre-Antoine said, his voice trembling with emotion. "I am honoured that you see such potential in me. I am more than willing to commit myself to this cause. I want to be a soldier in the army of God and fight for Christ. With your guidance and Our Saviour' wisdom, John and I could make a real difference in this world."

"Hear, hear!" clamoured one person before the whole assembly burst into cheers.

"What say you, John," solemnly asked Robert Kay, his eyes burning with expectations.

"The only answer coming to my mind is quoting Ecclesiastes 4," John answered, taken by the intensity of the moment. *"Two are better than one because they have a good return for their labour: If either of them falls down, one can help the other up. But pity anyone who falls and has no one to help them up. ... Though one may be overpowered, two can defend themselves. A cord of three strands is not quickly broken."*

"Well said," Robert Kay heralded, his authoritative voice commanding their full attention. "I've brought you two together because I believe your combined spirit and passion for our principles can help us create a brighter future for all those who seek the truth. Your journey will not be easy, paved with traps and doubts testing your resolve and your faith. But because you are servants of the Word and Jesus told us *I have not come to call the righteous but sinners to repentance*, I believe you have the strength to overcome any challenge that comes your way."

"Thank you, sir," the two young men responded, feeling both humbled and empowered by Bob's confidence in them.

"Let's make a pact, Pierre-Antoine" John suggested suddenly, his eyes shining with determination. "To always support each other in our pursuit of knowledge and service to the Covenant's ideals."

"Agreed," Pierre-Antoine said without hesitation, extending his hand across. John clasped it firmly, sealing their unspoken commitment to one another and the Covenant.

Robert Kay, observing their exchange, nodded in satisfaction. "This is precisely what I hoped for when I brought you two together. Your combined strengths will make you formidable advocates for our cause. Now, let us pray," he declared to the surrounding assembly while opening his Bible. "Let us delve together into the teachings of Jesus and be blessed by his wisdom."

As he started reading the verses, the young Frenchman found himself increasingly drawn to John's insights. The American seemed to possess an intuitive understanding of the scripture that complemented Pierre-Antoine's more analytical approach. *I never thought I would meet someone who shares my fervour for the Word,* Pierre-Antoine mused. *Together, we will accomplish great things under Bob's guidance.*

4

Pierre-Antoine could feel the weight of history in each step as he and John peregrinated the hallowed halls of Arcturus Lodge. Weeks had passed since his arrival, and within this sanctum of conservatism, a camaraderie had sprouted between the two men—an alliance rooted in shared ideals and fortified by mutual ambition. Members of the Covenant were instructed to form a publicly invisible but privately identifiable pair of companions, mirroring the way Jesus organised his disciples. Each companion served as a moral compass to the other against any possible deviation from the doctrine of Christ. Only through such commitment would they strengthen their bonds, committing themselves to the sole service of the Covenant and Christ's glory.

And so, their friendship blossomed in quiet corners and during long walks amidst the forest that cradled the mansion. They exchanged visions for their respective nations, Pierre-Antoine's fervour for France's future intertwining with John's staunch American patriotism. Conversations delved into the philosophies of great statesmen, the stratagems of ancient generals, and the immutable words of scripture that they believed should guide the hand of governance.

"True leadership," Pierre-Antoine mused one crisp morning, "is akin to a shepherd's vigilance—ever watchful, guiding his flock."

"Indeed," John concurred, his blue eyes reflecting a resolve as firm as the surrounding oaks. "A shepherd must protect against the wolves of liberalism and moral decay."

The daily activities at Arcturus Lodge were meticulously structured, a regimen designed to mould the minds and bodies of its residents.

Each day began with a study of the Gospels; the air filled with recitations from evangelical texts, discussions on the life of Jesus, and how His teachings could be applied to modern governance. Members of the Covenant were scripturally literate but did not care much about the whole Bible. On his first day, the Frenchman was given a small book called Words of the Saviour regrouping the four Gospels and the Book of Acts — referred as Book of Emissaries. Nothing else. Pierre-Antoine found himself absorbed in these dialogues, his intellect challenged by the theological nuances and historical contexts presented by his peers.

Afternoons were dedicated to stewardship of their temporary home. Pierre-Antoine, alongside John and the residents, tended to the upkeep of the house and the verdant expanses of gardens. They laboured shoulder to shoulder, their hands nurturing the soil, a symbolic act that Bob often remarked was akin to cultivating the seeds of their burgeoning careers.

"Through toil, we find humility," Bob told them once, watching over like a sentinel, "and through humility, strength."

As dusk approached, the residents congregated on the field behind the mansion for an hour of team sports. The games, though competitive, were less about victory and more about reinforcing the bond of brotherhood among them. Sweat glistened on Pierre-Antoine's brow as he passed the ball to John during a vigorous match of football, their synchronization on the field a testament to the trust developing off it.

Evenings ushered in political discourse, the large wood-panelled reception room serving as their agora. It was there that Robert Kay, along with guests from various echelons of society and countries, would engage the residents in debates and discussions that stretched into the night. The flicker of the fireplace cast animated shadows upon their faces as they dissected policy, ethics, and strategy—each topic a stepping stone towards their envisioned ascendancy. Seeing so many influential figures gathering week after week under the mantle of Arcturus Lodge reinforced the young Frenchman's conviction about the extent of the Covenant's influence and the need to be part of it to achieve his future goals.

The days melded into one another, each setting sun marking not an end but a continuation of their journey. Within the confines of Arcturus Lodge, Pierre-Antoine felt the metamorphosis from ambitious politician to devoted acolyte of conservative doctrine. And at the heart of this transformation was the kinship with John—a friendship that promised to endure beyond the iron gates of their temporary Eden.

Once a month, Robert Kay would gather the ten residents for an open reflexion, a way to assess their progression and commitment to the Covenant's cause. However, usually, the exchange turned into a long virtuous monologue from their figurehead, nicknamed by John as *the vigorous Sermons of the Mount*. That day was no exception as Bob Kay, his eyes blazing with the fires of heaven, opened the discussion with a controversial statement.

"You are here to learn the how to rule the world", he declared unwavering, scrutinising their reaction. The young men remained silent, expecting a few more fiery words. Instead, he decided to challenge them. "How does that make you feel? Anyone?"

"Why... me?" adventured Felipe, a resident from Spain.

"Yes, young man." replied Bob eagerly, his voice hissing like a snake ready to strike. "Why you? Or him?" He pointed his finger to another resident. "Or anyone else here?"

"Because we are Christians" answered boldly Piotr form Russia.

"Wrong!" the reply fell as sharp as the blade of a guillotine. "Being Christian is accessible to anyone. In that you are no different from the people outside in the world." He paused to let the argument sink deep in their minds. "Someone else?"

"Because we follow Jesus," said John spontaneously.

"Yes, John. But more precisely?"

"Because... He chose us," hazarded the Frenchman.

"Yes, Pierre-Antoine! Because he chose YOU!" Bob Kay's voice exulted in triumph. "Because he chose you, you, and all of you." His finger aimed at each of them like an implacable sentence. "You are Jesus' chosen ones."

"Excuse me for saying this, Sir," replied William, a resident form Minnesota, "but how sure can you be? What makes us so different?"

"Nothing William, absolutely nothing. And that's what make you so valuable."

"I…, I don't understand."

"William, what comes in your mind when thinking about Kind David?"

The young American hesitated a moment before answering shyly: "He was a great king, if not the greatest king of Israel. An accomplished warrior, a protector of his people and his nation, and a bringer of justice. The epitome of what a righteous ruler should be."

"Indeed." The elder stepped forward, confronting his objector. "But you seem to forget that this man broke several of God's commandments. He was an adulterer and a murderer! How can such a despicable sinner could become God's anointed?" he proclaimed, slowly crooking his fingers together in the air as if trying to catch some impalpable truth. The ten young men stood paralysed, terrified at the sight of Bob's menacing fist. "Simply because … he…was…chosen! If you are chosen, it doesn't matter what you do, God and Jesus will always be with you. We elect our leaders, Jesus elects his. And you, young men, are Jesus' future leaders because you are the chosen ones."

"But how can we be certain we have been chosen?" asked William, still unconvinced.

"By coming here willingly, in the heart of the Covenant, you have answered Jesus' call to destiny," Robert Kay intoned. "Consciously or unknowingly, you were all chosen to serve Jesus' greatest interests. I will end today's talk by asking you to reflect on Matthew 11:27: *All things have been committed to me by my Father. No one knows the Son except the Father, and no one knows the Father except the Son and those to whom the Son chooses to reveal him.* Dismissed."

Pierre-Antoine and John took the grand spiral staircase to reach their respective rooms.

"Phew!" declared the American, circumspectly, "Bob was on fire tonight. I've rarely seen him so offensive."

"I admit I've never thought of King David in such a way," replied the Frenchman, thoughtful. "That sheds light on many things about the events that occurred a decade ago. Isn't it true that the Covenant, at the time, supported Tr—

"Be quiet!" John suddenly interrupted him, his gaze fearful. "There are topics that should not be discussed here. That man's incompetence has caused the current predicament we find ourselves in. His second term marks a dark period in our movement's history, with all its failures. It is forbidden to even utter his name."

"But I thought that—"

"It took the Covenant nearly a decade to regain credibility and make any real headway in the political arena." John spoke in a low, almost inaudible tone. "But let's not mention it. I say this for your own good."

— Very well, I'll avoid the subject in future. Good night, John.

— Good night, Pierre-Antoine.

5

The morning sun spilled through the stained-glass windows of Arcturus Lodge's parlour, casting kaleidoscopic patterns on the polished wooden floor. It was a warm summer day, the kind that promised the heat would linger well into the evening, leaving the air thick and still. Pierre-Antoine sat cross-legged on a plush cushion among the other nine residents, their heads bowed in reverence as the common prayer began. There was a comfort in this routine, in the shared spirituality that wove them all together in a tapestry of belief and brotherhood.

"Good morning, everyone," John said, standing at the front of the room with the Words of the Saviour in hand. His voice was gentle yet firm, commanding the respect and attention of those gathered before him. "Today, we shall read from the Gospel of Luke, chapter 12, verses 22 to 31."

Pierre-Antoine raised his head and listened intently as John began reciting the scripture. He couldn't help but admire his skill in leading the prayers; his deep, resonant voice gave life to the words, making them feel more profound and meaningful than they might have sounded if read silently on the page.

"*Then Jesus said to his disciples: Therefore I tell you, do not worry about your life, what you will eat; or about your body, what you will wear,*" Heider continued, his gaze never leaving the pages.

As John's lips moved with the verses, Pierre-Antoine found himself drawn not just to the familiar cadence of the scripture, but to the man himself. He observed, almost detachedly, the way his friend's jaw tensed slightly with each enunciation, the gentle bob of his Adam's apple as he spoke. His gaze traced the curves of the young man's silhouette, noting the tight cut of his clothes imperceptibly revealing the subtle strength that lay hidden beneath.

"*Consider the ravens: They do not sow or reap, they have no storeroom or barn; yet God feeds them,*" John read on, his voice steady and sure. "*And how much more valuable you are than birds!*"

In the stillness of the parlour, Pierre-Antoine's thoughts meandered through the recent weeks, recalling how his bond with John had deepened. They had shared confidences, debated theology, their minds often mirroring each other's in a harmony that transcended mere friendship. Around him, the murmurs of affirmation from the other residents rose and fell like the ebb and flow of the tide.

Yet, as the Frenchman sat there, enveloped in the communal reverence, his perception shifted. The sun-tinged air seemed to cast a spotlight on John, revealing contours and shadows that beckoned Pierre-Antoine's gaze like forbidden fruit. The American's forearm flexed subtly as he lifted the Covenant's book, and something primal within Pierre-Antoine responded, a craving to trace the landscape of muscle and sinew beneath those clothes.

"*Who of you by worrying can add a single hour to your life?*" Heider asked, looking up from the digest for a moment to address the assembled residents. "*Since you cannot do this very little thing, why do you worry about the rest?*"

The Frenchman's eyes fixated on John's lips, watching them shape divine words. But now, they whispered secular temptations into Pierre-Antoine's soul. He imagined the warmth of those lips, their pressure against his own, a craving for contact so intense it bordered on pain. He blinked, attempting to banish the distracting thoughts from his mind, but they persisted, like a nagging itch that refused to be ignored.

A pang of horror sliced through him as he recognized the nature of these desires. They were not merely carnal; they were profane, an affront to the very tenets he had vowed to uphold. How could such longings emerge, unbidden, towards another man?

Lord, he implored silently, a desperate plea for understanding, *why do you test me so?*

Tormented by the dissonance between flesh and faith, a battle raged within him. In a moment of frantic self-discipline, Pierre-Antoine's hand shot down, smacking his thigh with a force that echoed in the quiet room. Heads turned; eyes widened in puzzlement at the disruption.

"Pierre-Antoine?" John's voice, laced with concern, cut through the tension. "Are you alright?"

The Frenchman's heart thundered against his ribcage, fear mingling with the shame of what his soul harboured. Sweat beaded on his forehead, a physical testament to the turmoil that clawed at his insides.

"Forgive me," he stammered, rising shakily to his feet. "I—I am not well. Please, excuse me." Without waiting for a response, he stumbled toward the refuge of the nearest bathroom, fleeing from the bewildered gazes of his fellow residents.

After locking himself in, Pierre-Antoine's palms pressed hard against the cool ceramic of the sink, the chill seeping into his skin as he leaned forward, gasping for breath. He twisted the tap violently, and water cascaded from the spout, splattering against the basin before he scooped it up in trembling hands. The coldness shocked his flushed skin, droplets careening down his cheeks, mingling with the sweat that had broken out across his forehead. He looked up, catching his reflection in the mirror—a man on the brink of unravelling, eyes wild with confusion and fear.

"Leave me be, Satan," he whispered to his image, as if by labelling his desires, he could exorcise them. *These thoughts... they are not mine. They are but a trial, set upon my path to test my resolve.*

His mind spun, weaving rationalisations as fast as doubts sprouted. Pierre-Antoine clung to the notion of a divine test, an ordeal sent to fortify his spirit. It was inconceivable, unthinkable that he might be gay. His life, his faith—they hinged on the certainty of his righteousness.

"Lord," he murmured, the words lost amid the sound of water swirling down the drain, "grant me strength. Let this poisoned chalice pass from me."

A soft knock at the door jolted him from his reverie.

"Pierre-Antoine?" John's voice, muffled by the door, was tinged with concern. "Is everything alright?"

"Y-Yes," the Frenchman managed, steadying his voice as best he could. "I'm just... I didn't sleep well last night because of the heat. I just need some rest. Please excuse me to the others for the morning. I'll join you in the afternoon."

"Of course," replied John replied benevolently. "Please let me know if you need anything."

Pierre-Antoine waited, holding his breath, until the sound of his friend's retreating footsteps assured him of privacy. Only then did he allow himself to crumple, his knees buckling as he slid down against the door. His head fell back with a soft thud, the cool wood a small comfort against the storm raging inside. After a long moment spent gathering the shattered pieces of his composure, Pierre-Antoine rose and made his way quietly to his room, the sanctuary where he could confront his turmoil without prying eyes. Once inside, he closed the door and sank onto the edge of his bed, the mattress creaking softly under his weight.

"Father," he began, "guide me through this darkness. Cleanse my thoughts, purge these... unnatural inclinations. I am your servant, wholly devoted to your will. Lead me not into temptation," he implored, the words a lifeline thrown into the tempest of his soul. "Deliver me from evil."

The light filtering through the curtains warmed his face, but Pierre-Antoine felt only the cool resolve settling in his chest. He would overcome this ordeal. He had to. For in the battle between desire and devotion, there could be only one victor.

The sun hung high in the sky, bathing Arcturus Lodge's gardens in a warm, golden hue. Pierre-Antoine stepped outside, his steps measured, his face betraying nothing of the tempest that had raged within him only hours before. The other residents were already at work, scattered across the verdant expanses, their hands and tools shaping nature's wildness into manicured beauty. John was there among them, stripped to the waist, his skin shimmering with sweat as he bent to pull weeds from the flowerbeds. Pierre-Antoine caught himself staring at the play of muscles along John's back, the way they shifted with each movement, sinewy and alive under tanned skin. He felt the familiar stirring within, a flame he thought he had doused with prayer now licking at the edges of his resolve.

Jesus, be my shield, Pierre-Antoine urged silently, a mantra to ward off the unwanted desire. He turned away, busying himself with pruning shears and the overgrown rose bushes, trying to focus on the task at hand. But his gaze betrayed him, drawn inexorably back to John.

"Hey, Pierre-Antoine!" hailed John suddenly noticing his presence. "Glad to see you're feeling better. Care to help with watering this flower bed other there?

"Of course," the Frenchman replied, focusing on the task at hand, determined not to let his gaze linger on the tantalizing sight before him.

When the hose twisted in his grip, sputtering to life, Pierre-Antoine seized the chance for distraction. He aimed the stream at the base of the plants, watching the soil darken as it drank thirstily. Unexpectedly, John approached, his own hose in hand, and without a word, they fell into a rhythm—watering, weeding, and tending to the earth. A mischievous glint sparked in Heider's eye, a silent challenge. Pierre-Antoine hesitated, then with a lightness he hadn't felt since morning's ordeal, he angled his hose slightly, sending a playful spray towards John's feet. Laughter bubbled up from his friend's throat, rich and unguarded as he retaliated, a gentle arc of water catching the Frenchman across the shoulder.

Their eyes met, a shared moment of innocent mischief amidst the labour, but Pierre-Antoine could feel the weight of the Covenant pressing down upon them. They treaded carefully, their game never crossing the invisible line dictated by the strict beliefs that ordered their lives within the Lodge. Discreet touches passed between them under the guise of handing over tools or steadying a ladder—a brush of fingers here, a supportive hand there. Each contact sent a jolt through the young French, a thrill of connection that was dangerous in its sweetness. He kept his smile humble, his laughter subdued, all the while feeling the eyes of the other residents like whispers on the breeze.

As the afternoon wore on, the sunlight softened, and the patch of garden transformed under their care. Pierre-Antoine found solace in the work, in the simplicity of soil and sweat. Yet, even as he knelt among the flowers, hands stained with green, his heart was elsewhere—hovering around John, seeking the warmth of his presence like a craving worthy of Tantalum's torture.

Stay strong, he told himself silently, the prayer no longer a plea but a vow. *Stay true.*

And for now, amid the splash of water and the rustle of leaves, the Frenchman held on to control, his faith a bastion against the tide of forbidden longing washing against its walls.

As the evening grew darker, Pierre-Antoine's silhouette melded with the shadows of the French gardens, a solitary figure against the backdrop of the dawning night. The air was fragrant with the scent of lavender and rosemary, the enclosing coolness a soothing balm to his fevered thoughts. Above him, the Milky Way arched grandly across the sky, a celestial river strewn with stars that shimmered like tiny diamonds scattered on velvet.

He had always found solace in the stars—their eternal presence a silent testament to the vastness of creation. In the quietude, Pierre-Antoine couldn't help but wonder if somewhere out there, beyond the confines of this world, there might be a place where people could live free of religious constraints – where love and desire weren't shackled by doctrine or dogma.

"Beautiful, isn't it?" John's voice broke the silence, close enough to send a shiver down the Frenchman's spine.

"Truly," he responded, looking over to see Heider standing just a few inches away.

"Mind if I join you?" John asked, his eyes reflecting the stars above them.

The young man settled beside him, close enough for his warmth to radiate between their bodies, reigniting the embers of desire that had smouldered within Pierre-Antoine throughout the day.

"Sometimes I wonder," John said, gazing upwards, his face softened by the glow of the heavens, "what God might be thinking of us, seating on his eternal throne, somewhere in that vastness. Could he be playing with us and mocking our vain ambitions?"

"Hopefully not, Pierre-Antoine answered, his gaze shifting from the star field to the profile of the man beside him as a flawless full moon appeared in the distance. "Or he has a very peculiar sense of humour that mankind as yet to apprehend."

"Indeed…"

The silver light played upon the American's features, highlighting the curve of his jaw, the gentle furrow of concentration between his brows. It was as if Pierre-Antoine were seeing him for the first time, really seeing him, not just as a friend or confidant but as the very embodiment of his deepest desires.

With a start, Heider grabbed the Frenchman's hand and said, "Come on, walk with me."

Hand in hand, they wandered side by side along the cobblestone path. It was an innocent gesture to any onlooker, yet, charged with unspeakable meaning—a fleeting connection in defiance of a world that would never understand. As they paused beside a fountain, the murmur of water mingling with their shared silence, Pierre-Antoine felt the pull of something deeper. Here, away from the prying eyes of the Covenant, the veneer of composure began to crack, revealing the raw edges of a yearning neither could fully suppress.

And then, as naturally as the dawn follows the darkest night, John leaned in, their lips meeting under the silver celestial body. The kiss was a revelation, a fusion of longing and truth that seared through Pierre-Antoine's being. As their mouths moved together, the world around them faded, leaving only the sensation of John's lips, the press of his body, the mingling of their breaths. In this sacred space of surrender, the Frenchman's fears dissolved, replaced by a fierce joy that bordered on the divine.

"John," he whispered, the name a prayer on his lips, "what are we doing?"

"Something dangerous," he admitted, pressing Pierre-Antoine's quivering body further against his. "Maybe God is just playing with us. Who knows?"

And in the shadow of Arcturus Lodge, under the watchful gaze of a slivered moon, two souls danced upon the precipice of the forbidden, the gravity of their affection inexorably pulling them into the abyss of the senses.

6

Pierre-Antoine stood by the towering window of his opulent room at Arcturus Lodge, the gilded hues of dawn casting long shadows over the gardens below. The Potomac River lay beyond, a serpentine ribbon of water reflecting the nascent light. He watched as John Frederick Heider, tall and statuesque against the burgeoning day, strode purposefully along the gravel paths doing his morning exercises. They were now in the fourth week of their covert affair, and every stolen moment seemed more real than the last. Even from this distance, the sight of his lover stirred an unsettling alchemy within Pierre-Antoine's breast, a mixture of admiration and something more fervent, more perilous. *It must be what love feels*, he thought laconically. Before each of their clandestine encounters, the young man experienced an adrenaline rush, like a voracious appetite that would have made Tantalum suffer. He had never felt anything like the intensity of their physical interactions in the past. This was unchartered territory for him.

The Frenchman gently traced his lover's jawline with his finger, his voice tinged with content. "I should have known there was something different with you," he told to John in the quiet of his room the night before. "That first evening, when you quoted Ecclesiastes 4... You seemed to have omitted a verse."

John leaned in, their lips barely touching as he whispered back, "*Also, if two lie down together, they will keep warm. But how can one keep warm alone?*" His eyes shone with desire as he pressed closer to Pierre-Antoine. "My little Frenchie," John murmured before kissing him deeply. "You're slow to catch a hint. I felt it from the moment I met you at the airport."

Pierre-Antoine pulled back slightly, his expression softening. "Speak for yourself," he berated playfully. "I'm new to this. And this is the last place on earth I would have imagined—"

"Say no more," John interrupted, his expression suddenly turning serious and grim.

The Frenchman could still recall the faint look on his lover's face, the silent manifestation of a screaming conflict echoing inside his secret boyfriend's mind. A shadow mirroring his own ambivalence and struggles. But while his doubts were slowly fading with each passing week, bolstering his belief in their love and its godly essence despite the Covenant's disapproval, John's seemed to grow bleaker and more uncertain by the day.

The touch of cold glass against his fingertips brought Pierre-Antoine back to the chilling reality of his circumstance. He retreated from the window and settled into the armchair beside the dormant fireplace. The mahogany desk before him bore the weight of a phone, its presence a lifeline to the world beyond these seamless confines. He dialled Monika's number, his hands trembling with a mix of anxiety and anticipation. When her familiar voice greeted him from the other side of the connection, he could no longer contain the torrent of emotions that threatened to drown him.

"Monika," he began, his voice a mere whisper, betraying the tumult within, "I find myself in uncharted waters."

"Oh God!" she replied in panic. "What happened? Is everything OK?"

"*Je dois te dire quelque chose d'important.*[4]" Pierre-Antoine took a moment to gather his thoughts, his eyes closed and his hands trembling slightly. "I am in love," he finally spoke, his voice filled with both excitement and apprehension.

"Are you? *Aber es ist wunderbar!*[5]" she exclaimed with genuine joy. "But wait… how did you find love in a place you cannot leave and where women are not allowed— Oh!… I see…"

"Monika, I… I have discovered something about myself," Pierre-Antoine continued, his words spilling out like a flood that could no longer be contained. "I believe I am… gay."

Silence hung in the air for a moment before Monika's calm voice broke through. "I see, I see…" She paused, carefully

---

[4] I must tell you something important.
[5] How Wonderful!

measuring her words before speaking again. "But tell me, do you believe or are you sure?"

Pierre-Antoine hesitated, unsure of how to answer. "I... I am sure," he finally declared with conviction.

Monika's response was immediate and filled with relief. "Finally!" she exclaimed with a sigh, as if a weight had been lifted off her shoulders.

"What do you mean by *finally*?" the young man asked, frustration creeping into his tone at her seemingly nonchalant reaction.

"*Mein lieber freund* [6]," she answered, her voice soft yet cautious, "I always knew. Ever since you invited me to sit next to you on the university bench. I never brought it up until now because I wanted to give you enough time to come to terms with it."

Pierre-Antoine scoffed in frustration. "How condescending," he retorted.

"Please, let me explain," she pleaded. "Our friendship has always been based on mutual respect and understanding of each other's boundaries. Your sexual orientation is not something I have any right to pry into."

"But still," Pierre-Antoine argued, "why is it that in situations like this, the person in question is often the last one to know?"

"I don't know... call it a woman's intuition?" Monika replied with a laugh.

---

[6] My dear friend

"Oh, please, spare me the clichés," the Frenchman shot back.

"Well, cliché or not, it's true," she declared. "Anyway, I'm glad you felt comfortable enough to come out to me first. So, who's the lucky guy?"

Pierre-Antoine took a deep breath before whispering his answer, as if confessing a secret sin: "John Frederick Heider…"

"Wait, what? THE John Heider?" Monika's incredulous reaction caused Pierre-Antoine to pull his phone away from his ear.

"Yes," he confirmed quietly. "We've been seeing each other secretly for over a month now."

Monika's voice rose in volume as she exclaimed, "Pierre-Antoine, are you out of your mind? This is Robert Kay's protégé we're talking about! Not just some insignificant resident!"

Tears welled up in Pierre-Antoine's eyes as he shouted back in defence, "I love him, that's all that matters!" His words came out in an unfiltered stream of realisation and anguish, as if they had been pressing against his chest for too long. "How dare you judge me after what happened between Anton and you?" he sobbed.

His best friend's tone softened as she tried to calm him. "Please, Pierre-Antoine, don't take it wrong. You caught me off guard, that's all." She paused a moment before continuing, "This is a lot to process all at once."

Pierre-Antoine wiped away his tears as he said, "I just… I love him."

There was a pause, laden with the gravity of his admission. "This is no trivial matter," Monika intoned gravely. "You are ensnared in a den of conservatism. Any revelation of such nature could be your undoing."

"I am aware of this," he replied, his gaze drifting to the crucifix adorning the wall on his left, "yet my heart yearns with a truth I cannot suppress."

"Then guard that truth closely, for it wields the power to shatter your world," she warned. "The Covenant will not abide by love that it deems unnatural. Just promise me," she implored, her voice tinged with urgency. "Promise me that you will be cautious, and not let this love destroy everything you have worked so hard to achieve."

"I promise," Pierre-Antoine whispered hoarsely, the words tasting bitter on his tongue. How could he reconcile his desire for John with the knowledge that their love was forbidden, destined to remain hidden in the shadows of the very institution that sought to bind them together? After they bid each other a careful farewell, he stayed seated, ensnared in contemplation. The internal struggle that besieged the Frenchman was akin to the Biblical tales of temptation and tribulation. His faith, once the bedrock of his existence, now seemed to clash with the very essence of his being. Could the divine teachings he revered coexist with the love he harboured for another man? He returned to the window. His gaze met John's once more, who furtively waved at him before disappearing under the colonnade. In that brief moment, amidst the blooming lights of the emerging sun, Pierre-Antoine knew he would carry this secret love like a cross upon his back, bearing its weight with quiet dignity as he navigated the treacherous waters of the Covenant's teachings.

John gave Pierre-Antoine a fleeting glance. In that moment, he felt like a modern-day Romeo, torn between his loyalty to the Covenant's strict principles and his forbidden love. The inner turmoil consumed him as he hurried to his room and sought refuge in the warmth of a long shower. But even as the water cascaded down his body, the conflict continued to gnaw at his soul, its grip tightening like a serpent coiling around his heart. He sought solace in prayer, imploring God for guidance and strength to navigate the treacherous path before him. Yet even as he whispered desperate pleas into the darkness, images of Pierre-Antoine's smile, the warmth of his touch, and the depth of his gaze haunted the young man. John wrestled with his own demons. Under the vigilant tutelage of Robert Kay, his political aspirations swelled like a tide against the shore. Each lesson, each biblical parable twisted to serve the Covenant's cause, was a brick in the edifice of his ambitions. Yet, amidst the fervour of his pursuit, a serpent of paranoia slithered into his thoughts. After putting fresh clothes on, he decided to go for a little stroll to clear up his mind before the morning prayer. A moment later, while wandering the hallowed halls of Arcturus Lodge, he observed the way eyes seemed to linger on him for a fraction too long, the weight of gazes he felt even when none were cast his way. The atmosphere itself felt heavy with unspoken accusations, suffocating him with its weight. His mind became a breeding ground for spectres of judgment and disgrace, though he knew deep down they were merely products of his own fear and insecurity. The ghosts of doubt and shame danced around him, taunting and tormenting his troubled thoughts.

"John?"

The American recoiled with surprise before recognising one of the residents.

"Yes, Mark?" he replied, trying to calm his racing heart.

"Apologies for startling you, John. Bob wishes to see you in the library."

"Oh? I... I'm going right away. Thank you for telling me, Phillip." The young man stammered, feeling a sense of dread wash over him.

"You're welcome." Mark said with a smile before walking away.

As John walked, fear consumed his thoughts, making his steps quicken and his palms sweat. What if Bob knew? What if someone had talked? All his hopes would be dashed, and the same man who had taken him under his wing would not hesitate to ruin his reputation within the Covenant. The very thought sent shivers down his spine. *Shame! Sinner!* howled invisible ghosts that seemed to be circling him, taunting and condemning him. He could almost feel their icy fingers gripping at his soul. With each step, he felt like he was coming closer to his downfall. *My God, what have I done?* John silently prayed as he approached his destination, unsure of what awaited him inside.

The grandeur of the Covenant's library, with its vaulted ceilings and shelves laden with ancient tomes, was a sanctuary of contemplation. Here, among the silent witnesses of history,

John Frederick Heider felt the gravitas of his existence weighing heavily upon him. His heart throbbed with a discordant rhythm as Robert Kay entered, the echo of his footsteps an ominous harbinger.

"John," began Bob Kay, his voice sharp like a knife, "I have heard troubling rumours regarding your... association with our French guest. And, indeed, I've noticed a... particular affinity between the two of you. Such bonds can be fortuitous, but they may also lead astray. I consider you like a son, John, and you know you can confide in me with no fear. So, tell me, what is the nature of your friendship with Pierre-Antoine?"

The question, innocuous as it seemed, pierced John's façade like a lance. Sweat beaded on his brow as he wrestled with the serpent of truth coiled within his bosom. The shadows of the library seemed to close in around him, each book a judge awaiting his confession.

"Sir, I..." The young man hesitated, the words congealing in his throat. He envisioned Pierre-Antoine's face, the warmth of their stolen moments, and felt the bitter sting of betrayal on his tongue. But the spectre of his aspirations loomed larger still, a colossus casting its shadow over his love. With the gravity of a martyr, John capitulated to his own ambition.

"Forgive me, for I have sinned," John proclaimed, his eyes cast downward in feigned penitence...

"Pierre-Antoine, Bob has called for an urgent meeting," William heralded through the heavy oak door. His voice echoed in the spacious hallways of the ancient mansion, causing a sense of foreboding to settle in the Frenchman's stomach. "We are to meet in the grand parlour in five minutes."

"Understood, I'll be there.". *An urgent meeting? What could that be about?* Fear mingled with curiosity, sending a shiver down his spine.

As he arrived, he found all the residents already gathered, their faces etched with suspicion and tension. The air crackled with unspoken words and unease. In the centre of the room stood Robert Kay, flanked by John, his once-confident lover, who now seemed to shrink under the penetrating gaze of the elder statesman.

"Ah! Pierre-Antoine", greeted Bob with a strained smile, "please join us. We have much to discuss—"

"My brothers," John suddenly interrupted, his voice betraying a tremor. "I come before you with a heavy heart. For the integrity of our mission, I must expose a serpent in our Eden." The room stilled, and every breath seemed to hang suspended in time. John turned to Pierre-Antoine, his blue eyes now icy mirrors reflecting a chilling resolve. "Pierre-Antoine has strayed from the path. His affections… are unnatural, misaligned with our sacred principles."

A collective gasp rippled through the assembly. The Frenchman's vision blurred at the chock of the dire revelation. He stood, exposed and alone, the target of accusing stares that were once warm with camaraderie.

"Forgive me, for I have sinned," John then proclaimed, his eyes cast downward in feigned penitence. "I allowed myself to be tempted, seduced by evil's whisper. Like Eve in the Garden of Eden, I tasted the forbidden fruit."

A hush fell over the room, the air thick with the scent of old leather and unspoken judgments. Robert Kay's countenance softened, the lines of age drawing a map of understanding upon his visage.

"What say you, Mr Lascombes," he asked, his voice as terrible as a command from the heavens.

"I... I..." Pierre-Antoine stammered, his body frozen in fear and unable to form coherent words.

"Your silence and lack of denial are undeniable proof of your guilt," Kay declared, his words landing like hammer blows in the quiet parlour. "Unnatural tendencies," he intoned with disdain, "have no place in our fellowship. You will retire to your room until a decision is made about you," he concluded, leaving no room for argument or defence.

Pierre-Antoine spent the next hour in seclusion, his room a prison of shame and self-doubt. Mocking laughs reverberated through his mind, taunting him for his past ambitions and present disgrace. Arcturus Lodge, once a haven for his conservative ideals and political aspirations, now reeked of disdain and rejection towards everything he stood for. He couldn't understand why this was happening — why would God punish him for simply being who he was. As he sat there, lost in despair, he suddenly heard a faint noise and saw a white envelope slide surreptitiously under the door. With trembling hands, he retrieved the note and as he read its words, they struck a fatal blow deep within his soul.

Greetings in Christ!

We are notifying you at this time, based on your unwillingness to reconcile with the words and principles enacted by Our Holy Savior, that the assembly of the Covenant Foundation, called today, unanimously voted to dismiss you from his membership as a disciplinary measure. By your actions, you have demonstrated that you are a person lacking saving faith and, as such, brought shame to our venerable institution.

Therefore, you have one hour to gather your belongings before being taken to the airport, where private transportation has been arranged to return to your home country.

We pray that God, in His providence, will grant you repentance, acknowledgement of the truth, and be brought to your senses so as to escape the snare of the devil (2 Timothy 2:25-26).

May the peace of God be always with you.

Yours sincerely,

Robert William Kay
Associate Director of the Covenant Foundation.

My unwillingness? I was not even given a chance to justify or defend myself! Cast out from the sanctuary of Arcturus Lodge, Pierre-Antoine found himself adrift in a sea of uncertainty, the dreams he had nurtured and the love he had discovered slipping through his fingers like grains of sand.

The expulsion was swift, merciless. The Frenchman, stripped of his dignity, was unceremoniously escorted from the mansion. The grand spiral staircase, which he had ascended with such hope, now bore witness to his descent into disgrace. As he made his way through the grand main corridor, he caught a quick glimpse through the ornate parlour door. Inside, the other residents were gathered in a tight circle around Robert Kay and John Heider. The two men stood clasping each other's hands, their heads bowed in deep concentration.

"Brother John," Kay intoned, his voice suffused with compassion that belied the steel beneath. "Your honesty honours you. Just as God forgave King David, so do we forgive those led astray but who return to the flock."

"We forgive you," answered the others solemnly."

Pierre-Antoine's gaze lingered upon John, searching for a sign of the love once professed in the quietude of night. But the visage that returned his look was a mask of contrition, a facade betraying no hint of their shared passion. Within the hollow chambers of his heart, where once blazed the fire of their clandestine love, there was naught but the cold ashes of despair. Silently, the young man collected the remnants of his dignity, each step toward the exit a descent from the heights of elation to the nadir of abandonment. The Covenant's house, Arcturus Lodge, had been more than a political steppingstone; it had been the crucible of his heart's awakening. Now, it was but a mausoleum of dreams unfulfilled.

With the closing of the great oak door behind him, Pierre-Antoine stepped into the chill of the Virginian dusk. The sky above, streaked with the dying light of day, seemed to mourn along with him, bearing witness to the end of an epoch in his soul's odyssey.

***

The engines of the private jet roared to life as Pierre-Antoine Lascombes settled into the supple leather seat, his gaze affixed to the window where the world outside began a slow retreat. The tarmac gave way incrementally, like the shedding of old skin, each line and marker slipping from view as the aircraft jockeyed for position along the runway at Dulles International Airport. His fingers traced the window's edge with the rhythmic precision of a metronome marking the tempo of his heartbeat, a tactile affirmation of his presence at this moment of departure. His tall, slim form, usually the epitome of poised authority, was now a bastion of solitude amidst the opulence of his private aircraft. The piercing gaze that so often commanded attention was turned inward, searching through the nebulous shadows of his own thoughts. Like a stoic philosopher contemplating the ruins of Carthage, the Frenchman pondered the empire of his aspirations, now imperilled by the vicissitudes of fate. His ambition, once a blazing chariot racing toward the sun, seemed to dangle precariously on the strings of Icarian folly. Each beat of his heart a silent litany, an invocation for clarity in the labyrinthine corridors of his soul.

"Mr. Lascombes," the voice of the captain crackled over the intercom, "we are cleared for take-off."

A nod was his only reply; words felt superfluous—a mere profanation of the cathedral-like silence that enveloped him. The plane surged forward, the force pressing him gently back into his seat. Pierre-Antoine's senses awakened to the symphony of acceleration—the hum of machinery, the whisper of wind against the fuselage, and the subtle shift of gravity that heralded ascent.

With the earth fading away beneath them, the landscape transformed into a gleaming patchwork quilt woven by the hands of an unseen Demiurge. It was a mosaic of history and modernity, where the pillars of Jeffersonian democracy stood sentinel over the ceaseless march of progress.

The plane pierced the veil of clouds, ascending into the empyrean realm where the gods of old were said to dwell, arbiters of mortals' fates. Pierre-Antoine's mind grappled with the gnostic dualism that cast light upon the darkness of his recent tribulations. The spark kindled within him at the Covenant's threshold now smouldered with the intensity of forbidden knowledge, the Gnosis of love found and lost in the shadowed halls of Arcturus Lodge.

"Where do the forsaken find solace?" he murmured, the question hanging in the air like the echo of a forgotten prayer. The answer eluded him, much like the ephemeral nature of power and influence that he had so deftly wielded. The image of John Frederick Heider, now both Judas and beloved disciple, haunted him—a spectral reminder of the fragility of human connections. As the jet reached its cruising altitude, the young man closed his eyes against the surrounding shadows, retreating into the sanctuary of his mind. His thoughts danced around the possibility of redemption, of a future unshackled from the chains of tradition.

As Dulles International Airport vanished from sight, swallowed by the vastness beneath him, Pierre-Antoine Lascombes accepted the unresolved tension of his existence, his future actions and decisions shrouded in the mysteries that laid beyond the horizon.

FIRST INTERLUDE

Year 2069

7

Amidst the sombre shadows of an antiquated chamber, silent witness to centuries of whispered confessions and fervent prayers, five men of faith gathered. Their visages, illuminated by the haunting glow of flickering candlelight, were as taut as the strings of a lute awaiting the touch of a master's hand. The air was thick with discord; the Council of Istanbul had stirred the tempestuous seas of theological contention, threatening the age-old anchors of their beliefs.

"Brothers," intoned Pope Benedict XVII, his voice resounding with the gravity of Rome, "this abomination, this Shenouda's reformation, it festers like the wounds of our blessed saviour unattended. Its malignancy spreads through the body of the faithful, yet we stand shackled, beholding its unholy proliferation."

Russian Patriarch Alexy III, his eyes like coals smouldering beneath furrowed brows, nodded in solemn agreement. Grand Mufti of Egypt Suleiman al-Nawawi's fingers danced restlessly over the polished surface of the mahogany table, while Chief Rabbi of the Conference of the European Rabbis Solomon Goldsmith pressed his lips into a thin line, the weight of history pressing upon his shoulders. Archbishop of Canterbury Geoffrey Tenison, his countenance etched with lines of concern, shifted uneasily in his chair.

"Indeed, Holy Father," the Patriarch said, his Russian accent curling around his words like incense smoke at vespers. "But how do we quell this insidious tide? The very fabric of our congregations is being unravelled by this…this heretic."

"Shenouda speaks not but with the forked tongue of a serpent," Pope Benedict declared, his eyes blazing with a fire that might have been kindled in the sacred heart itself. "He cloaks his blasphemy in the guise of unity, yet there is no sanctity in his confluence of creeds. It is a chimerical pursuit, one that would see the pillars of St Peter crumble into dust!"

The Grand Mufti leaned forward, his voice a soft yet steely whisper, "Shall we then let the shepherd be led astray by the wolf in sheep's clothing? We must shepherd our flocks with wisdom and vigilance."

"His words are as honey to the masses, sweet to the ear, yet poison to the soul," the Pope continued, his hands clenching on an ancient bible—a silent testament to the unyielding doctrines within. "We must act, lest this false prophet's shadow eclipses the light of truth."

"Action, yes—but what form shall it take?" inquired the Archbishop, his English reserve belied by the urgency in his tone. "Surely, there must be a path through these darkened woods that does not lead us to further schism."

"Indeed," murmured the Chief Rabbi, the silver threads in his beard catching the light as if holding fast to fragments of wisdom from ages past. "Yet, we must navigate with care, for in our zeal to extinguish this flame, we must not set the world ablaze."

"But what about President Lascombes' despicable act?" asked the archbishop.

In the dimly lit chamber, draped in the gravitas of centuries-old tapestries and the weighty scent of incense, the religious leaders' horror was palpable—a visceral entity that coiled around each man like a serpent. The Old City of Jerusalem, a sacred reliquary of their shared faiths, now lay marred by the clandestine machinations of Pierre-Antoine. The European president, now self-proclaimed leader of the free world after his stupendous re-election, had orchestrated devastation upon the city's ancient stones, yet they could not reveal the sacrilege to the world.

"His threat hangs over us like the sword of Damocles," Patriarch Alexy murmured, his eyes glistening with unshed tears for the desecration. "Dare we expose the truth, Akhenaten's artefact would be laid bare for all to see, and our grip on the faithful would unravel."

"Indeed," Grand Mufti al-Nawawi agreed, his voice strained as if speaking pained him. "Pierre-Antoine commands shadows that move with the silence of the desert wind. We are but men against a storm that erases the footsteps of those who walk before us."

"Then let us find unity in our plight," Chief Rabbi Goldsmith proposed, his hands clasped tightly together, fingers white-knuckled. "For now, we must set aside the discord sown by our doctrines. In the face of such peril, our divisions are a luxury we cannot afford."

"Let us not forget, my brethren," Pope Benedict intoned with a finality that brooked no dissent, "that the cornerstone of our actions must be rooted in preserving the sanctity of our traditions. For if we falter, the very stones upon which our faiths are built will cry out against us."

The chamber, steeped in history and echoing with the whispered prayers of centuries, felt suddenly close, as if the ancient walls themselves pressed in upon the gathering of prelates. Their faces, an array of furrowed brows and tight lips, spoke volumes of the burden they bore—a weight that had nothing to do with theology and everything to do with the preservation of their power.

"Brothers," Patriarch Alexy III began, his voice resonant yet tinged with a rare note of trepidation, "we stand at the precipice of chaos. The artefact—the very mention by Pierre-Antoine could unravel the delicate fabric we have woven so painstakingly over centuries."

Grand Mufti Suleiman al-Nawawi nodded gravely, his eyes dark pools reflecting the gravity of their situation. "It is not merely our authority at stake, but the bedrock of faith that cradles our people against the tides of disillusionment."

Chief Rabbi Solomon Goldsmith's fingers traced the lines of an ancient text before him, as if seeking counsel from the silent ink. "Our shared history, though fraught with divergence, finds us united in peril. We must, for now, lay aside our doctrinal disputes and contend with this common threat."

"Indeed," Archbishop Tenison added, his voice carrying a hint of steel beneath its polished veneer. "Yet, where does one begin when the enemy wields truth as a weapon? Our unity must be our shield against the unveiling of secrets best left entombed."

The Pope, a figure of stoic resolve amidst the storm of concern, cast his gaze downward in contemplation. "We are shepherds without a staff, guardians of a flock beset by wolves. Our path must be shrewd, our actions concealed beneath the mantle of deception."

As if on cue, the shadows themselves seemed to coalesce into form; where darkness had lain, now stood a man who emerged with a poise that belied his sudden appearance, a figure cloaked not just in physical obscurity but in the mystique of his organisation's far-reaching influence. The chamber, a silent witness to the clandestine gathering, seemed to contract as the man stepped forth, his form an opaque silhouette against the dimly lit alcoves. The air was thick with trepidation, and every breath carried the weight of centuries, the scent of old books and sanctity mingling with the tension that clung like cobwebs to the gilded cornices.

"Esteemed leaders," he greeted them, his voice a harmonic blend of authority and calm assurance. "Your concerns, while deeply rooted in the soils of antiquity, need not grow into insurmountable oaks. The organisation I represent has long stood vigil over the sacred and the profane alike."

"Mr. Kay," the Pope acknowledged, his voice a measured cadence that matched the newcomer's composure. "Your presence here is... timely. Pray, share with us the insight that stirs from within the wells of your vast network."

"Be assured," Mr. Kay began, his voice reverberating off the vaulted ceiling, "The Covenant has long stood as the bulwark against the tempests of change. We will not falter at this juncture." His gaze, piercing and resolute, held each leader in turn, as if to impress upon their hearts the gravity of his words. "The council's ambitions shall find themselves adrift upon rocky shores. However," he continued, the timbre of his voice deepening, "the linchpin to our success lies buried with the secrets of Akhenaten. The artefact must be found."

Pope Benedict XVII, seated at the head of the oaken table, adorned in vestments that spoke of faith's solemn grandeur, digested the implications with a nod. His fingers carved steepled arches, resembling the very edifice that ensconced them.

"Understood," he intoned, his response not merely verbal but visceral, the echo of St. Peter's own resolve. "It is incumbent upon us to unearth this relic before it can dismantle the pillars of our belief. I shall commit the Society of Jesus to this task. Their acumen in matters both spiritual and temporal is unparalleled, and they shall operate under my direct supervision."

The assembly could almost hear the gears of history grinding, setting in motion events that would unfold in the cryptic language of spies and scholars. The Jesuits, known for their erudition and cunning, were the Holy See's elite guard, the vanguard in a war waged in shadows and whispers.

"Time is the essence we must distil with great care," the Pope added, his tone laced with the urgency that gnawed at his soul. "The artefact's revelation would not only illuminate pathways to forgotten truths, but cast light on our own vulnerabilities. We cannot, we shall not allow it to unravel the tapestry of devotion woven over millennia."

Mr. Kay stared at the religious leaders, his eyes briefly alighting on each of the assembled figures like a benediction. "The artefact, while potent in implication, remains but a piece in a larger mosaic. My counsel is thus: to seek it with wisdom, to guard it with prudence, and to wield it with discretion."

"Discretion," echoed the Grand Mufti, the word hanging in the air like incense. "A virtue that has served us well through the annals of time."

"Then let us be discreet in our endeavours," concluded the Patriarch, a note of finality resonating in his declaration. "For the eyes of the world must remain blind to the hands that guide its fate."

With a nod that was both acknowledgement and dismissal, Mr. Kay retreated once more into the comfort of shadow, leaving behind a renewed sense of purpose among the prelates. They knew the road ahead would be fraught with clandestine manoeuvres and veiled machinations, but the necessity of their mission lent them an unspoken camaraderie. This alliance of necessity, born of fear and desperation, would serve as their crucible as they sought to quell the rising tide of revelations that threatened to sweep away all they held sacred.

Once the echo of the shadow's departure had faded, the room burst into fervent discourse. Archbishop Geoffrey Tenison spoke first, his British reserve barely containing the undercurrent of alarm. "We must act with both discretion and haste. The council stands in the way of our designs, and if we do not stifle this movement, it could rend the very fabric of our institutions."

"Agreed," Chief Rabbi Solomon Goldsmith chimed in, his hands clasped before him as though in prayer. "We need to send emissaries immediately and collect intelligence about the artefact's hidden location."

Russian Patriarch Alexy III's deep voice resonated with authority. "And what of the faithful? They must not know the depths of our concerns, else panic will spread like wildfire through the pews."

"Again, discretion shall be our watchword," Pope Benedict intoned, the weight of centuries bearing down upon his shoulders. "Our operatives, whether cloaked in monastic robes or lay attire, must remain shadows among shadows."

As the prelates exchanged ideas and stratagems, the air grew dense with the gravity of their task. They spoke of ancient texts and modern espionage, of faith and subterfuge, intertwining like ivy around the pillars of their power. Each leader, despite the divergent paths of their doctrines, understood the magnitude of the threat posed by Shenouda's unifying call—a siren song that could lead their flocks astray.

"Let us then weave our own web," Pope Benedict declared, his voice infused with a resolute calm that belied the storm brewing within. "One that will ensnare our enemies in their own hubris."

"May wisdom guide us," whispered Archbishop Tenison, "and may history judge our actions kindly."

The chamber was a crucible of ambition and fear, each man acutely aware that the coming days would test their resolve, their cunning, and the very foundations of their beliefs. The Council of Istanbul loomed on the horizon, a gathering that promised to shake the pillars of heaven and earth with the clamour of reformation. And amidst it all, the hunt for the artefact became not merely a quest for an object of power but a battle for the soul of the world.

Pope Benedict XVII's gaze swept across the faces of his fellow prelates, each countenance a mask of sombre reflection. The gilded room, illuminated by the subdued light of antique chandeliers, seemed to close in on them as if the very walls were pressing down with the weight of centuries. The Pope's heart beat with the rhythm of an ancient war drum, calling forth the spectres of ecclesiastical history—crusades, schisms, and martyrs' blood—all whispering from the crypts of bygone eras.

"Brethren," he began, his voice reverberating off the frescoed ceiling, "we stand upon the precipice, our every choice resounding through the annals yet unwritten."

Grand Mufti al-Nawawi's brow furrowed deeply. "Indeed, Your Holiness," he concurred, "the eyes of Providence watch over our council, and we must tread with a discretion most divine."

"Secrecy," intoned Chief Rabbi Goldsmith, his voice a solemn canticle, "must be the guardian of our covenant. For words spoken in haste may become daggers in the hands of our adversaries."

"Agreed," said Patriarch Alexy III, his fingers tracing the ornate embroidery of his vestments, as though seeking solace in their complexity. "We must move with the stealth of serpents, lest our purpose be betrayed before its fruition."

"Let us then depart from this sanctum with lips sealed," Archbishop Tenison declared, his eyes alight with a fervour that belied his measured tone. "And let our trust be bound by the shared sacrament of our sacred duty."

Each nod that followed was a seal upon their pact, a silent oath forged in the crucible of necessity. They rose from their seats, their movements deliberate, and exchanged glances that held volumes of unspoken strategy. With the finality of a benediction, they parted ways, their minds riddled with the labyrinthine plots they must navigate.

***

The night had draped the Vatican in a velvet shroud, pierced only by the faint glimmer of stars that seemed to gaze down with celestial curiosity upon the unfolding human drama. Within the Pope's private office, a sanctum of sacred solitude, Benedict XVII sat enshrouded not only by darkness but also by the gravity of his charge. His silhouette was a stark contrast against the opulence of his surroundings, where art and history whispered echoes of eternal struggles.

"Father General Ricci," the Pope began, "time is the essence we cannot afford to squander. The artefact—Akhenaten's legacy—must be found. Our very foundations tremble at the prospect of its revelation."

Pope Benedict's eyes, alight with an inner fire, met those of Francisco Ricci, Father General of the Jesuit Order. The room was steeped in the musky scent of antique leather and the soft rustle of cassocks as the Admonitor, Giovanni Puglisi, and the Jesuit priest, Luca Calleja, leaned in, their attention rapt upon the Pontiff's words.

"Your Holiness," responded Ricci, his tone imbued with reverence and resolve, "the task you entrust requires a blend of erudition and tenacity. One name alone ascends above all others, as sure as the morning star heralds the dawn."

"Speak it," urged the Pope, his hand gesturing with papal authority, commanding the revelation as though summoning scripture from silence.

"Father Luca Calleja," declared Ricci, his gaze shifting towards the man in question. "His triumphs are etched into the annals of our order, and his acumen for the arcane is unparalleled. His voyage through the cryptic corridors of history has prepared him well for this undertaking."

The Pope nodded, the lines of his face etching deeper with the solemnity of the moment. He acknowledged the presence of Calleja with a look that bore the mantle of responsibility and expectation. The shadows seemed to gather around them, as if to shroud their conclave from the prying eyes of the world beyond these hallowed walls.

"Then let it be so," decreed Benedict XVII, his command resolute as the stone of St Peter's Basilica. "Father Calleja, the mantle falls once more upon your shoulders to unearth what is hidden and to shield it from those who would wield it as a weapon against us."

In the quiet that followed, only the subtle sounds of breath and the occasional crack of ageing vellum disturbed the air.

Father Luca Calleja stood erect, the soft glow of candlelight playing upon his features. His dark blue eyes met the Pope's with an unwavering gaze that bespoke a fortitude born not of flesh but of spirit.

"Your Holiness," he began, his words measured, "the charge you bestow upon me is one I embrace with a heart both steadfast and contrite. I shall navigate the meandering paths that history has veiled in secrecy, and with God as my guide, I will reclaim that which has been lost to the sands of time."

The chamber seemed to inhale sharply at his declaration, the very walls echoing with the gravity of the mission laid before him.

As the silence rippled with contemplation, Father Ricci turned his attention back to the Pope, his voice low, tinged with concern for matters that transcended the present discourse.

"Your Holiness, if I may inquire," Ricci began, his eyes seeking truth in the depths of the Pope's solemn visage, "have there been any tidings regarding your esteemed predecessor, Pope Emeritus Urban IX? The circumstances of his sudden departure have left many questions in their wake."

Pope Benedict XVII's gaze momentarily faltered, the weight of Father Ricci's question pulling him down into an abyss of sorrow. His lips parted, but the words seemed to catch in his throat, entangled in a net of grief and unease. The pontiff drew a deep breath, steadying himself against the tide of emotions that threatened to wash over the sanctity of his office.

"Brothers," he began, his voice barely more than a whisper, echoing through the hallowed chamber, "the truth about our brother Urban is far graver than the official proclamation suggests." He paused, the gravity of his imminent confession pressing heavily upon the room. "Despite what has been communicated to the faithful, Pope Emeritus Urban IX resides not in a cloistered retreat for peaceful contemplation but rather...
—the Pope hesitated, his eyes clouding with sudden sadness—
...within the walls of a private asylum, his mind lost to the insidious grip of dementia."

A collective gasp resonated among the gathered, the revelation striking them with the force of a mallet upon a chisel. The air grew thick with consternation as the implications of the Pope's words settled upon their shoulders like a shroud.

"Allow me to show you," Pope Benedict said, moving towards his desk, and opening one of the antiquated draws. With a reverence befitting a sacred artefact, he produced a thin transparent tablet which he turned on with trembling hands. The chamber lights dimmed as the screen flickered to life, casting a pale glow that seemed to cast shadows across their very souls. There, in stark, unyielding clarity, was Pope Emeritus Urban IX, his once-commanding presence now diminished to a mere shadow of its former glory. The surrounding cell was stark and clinical, the antithesis of the opulence one might associate with the Vatican's inner sanctum.

"Behold," the Pope murmured, "the unseen burden of our Church."

Urban's voice, once a clarion call to the faithful, now trembled with delirium. "The end is nigh," he rasped, his eyes wide with terror that pierced the veil between sanity and madness. "The seals have been broken; the Four Horsemen set loose upon the world. The Antichrist walks among us, cloaked in deceit!"

The image of the once great leader, ensnared by the tendrils of madness, was a sight to rend the heart of even the most stoic observer. His hands clutched at the air, grasping for salvation amid his tormented prophecies.

"See how the mighty are brought low," Pope Benedict intoned, his voice a lamentation that mirrored the despair reflected in each prelate's eyes. "We must gird ourselves against the coming storm, lest we too succumb to the chaos that seeks to engulf us."

Silence enshrouded the chamber as the flickering luminescence of the monitor died away, leaving the faces of the prelates painted in shades of horror and disbelief. The Father General's hand trembled upon his rosary, his whispered prayers a thread fraying in the cacophony of dark prophecies. Admonitor Puglisi's lips moved in silent prayer, his gaze fixed upon the void where Urban's tormented visage had railed against unseen foes.

"May God have mercy on his soul," murmured Father Ricci, his venerable eyes reflecting a sorrow born of the shared understanding of leadership's lonely burden. "The devil preys on the minds of the righteous. We must stand firm."

Pope Benedict XVII, his jaw clenched, felt the weight of his responsibilities pressing upon his shoulders He rose, the very air around him seeming to bend with the gravity of his office. "My dear brothers," he began, his voice steady as the founding rock of St Peter, "let not your hearts be troubled by the shadows of madness. We are the bulwark against which heresy and despair shall break."

A quiet determination settled over the room like a mantle as each attendee drew strength from the Pope's resolve.

"Verily," intoned Pope Benedict, "our path is fraught with tribulations, but we stand united in our holy purpose. Akhenaten's artefact must be removed from the hands of those who would wield it for ill." His fingers traced the golden cross on his chest, feeling its reassuring solidity. "It is imperative that we secure this relic, safeguarding our congregations from the encroaching darkness of Shenouda's false unity."

"Indeed, Your Holiness," responded Admonitor Puglisi, his own countenance set with a fierce intensity. "Action," he went on, "must be swift and decisive. In the annals of history, let it be written that when faced with the abyss, we did not falter."

And so, they conferred, each voice contributing to the tapestry of strategy and faith, weaving through the night a plan to preserve the sanctity of their order. They spoke of logistics and alliances, plotting courses through treacherous political landscapes while contemplating the machinations of Pierre-Antoine Lascombes and his ilk.

"Very well," the Pope concluded with a satisfied look on his face. "I believe we have devised a solid plan of action. If we play our cards wisely, the European President will have no choice but to surrender the artifact, whether willingly or not. The success of our mission falls mainly on your shoulders now, Father Calleja. Your main target is that heretical Prophet

Shenouda. Failure is not an option, as it would mean all our hopes of regaining control of events would vanish."

"I understand the importance of my mission, Your Holiness," the priest responded with reverence. "But if I may ask, Holy Father, what about Mr. Kay? Should we inform him?"

"Be cautious of that man; his help often comes at a steep price," the Pope warned with a shiver. "And let us not forget that President Lascombes was once under his influence. We cannot disregard the possibility that they may be working together behind doors. Remember what happened in the United States due to their involvement. I only agreed to accept his assistance because the existence of the artifact poses an immediate threat. But, make no mistake, Kay is the devil incarnate and *He who justifies the wicked and he who condemns the righteous are both alike an abomination to the Lord*. Whatever was discussed and agreed upon during these past hours must remain strictly between us at all costs. That man should have no part in this, or we will pay dearly for it. Once the artifact is retrieved, I will personally handle Mr. Kay."

As dawn threatened to breach the stained-glass windows, casting light upon the hallowed conclave, the four protagonists stood—a phalanx of devotion and power, bound by a sacred oath. The urgency of their mission was etched upon their faces, in their clasped hands, and in the silent prayers that filled the space between words.

"Now go forth with the armour of righteousness," the supreme pontiff declared, his eyes alight with a fire that burned with divine purpose. "For the world may change, nations may rise and fall, but the Word endures forever. We shall find the artefact and, by God's grace, shield humanity from the tempest that seeks to ravage our faith."

With a final benediction, they parted, each to marshal their forces against the tide of heresy, their resolve a bastion against the coming storm.

PART TWO

Intrigues

Years 2052 - 2053

8

Within the solemn splendour of his office at the Quai d'Orsay, Pierre-Antoine, France's soon-to-be former Minister for Foreign Affairs, sat ensconced behind a mahogany desk that bore the weight of many decisions. His fingers traced the intricate carvings on its surface, a silent testament to the bygone era of meticulous craftsmanship—a stark contrast to the synthetic aesthetics that pervaded modern Parisian life. The room, steeped in the gravitas of diplomatic history, seemed to echo with the whispers of statesmen past. Pierre-Antoine's gaze wandered over the Seine, where the waters, more than just the reflection of the City of Lights; bore witness to the ebb and flow of political tides.

The stunning victory of the opposition's coalition in the recent general elections had sent shockwaves through France's political landscape, defying all polls and expectations. As the new government took its place, Pierre-Antoine remained prostrated in the midst of the gold of the republic, his mind churning with disbelief and regret. With a heavy heart, he scanned the ornate room that had been his for the past four years, each memento and decoration now a cruel reminder of his impending vacation. His gaze fixated on the clock before him, as if by sheer willpower he could freeze time and cling onto his fading power and influence. The new majority's agenda weighed heavily upon him—an agenda that could unravel the tapestry of policies he'd so diligently woven. The air felt thick with change, the kind that alters the course of nations, and there stood Pierre-Antoine Lascombes, at the precipice of obsolescence, pondering the relics of his tenure.

The sound of his phone ringing snapped him out of his daydream.

"Yes, Martial?"

"My apologies, Monsieur le Ministre, but there is a gentleman here who insists on being received."

"Who is it?"

"A Mister Kay ... Robert Kay."

Pierre-Antoine's body tensed at the mention of a name he thought he had buried deep in his past. He grits his teeth, fighting against the flood of emotions threatening to overwhelm him. After what felt like an eternity, he finally managed to whisper through clenched jaw:

"Fine, let him in."

The creak of the door—a sound ordinarily inconsequential—resonated like the crack of an ancient tomb being opened. The Frenchman's heart seized as his former American mentor, a spectre from a chapter of life long closed, stepped across the threshold of his sanctum. The room, once a bastion of order, became a theatre of tension, each footfall of the American evangelist reverberating against the silence.

"Good afternoon, Pierre-Antoine," Kay said, his voice a low timbre that seemed to carry the weight of prophecy. His grey hair, once vibrant, now stood as a crown of wisdom—or deceit.

Pierre-Antoine's throat constricted, and the words struggled to form. "Monsieur Kay," he managed, his tone betraying a cocktail of emotions. It had been eighteen years since their paths diverged amidst the dire events of 2034. In those days, he had been captivated by Robert's vision of a utopian world governed by God and Jesus, a world where morality would reign supreme. But as the years passed, witnessing from afar the insidious machinations of the Covenant, Pierre-Antoine had long realised that what glimmered like gold was often laced with lead.

"May I?" Kay gestured toward a chair with the casual assurance of one who has grown accustomed to doors opening at his mere presence.

"Please," the Frenchman relented, though his mind raced with trepidation. What could bring this man, the associate director of the Covenant Foundation—the very embodiment of veiled agendas—to suddenly reach out to him after all these years?

"Your office... holds some timeless charm," Kay observed, his eyes steadily scanning the room. But there was something predatory in his scrutiny, akin to a seeker of concealed evidence sifting through the sands of time for a hidden truth. "I can see that France has treated you well."

"Charm is often the veneer over complexity, Monsieur Kay," Pierre-Antoine replied, reminiscing the verbal games that often laced their exchanges. "To what do I owe the pleasure of this unexpected audience?"

The American put on his enigmatic smile, the one that had once inspired the Frenchman, but which now only aroused his suspicion. "I have come bearing olive branches and opportunities," he declared, his eyes locking onto the ones of his former disciple with the intensity of a zealot.

Pierre-Antoine's pulse quickened, his mind racing to decipher the cryptic message concealed within Kay's proclamation.

"I thought," his former mentor carried on, "that in your current situation we could have a little chat." He paused a moment before continuing. "I understand you're about to step down from politics. That must be quite a decision for you.

"Indeed," Pierre-Antoine said, struggling to keep his voice steady. "But I assume you didn't come all this way just to discuss my political resolutions."

"True," Robert conceded, leaning forward in his chair. "I actually came because I believe this is the right time for us to put the past behind and work together once more towards our common goals. In other words, I came to offer you forgiveness and redemption"

Pierre-Antoine's breath caught in his throat. He studied Kay's face, searching for any hint of sincerity or deception. As much as he wanted to believe+ the man before him, the wounds of their shared past still festered within him.

"Forgiveness?" he managed to stammer, incredulous at the suggestion. "What makes you think I would even consider such an odd offer?"

"Because," Robert said, his voice steady and confident, "I know that deep down, you still believe in our mission. I have been following your career closely for years, Pierre-Antoine, and I can confidently say that you are not one to give up easily. I also know that you are the type of person who would seize a once-in-a-lifetime chance to assist us in achieving our shared objective.

"And what would that be?"

"Electing John as the next President of the United States."

Pierre-Antoine hesitated, his mind racing with conflicting emotions. He remembered all too well the passionate nights he had spent with John Heider, their love a fleeting flame that had burned bright but ultimately left him with only ashes and heartache. To be involved in his bid for the presidency would mean confronting those long-buried memories, and perhaps reopening old wounds.

"John Eider?" Pierre-Antoine asked, struggling to keep his voice from faltering. "You want me to help elect someone who is not even the Republicans' official candidate? "

"With only three weeks until the Republican National Convention, John has secured enough delegates to ensure his nomination. The rest of the process will be a mere formality. At this point, John can confidently call himself the official Republican candidate for the upcoming election."

"Fair enough," the Frenchman hissed, narrowing his eyes at his former mentor with suspicion. "But why me? I am

French and barely knowledgeable in American politics. What could I possibly contribute to John's campaign?"

"Don't play the false modesty card with me, Mr Lascombes," Kay retorted with a sardonic smile. "You were named diplomat of the year by Newsweek just a few months ago. Everywhere I go, I hear nothing but praise for how you deftly handled the volatile situations in Lebanon and Iran. There's even talks of you as a possible Nobel Peace Prize Laureate. While John may excel in domestic affairs, he pales in comparison when it comes to international matters, especially in European affairs. Having someone of your calibre on our team would make John more palatable to foreign leaders."

"Flattery won't get you far with me, Bob," Pierre-Antoine replied with a blunt tone. "And I can't shake off the feeling that your proposal has ulterior motives."

"I understand your reluctance and would probably react the same under the circumstances. But you must understand that this election is essential to our goals," Robert explained, leaning forward intently. "John is a man who understands the importance of faith and tradition, and he is willing to stand against the liberal tide that has swept across our country long enough. Your assistance, Pierre-Antoine, could prove… pivotal," Kay continued, his voice low and persuasive. "John Eider's ascension to presidency hinges not merely on political manoeuvring but on the alignment of powers both terrestrial and celestial."

"Why should I aid you and the man who…"

"Who has been chosen," Kay interjected, his eyes alight with the fire of conviction. "He is the vessel through which our vision will be realised. And your role, my dear Pierre-Antoine, is inscribed in the annals yet unwritten."

"Publicly helping John would mean betraying everything I've worked for during my political career since you ostracised me," Pierre-Antoine murmured, his voice heavy with the weight of his internal struggle. "And it would mean allying myself once more with the Covenant… with you."

"Ah, but my dear Mr Lascombes," Robert countered softly, his eyes locked on the conflicted man before him, "sometimes the greatest betrayals are those we commit against ourselves. By denying your true nature and your deepest convictions, you have been living a lie. You know that our cause is righteous, and now you have a chance to redeem yourself in the eyes of God and our brotherhood."

Pierre-Antoine stood motionless, the weight of the past pressing down upon him like the walls of an ancient temple threatening to entomb. He gazed out the window, where the Parisian skyline lay draped in the hues of an indifferent dusk. In the distance, the Seine flowed—a placid witness to the passions of men.

"Within these hallowed halls, you have forged alliances, weathered diplomatic tempests," Kay said, moving closer, his shadow stretching across the hardwood floor. "Consider this not an end, but a genesis. Your influence, though momentarily eclipsed, shall rise again."

"Rise again?" Pierre-Antoine echoed, the words laced with both scepticism and an undercurrent of yearning. The prospect of a political renaissance was alluring, a siren's song amidst the shipwreck of his career.

"Indeed," Kay affirmed. "As the morning star heralds the dawn after the darkest hour of night."

The Frenchman turned to face the American evangelist, his expression enigmatic. The offer laid before him was a chalice brimming with both promise and poison. To accept would mean intertwining his fate with a man who had once possessed his heart, only to have it crushed beneath the heel of ambition.

"Give me a few days," Pierre-Antoine finally said, his voice barely above a whisper. "I need some time to think about this."

"Time is the river that erodes all certainties," Robert replied, his smile unfaltering. "But even rivers can be redirected by the hands of the faithful."

With that, Kay took his leave, his departure as sudden and enigmatic as his arrival. Pierre-Antoine remained alone, the shadows lengthening around him, the whispers of history and the ghosts of love long lost murmuring in the recesses of his soul.

***

Hours later, the court of honour at the Quay d'Orsay bristled with the pageantry befitting a changing of the guard. Pierre-Antoine slowly walked down the grand staircase, each step a descent from the zenith of power. His collaborators, arrayed like sentinels of a fallen regime, awaited his approach.

"*Merci*," he whispered to each, hands clasping theirs in turn. His gratitude, genuine and profound, was a balm to the melancholy etched upon their faces. Their loyalty had been his bastion; now, it felt akin to a relic of bygone days.

"*Mes chers amis*," Pierre-Antoine addressed the crowd gathered before him, his voice tinged with emotion. "It has been my absolute privilege to serve alongside you during my term as Minister for Foreign Affairs. Your unwavering commitment to advancing the goals of our esteemed institution over the last four years, even during challenging moments, shall be the legacy we share. I stand before you, humbled and honoured by your unwavering dedication to the service of the State."

The crowd responded with resounding applause, their admiration for their now former chief evident in their eyes. Turning to his successor, Pierre-Antoine mustered a smile both magnanimous and tinged with sorrow. "I entrust you with the keys of this noble house, he said, extending a hand that was clasped with fervent respect. "May your tenure be marked by wisdom and success."

"*Je vous remercie, Monsieur Lascombes*," simply replied the new minister, the weight of the legacy he was inheriting evident in his grasp.

As the ceremony drew to a close, Pierre-Antoine afforded himself one final glance at the storied façade of the ministry. The stones held memories of triumphs and trials, whispers of secret negotiations and public declarations. Stepping into the car that would ferry him away from public affairs, he felt the keen edge of transition cut through the fabric of his being.

The official vehicle glided away, bearing him toward the verdant refuge of his home in the Southwest, where he would face alone angels and demons alike, pondering the choice laid before him—a choice that could exalt or expunge the very essence of his destiny.

9

Amidst the gentle embrace of his ancestral home, Pierre-Antoine found solace in the solitude that the outskirts of Toulouse offered. The familiar sights and smells of his rose bushes and peony flowerbeds brought a bittersweet mix of memories, some of past achievements, others of regrets and missed opportunities. Sitting in the quiet stillness of his garden, surrounded by the gentle dance of the willow trees in the wind, Pierre-Antoine grappled with the spectre of his political mortality. The recent election had been a devastating blow to his carefully constructed plans, and he was now left with nothing but time to contemplate his next move. But amidst the turmoil and self-doubt, there was a strange sense of peace that settled over him as he sat there, alone with his thoughts. The gentle fragrance of the flowers, the delicate rustle of the leaves, and the distant chirping of birds all seemed to whisper secrets to the wind, reminding him of the beauty and simplicity of life.

And, for a fraction of eternity, all his worries and fears faded away.

The peacefulness of his meditation was interrupted by the familiar sound of determined footsteps crunching over the gravel.

"Monika," he breathed, as the elegant figure of Monika Richter, now German Ministry for Economic Cooperation and Development, emerged from the kitchen. Their eyes met and she offered a warm smile as she approached him, a gesture that spoke volumes about their enduring friendship.

"Surprise!" she joyfully screamed before double-kissing her best friend on the cheeks.

"What an unexpected, pleasant surprise. How come?"

"I had some official meetings nearby, boring stuff. Then I told myself, why not make a slight detour before heading back to Berlin, so I could say hello to my dearest friend Pierre-Antoine?" she answered nonchalantly.

"I can't help but wonder how *slight* that detour was," the Frenchman responded in a scolding tone.

"Nothing that Helmut, my devout chauffeur, couldn't indulge. But let's stop here the pleasantries," she said, her voice filled with concern, "I needed to see how you were."

"Your presence is a balm for my weary spirit," Pierre-Antoine replied, touched by her show of support. "Come, let's speak inside."

Seated opposite each other in the intimate drawing room, Monika wasted no time addressing the events that had led to Pierre-Antoine's sudden departure from office.

"*Ich bin immer für Sie da, egal aus welchem Grund., mein Freund,*[7]" she replied. "Your recent misfortune is but an ebb in the great tide of your career," she assured him, her words steeped in the conviction of their shared history and long-forged camaraderie. "Your political career is far from over," she continued, her blue eyes resolute, "and I have no doubt that you will rise again, stronger and wiser than before."

"An ebb that may yet pull me under," her friend mused, allowing himself the vulnerability that only true friendship could foster.

"*Nein,*[8]" Monika countered with a strength that belied her compassionate gaze. "You are far too resilient, and the political theatre has a penchant for encores."

Her words were a soothing tonic, but Pierre-Antoine hesitated before divulging the true reason for his disquiet. "Robert Kay approached me," he confessed, feeling a shiver run down his spine as he uttered the name. "He asked for my assistance with the Covenant's plan in the upcoming US presidential elections."

"*Was?*[9] Robert Kay?" Monika echoed, a sense of stupor creeping into her voice. "You mean…?"

"Yes, THE Robert Kay" he confirmed. "The very same man who betrayed my trust all those years ago now seeks my help to elect John Heider as the next President of the United States."

---

[7] I'm always there for you, no matter the reasons., my friend.
[8] No.
[9] What?

A tense silence settled between them as she absorbed the implications of this revelation. Monika's expression hardened, her diplomatic tact giving way to uncharacteristic gravity.

"Have you considered the ramifications of accepting such a proposal? she asked, her voice firm. "The risks, the potential dangers? You would be placing yourself at odds with John Eider, a man you once loved and who sacrificed that love on the altar of his own ambitions."

Pierre-Antoine's gaze fell to the floor, his heart constricting at the mention of his former lover.

"I am well aware of the perils, Monika," he murmured, feeling the weight of the decision that loomed before him.

"Then tread carefully, my friend," she counselled, her eyes glistening with concern. "The Covenant is a powerful and insidious force. Choosing to align yourself with them again is to dance with the devil himself."

Pierre-Antoine nodded solemnly, knowing that he stood at a crossroads, his future hanging in the balance. The room seemed to close in around him, a cacophony of thoughts and doubts threatening to overwhelm him.

"Yet in the waltz of power, even devils may lead," he reflected, his thoughts adrift in a sea of moral ambiguity. "To refuse the offer is to court obscurity. To accept is to consort with shadows, casting my lot against a man whose heart I once held dear."

"But what about those *unforgivable sins* they cast you out for?"

"They would be ... forgotten and forgiven."

"So, that's what it's all about? Your redemption. The return of the prodigal son," she scolded. "How can, after all those years, still feel ashamed of what you are?"

"I ... I ..."

"If your sole motivation for returning to the Covenant is to seek absolution, Pierre-Antoine, you are delusional." She grasped his hands firmly, gazing into his eyes with intensity. "You are who you are, my friend. A beautiful man with a kind heart, as God intended. And no divine power on this earth can change this. Accept it, embrace it, and do not let the ashes of what was to cloud your vision of what must be."

"Must be?" he questioned, his gaze finding hers—a mirror reflecting the struggle within. "Or what may yet come to pass?"

"Consider the path before you," she urged, her plea etched with the sagacity of their shared past. "For every step taken in darkness, seek the light that will guide you back."

Pierre-Antoine's gaze wandered to the window, where a golden sun dipped below the horizon, casting long shadows across his quiet garden. The beauty of the moment failed to quell the turmoil within him, as he grappled with the possibility of rejoining the Covenant and the unease of facing his former lover once more.

"John Eider," Monika announced, as if she could read the thoughts running through his mind, "is no longer the man you once knew. In most European chanceries, he is considered a potential threat to not just the United States, but to the entire world. They view the man with great suspicion. Aligning yourself with him could have serious consequences."

"Yet the Covenant seeks my help in electing him. Surely, they see something in him that we do not," Pierre-Antoine replied, his brow furrowed in contemplation.

"Or perhaps they simply see a pawn, someone they can manipulate for their own ends," Monika countered. "You must be careful, *mein freund*[10]. The Covenant's influence has grown exponentially recently, methodically reclaiming all the grounds they lost in the aftermath of the Conservative party's crushing defeat in 2024. Their reach, once again, extends far beyond what most people realise."

"Are you suggesting I refuse their offer?" he asked, seeking her counsel.

"Only you can make that decision," she said gently. "But I would advise caution. Again, weigh the potential risks and benefits carefully before committing yourself."

Pierre-Antoine nodded, his mind racing with thoughts and questions. The idea of rejoining the Covenant both thrilled and terrified him, offering a sense of belonging he had long craved while also raising the spectre of past betrayals. And then there was John Heider – the man who had once held his heart, now a personification of all he abhorred.

"Whatever decision you take, know that I will support you," Monika assured him, placing a warm hand on his shoulder. "You are not alone in this, Pierre-Antoine. I will stand by your side, for better or worse, as I always have."

---

[10] My friend.

"Thank you, Monika," he whispered, his voice thick with emotion. "And so will I. Your friendship means more to me than I can express."

"Then let's close the subject, for now. Unfortunately, I must return to Germany for a special session at the Reichstag," she then said, her eyes filled with regret. "But please, do not hesitate to call if you need anything – advice, support, or simply someone to listen."

"I will. Godspeed, Monika," he called after her retreating figure.

"*Et cum spiritu tuo*[11], my friend," she replied without turning, her Latin farewell echoing softly in the halls.

Pierre-Antoine stood by the tall window, its panes a mosaic of twilight hues reflecting the sombre palette of his thoughts. The room's grandeur, once a testament to his esteemed position, now felt like an oppressive mausoleum of his aspirations—silent witnesses to the crossroads at which he stood.

The Covenant. A name that conjured images of ancient pacts sealed with blood and fire, resonating with the gravity of scriptural covenants. It was within this clandestine fraternity that Pierre-Antoine had once sought solace and purpose, only to find himself ensnared in a web of Machiavellian deceit, spun by none other than Robert Key—a man whose visage wore piety as a masquerade for power. He ran his fingers along the mahogany surface of his desk, feeling the cool wood under his touch—a stark contrast to the searing memories that besieged

---

[11] And with your spirit.

his mind. How young and fervent he had been, swayed by Kay's silver tongue, believing he could merge his political ambitions with a divine mission. But those days were sepulchral echoes in the crypt of his conscience, each whisper a reminder of innocence betrayed.

Pierre-Antoine's gaze drifted over the artefacts adorning his office: relics from his travels, each a fragment of the world's variegated beliefs. Amidst them sat an unassuming clay tablet, inscribed with the names of ancient kings who ruled by divine mandate. Did he, too, aspire to such heights, or would he become a mere footnote in the annals of history? The Covenant's offer dangled before him like a forbidden fruit, ripe with the promise of power resurrected from the ashes of his current disgrace. Yet, it was a fruit that grew from a tree with roots entwined around his very soul, reaching into dark soil fertilized by past transgressions.

"*Time is the devourer of all things,*" he murmured, the words of Ovid's Metamorphoses mingling with the scent of aged paper and leather-bound tomes that lined the walls. His eyes settled on a volume of Thucydides, its spine cracked with wisdom. *The outcasts are surely those who have the clearest vision of what is before them, glory and danger alike, and yet notwithstanding, go out to meet it.* A sense of urgency knotted the Frenchman's stomach. He could not dawdle at destiny's door, for the hands of the clock were relentless sentinels, marching forward to the beat of inexorable truth. To accept Robert Kay's offer was to forge anew the chains that once bound him; to reject it was to face an uncertain future, bereft of the influence he had so meticulously cultivated. His heart pounded in his chest, a metronome counting down the moments until he must choose. The consequences of his decision loomed large, casting their shadows over not only his political career but also his very soul. In his mind's eye, he saw the faces of those who had stood by him—Monika, loyal and steadfast, and the countless others who had placed their faith in his leadership.

"Is redemption found in the act of contrition or in the steadfast refusal to revisit one's sins?" he pondered aloud, the question hanging in the air like incense in a cathedral, heavy with the scent of introspection. Pierre-Antoine knew that with each passing moment, the scales of his fate tipped precariously, demanding a verdict. The Covenant awaited his response, a Goliath in the shadows, its silhouette cast long by the setting sun.

"*Libera me, Domine, de morte aeterna*"[12] he whispered, a plea to be delivered from the tempest of his own making. Tomorrow, he would choose—but tonight, he wrestled with the angels and demons that danced upon the chessboard of his legacy.

Pierre-Antoine woke up in the morning after a restless night, his mind consumed by the weight of the decision ahead. He had come to the conclusion that the path before him forked in two, each leading to vastly different horizons. To align with Robert Kay and the Covenant was to step into a familiar dance with power—a waltz that could elevate or ensnare. His political career had been a tapestry of triumphs and travails, and this choice would be the most indelible stitch yet.

---

[12] Free me, Lord, from eternal death.

"Is it vanity that whispers promises of grandeur or redemption that offers a chance for absolution?" he questioned, his heart caught in the thorny brambles of his past with John Heider—complications of the soul that defied simple resolution. "*Non[13],*" he concluded, the word escaping as a breath—resolute, final. "It is not vanity but necessity. The Covenant's reach extends far beyond the dominion of one man's ambition." Pierre-Antoine's desire to rekindle the ashes of influence burned with an intensity that surprised even him. Yet, intertwined with that aspiration was the trepidation of facing John Heider again—the bittersweet reminiscence of amorous warfare. *Je suis prêt[14]*. With a newfound determination, he had made his decision—a commitment forged in the crucible of his past experiences, his heartache, and his desire for retribution. It was time to act, to cast the die and let fate chart its course.

Pierre-Antoine reached for his holophone, its cold plastic a stark contrast to the warmth of his resolve. He slowly but unequivocally dialled the number etched into memory, a sequence of digits that summoned ghosts from the catacombs of his conscience.

"Robert, it's Pierre-Antoine," he announced crisply as the call connected. There was a pause on the line—a void where anticipation held its breath.

"Ah, Pierre-Antoine, your voice is the herald of good tidings, I trust?" Robert Kay's voice emerged.

---

[13] No
[14] I'm ready

"Indeed," the Frenchman replied, his tone cloaked in the armour of formality. "I have considered your proposal and… I accept."

"Ah, Pierre-Antoine!" Robert's voice was warm, almost paternal, though a trace of triumph lingered beneath the surface. "I knew you would see reason. We shall welcome you with open arms, brother. Together, we shall restore order and morality to a country that has been led astray by liberal depravity for far too long."

"Indeed," Pierre-Antoine replied, forcing a note of enthusiasm into his tone. "So, what is the next course of action?"

"Leave that to me," Kay assured him. "I'm sending my private jet immediately to deliver you from the land of Pharaoh to the shores of promise, just as Moses led the Israelites out of Egypt. With less than three weeks before the Republican National Convention, we have much to discuss, and time is of the essence."

"Very well," said Pierre-Antoine, his thoughts drifting back to that fateful day eighteen years prior when he had been unceremoniously expelled from the Covenant's ranks. The irony of his return to the United States via the same means did not escape him. And yet, he could not deny the allure of working alongside those who had once cast him aside—the opportunity to prove his worth and exact his own measure of justice. "Thank you, Bob," he declared at last, steeling himself for the trials that lay ahead. "I will be ready."

"Excellent," replied Robert, the satisfaction in his voice palpable. "I look forward to our reunion, my friend. Until then, may God be with you."

With those final words, the call ended, leaving Pierre-Antoine alone with the enormity of his choice. *Exodus or exile?* he pondered silently. *Only time will tell which I am destined to relive.* As he gazed out over the rolling hills of his beloved Southwest, he knew that the path he had chosen would test him in ways he could not yet imagine. But whatever the cost, he was resolute, determined to face the challenges that awaited him and emerge victorious—or perish in the attempt.

10

Pierre-Antoine stepped into the pulsating heart of the Dallas Convention Center, a cacophony of fervent chants and the thunderous applause of an assembled multitude washing over him like the roar of the ocean. The air was electric with hope and anticipation, saturated with the collective conviction of a Republican resurgence that had been a decade in the waiting. Around him, banners unfurled like the battle standards of old, emblazoned with slogans heralding a return to glory, a reclamation of values long besieged by what they called a corrupt establishment. Amidst the throng of fervent supporters, he found himself accompanied by Robert Kay and several other influential members of the Covenant, their presence both reassuring and unnerving as they navigated the storm of eager faces.

"Can you feel it, Pierre-Antoine?" Robert asked, his voice barely audible above the cacophony of cheers and applause. "This is the year the Republicans will win the Presidency and regain control of both Houses. The time has come to set our nation back on the path of righteousness."

The Frenchman nodded, his mind swirling with a mix of excitement and apprehension about his role in supporting John Heider's campaign. He had never before experienced such a spectacle, a sea of human devotion surging towards an unseen shore - an unstoppable tide of belief in a brighter future. The energy was intoxicating, and for a brief moment, Pierre-Antoine allowed himself to be swept up in the rapture.

"Look," Robert gestured toward the stage, where John, now Governor of West Virginia, stood bathed in a halo of light. Flanked by his wife and two children, he was delivering a passionate acceptance speech after the national delegates had officially endorsed him as the Republican nominee for president.

"… For far too long, we have cowered in silence as the Democrats have wielded their power to suppress our voices and manipulate our beliefs. But we will not be silenced any longer! We are not ashamed of standing up for what we believe in, even if it goes against the so-called '*official discourse*'." *We are not ashamed!* the crowd roared in agreement, their voices full of defiance. "No more will we stand idly by as they spew fear and hate against our values, disguising their own immoral actions. Enough is enough!" *Enough is enough!* "We are a strong and proud people, and we will not be bullied into submission. Our Republic stands for the majority, not for the manipulations of special interest groups seeking only their own gain." Heider paused for a moment, allowing his words to sink into the enthusiastic minds of the crowd. "My friends! Today, we stand on the precipice of greatness," he then proclaimed, his voice resonating through the vast arena. "Together, we will restore America's glory, fight against the decay that has festered within our nation's soul, and usher in a new era of prosperity and righteousness!"

His words were met with thunderous applause, a tidal wave of affirmation that shook the very foundations of the Convention Center, punctuated by chants of *Heider President!* Pierre-Antoine could not help but be impressed by John's magnetism, the way he seemed to weave a spell over the assembled crowd and draw them into his vision of a reborn America.

"Freedom is not merely a gift bestowed by providence," John declared with the confidence of one ordained for higher purpose. "America must stand strong and united against the forces that seek to undermine our founding ideals. We cannot allow our borders to be breached by those who would exploit our generosity. We cannot keep taking all the misery of the world!" His words ignited a fervent cheer from the crowd, many of whom had been stirred to a near frenzy by his rhetoric. "National security," he continued, voice resonating with the gravitas of ancient prophecy, "is not just about the strength of our military—it's about the sanctity of our values. Values that are under siege by those who would distort the fabric of our society. They claim they have rights. Indeed, they do. But so do we! The ones bestowed by our founding fathers to all of us, not solely to specific groups. We thought for those rights, and we stand ready to fight again to preserve them." *We stand ready!* answered the crowd.

Pierre-Antoine felt a chill at these words, recognizing the insidious subtext that underpinned the rhetoric. For within those carefully crafted phrases lay darker undertones: an insinuation of xenophobia that cloaked itself in patriotism, a veiled prejudice masquerading as concern for cultural integrity.

"Let us not be led astray by the false prophets of political correctness," John intoned, his voice a clarion call that resonated through the cavernous hall. "They would have you believe that all paths lead to heaven, that all lifestyles merit equal validation. But I say unto you, there are forces at work seeking to undermine the very cornerstones of our civilization."

The coded language did not escape the Frenchman. It was a masterclass in manipulation; a way to stoke the fires of bigotry without overtly fanning the flames, a nod to the conspiracies that whispered of shadowy cabals and moral decay.

"Remember," Heider's voice crescendoed, riding the wave of mounting fervour, "the fight for America is a crusade against the corrupt establishment that shackles the true patriots. We must unmask the deceivers, the usurpers of freedom! Will you stand with me, my fellow Americans? he cried out, his voice imbued with a passion that bordered on the messianic. "Will you join me in reclaiming our great nation, in restoring her to the pinnacle of righteousness and glory?

The response was deafening - a chorus of voices raised in affirmation, a cacophony of devotion that drowned out all else. And as the echoes of *John President!* swelled once more, filling the air with a resonance that seemed to transcend time and space, Pierre-Antoine understood the gravity of the game being played. The Covenant, with its labyrinthine machinations, had found its champion—a man whose public persona was as much a construct as the stage from which he now commanded the hearts and minds of a nation.

The Republican candidate descended the stage steps, his face beaming with confidence and determination, while cutting a path through the throng of fervent supporters that swelled like a tide around him. The Frenchman watched, almost in awe, as hands reached out to touch the hem of John's suit, as if brushing against something sacred. He moved among them with a messianic grace, bestowing smiles and handshakes, each gesture a benediction upon the faithful who had congregated in this modern-day temple of democracy.

"Governor Heider!" they called, their voices saturated with hope and reverence. "Lead us back to greatness!"

With a practised ease, Heider posed for selfies and photographs, his chiselled features alight with a fire that seemed to pierce the very soul of the camera lens. His charisma was palpable, an aura that drew the masses into his orbit, their chants rising in a frenzy that bordered on religious ecstasy.

Pierre-Antoine felt a firm hand on his shoulder. He turned to find Robert Kay at his side, his eyes gleaming with pride and excitement.

"Look at him," he gestured towards John. "He is young, handsome, intelligent, and God-fearing. Everything America needs to be led back onto the righteous track. Now, come," Kay enjoined, guiding Pierre-Antoine through the throng of jubilant supporters. "There's someone I'd like you to meet."

They navigated the sea of people, their fervour ebbing and flowing like the tide. At last, they arrived at a quieter corner of the convention centre, where a small group had gathered around a stout man in his late fifties. His grey hair was slicked back, and his piercing blue eyes scanned the room with a mix of scrutiny and disdain.

"Pierre-Antoine, let me introduce you to Edward Mac-Corkindale," Kay announced, his voice betraying a note of reverence, "the Governor of Louisiana and our esteemed nominee for Vice President. Edward, this is Pierre-Antoine Lascombes, former French minister for foreign affairs and a valued ally from across the waters."

"An honour, Mr. Lascombes," MacCorkindale intoned, his handshake firm, the clasp of a man who believed destiny was something to be firmly grasped, not merely awaited.

"Likewise," Pierre-Antoine replied, the formality of his accent contrasting sharply with the Southern drawl of his interlocutor. "But please, call me Pierre-Antoine."

"With pleasure," MacCorkindale replied, his voice cold and measured. "I've heard many songs of praise about you from Bob, here. We are grateful for your presence among us. I can only imagine the stark contrast to your previous surroundings," he remarked, gesturing around the arena with a sweeping motion of his arm.

"Indeed. This is not the type of pageant we are accustomed to in Europe."

"I assume so." Edward paused a moment, his gaze fixed on Pierre-Antoine in a calculated manner. "Bob told me about your misfortune in France. It must have been quite a blow for you. But, I guess, one man's misfortune is another man's gain."

"These are the principles of democracy," Pierre-Antoine responded with a hint of irritation. He was beginning to develop a strong dislike for the man.

"Democracy is beautiful in theory. In practice, it is a fallacy. We, at the Covenant, believe that the only way to achieve a fair and just government is by adhering to God's laws and principles. He then turned to the crowd devotedly cheering at John, who was taking the stage once more. "Look at them," MacCorkindale said. "See how they revere him. John is the messenger of our revival, a saintly figure they follow without hesitation."

"The history of saints is mainly the history of insane people. That's also from Mussolini," the Frenchman replied icily.

"Are you alleging our John might suffer from insanity, Pierre-Antoine?"

"One could argue that dedicating one's entire existence to the pursuit of power suggests a certain level of mental instability. After all, what is a politician if not someone who strongly believes in their own divine purpose?"

"Hmm. Interesting concept …"

"However, I look at Governor Heider and I see a strong leader, one who will no doubt usher in a new era of prosperity and righteousness."

"Ah, but it is not enough simply to have a strong leader," MacCorkindale countered, his gaze locking once more onto Pierre-Antoine's like a vice. "We must also ensure that our country is guided by the divine will of our Lord. Only then can we truly triumph over the forces of darkness that threaten to tear us asunder."

The Frenchman felt the air thicken, the palpable shift in the atmosphere as MacCorkindale expounded upon his vision—a regressive utopia where theocratic ideals overshadowed civil liberties. The vice-presidential nominee spoke of a new America, one where Christian dominion was absolute, and presidential decrees were divine mandates.

"Liberty," he proclaimed, no longer measuring his words, "is not the licence to act against God's will. It is the freedom to follow His path without the interference of mortal laws."

Pierre-Antoine's discomfort mounted, his senses assailed by the scent of zealotry mingling with the musk of ambition. Around him, a chorus of assent rose from the nearby delegates, their applause a thunderous affirmation of MacCorkindale's extreme doctrines. Women's autonomy, the sanctity of expression, the right to choose—all cast aside, sacrificial lambs on the altar of fanaticism.

"Imagine," the VP candidate continued, his voice swelling with exhilaration, "a presidency unbound by the fetters of the judiciary or legislature. One that answers only to the highest authority."

"But that would result in dictatorship," reacted Pierre-Antoine with stupor.

"Here comes the fancy language," jeered one delegate. "No, Mr Lascombes, we simply believe in a strong leadership guided by God's benevolence. And only until those deviant liberals are silenced once and for all."

"Hear, hear," approved several others.

The words hung in the air like a noxious cloud, and Pierre-Antoine found himself struggling for breath.

"Edward here has some...unorthodox views on certain issues," Kay interjected, detecting the Frenchman's uneasiness and attempting to defuse the tension. "But his passion and dedication are beyond reproach."

"Unorthodox?" MacCorkindale scoffed, his lip curling with disdain. "I call them necessary. This nation was founded upon Christian principles - it is high time we returned to them. Women's place is in their homes, just as our forefathers intended. Freedom of speech must be tempered with responsibility, lest it become a weapon in the hands of our enemies. And as for abortion, gender neutrality, transgenderism ...well, I hardly need to elaborate on the abomination that they represent."

Pierre-Antoine felt a chill running down his spine, his stomach churning with revulsion. And yet, he couldn't help but notice the approving nods and murmurs that rippled through the nearby crowd. These were not the ramblings of a madman, but the carefully considered beliefs of a politician who knew exactly how to appeal to his base.

"Edward speaks the truth," one woman whispered, her eyes shining with fervour. "He's the incarnation of the strong hand this country needs."

"Governor Heider may have charisma," another man agreed, "but it's MacCorkindale who will steer us back onto the path of righteousness."

And so it was that Pierre-Antoine found himself caught in a maelstrom of conflicting emotions, torn between the captivating allure of Heider's rhetoric and the chilling reality of MacCorkindale's vision. Before him laid the machinations of power, the convergence of politics and piety—a nexus where the covenant of old would shape the destiny of nations.

"May God help us all," he murmured under his breath, as the chant of *Heider-MacCorkindale!* thundered through the hall like a harbinger of doom.

***

Backstage of the Dallas Convention Center, Pierre-Antoine threaded through a labyrinth of corridors, the cacophony of the crowd fading into a distant echo. He moved with purpose, but not without trepidation, for he was about to have his first face to face with John Heider since his return to America. He had not seen John in over a decade, and yet, the memories of their time together remained as vivid as a fresco painted upon the walls of his mind. It was a strange sensation, to be both drawn and repelled by the prospect of their reunion—a testament to the complexities of the human heart.

As he approached the designated meeting point, Pierre-Antoine stopped short. Through the slightly ajar door of a dressing room, he glimpsed his former lover, his composure as impeccable as his tailored suit, leaning in with a conspirator's intimacy towards a youthful campaign aide. The young man, doe-eyed and flushed, absorbed John's honeyed words like a thirsty flower soaking up rain. It was a fleeting flirtation, deftly executed, leaving Pierre-Antoine unsettled by the familiar charm that now ensnared another.

Gathering his composure, the Frenchman stepped into John's line of sight. Their eyes met, and a decade's worth of history flashed between them.

"John," Pierre-Antoine began, his voice even but tight with unspoken emotion.

"Pierre-Antoine," he responded, quickly dismissing the aide, his grin a practised facade. "How wonderful to see you again after all these years."

"Likewise," the Frenchman replied, his mouth suddenly dry. "I must say, your speech was… electrifying."

"Thank you," Heider said, his smile not quite reaching his eyes. "And thank you for lending your support. Your presence strengthens our cause," he added, clapping a hand on Pierre-Antoine's shoulder, a simulacrum of camaraderie. "We are poised to reclaim this nation's glory."

"Indeed. To restore what has been lost."

"Now, if you'll excuse me, I should get back to the convention floor," John said abruptly, a glance at his watch prompting the end of their reunion. "It was nice seeing you. We'll speak again soon."

As Pierre-Antoine watched the Republican candidate walking away, a gnawing unease settled within him. It was clear that John's public image of a devoted husband was but a mask hiding forbidden desires. How could he reconcile his support for such a man with his own moral compass? And what of the Covenant, the shadowy organisation that had brought them all together?

11

Pierre-Antoine slunk his way through the crowds of delegates and participants, moving as quietly as possible to avoid drawing attention. He needed a moment of peace and quiet to carefully consider his options. Despite his desperate attempts to find a way out, he was constantly pushed back by the unyielding multitude in the arena, like a skiff struggling desperately against the tide. Just as the Frenchman was about to give up hope, a side door abruptly swung open, giving way to a group of delegates. Without hesitation, he darted inside and found himself in an empty corridor, where he took a moment to catch his breath before moving on. As he rounded a corner, Pierre-Antoine's ears caught the murmurs of a hushed conversation emanating from a dimly lit room. He hesitated, gripped by an inexplicable instinct that compelled him to draw closer and listen in. He instantly recognised the distinct Southern twang of Edward MacCorkindale.

"John may have managed to charm these simple-minded delegates," whispered the VP nominee, his voice dripping with disdain, "but we both know he's far too soft on certain matters. At one point, his convictions will need to be *strengthened*."

"Indeed," replied the shadowed figure of a high-ranking Covenant member, his tone conspiratorial. "But rest assured, we have ways of ensuring his compliance once he takes office if he decides to go astray."

The chill in Pierre-Antoine's spine deepened as he heard the unmistakable threat in their words. He held his breath, straining to hear more.

"His little... indiscretions," the voice continued with palpable malice, "would undoubtedly bring his house of cards crashing down around him if revealed. Remember, the organisation is relying on you to be the power behind the throne."

"And so will I," replied MacCorkindale without an ounce of hesitation. I'll make sure he remembers where his loyalty lies—or the world will know of his... depravities."

A sickening realisation dawned upon Pierre-Antoine; these men knew of John's sexual inclinations, yet they not only turned a blind eye but sought to exploit them for their own nefarious purposes. With this revelation seared into his consciousness, the Frenchman sought out John, navigating the labyrinthine backstage corridors until he found him alone, staring at his reflection in the mirror—a modern-day Narcissus entrapped by his own visage.

"John," he called softly, catching his former lover's attention. "May we speak privately?"

Heider turned and glanced at Pierre-Antoine with a guarded expression, his eyes flickering like candle flames in the darkness. "Very well," he conceded, leading them to a secluded corner.

"John, we must address the past between us," said Pierre-Antoine, his voice wavering.

John's gaze remained fixed on the distant horizon, unwilling to face the Frenchman's eyes. "There is nothing for us to discuss," he replied coldly.

"Ah, but there is," Pierre-Antoine insisted, his voice cracking as he continued. "Your betrayal and rejection left me heartbroken, John. I thought what we had was real."

"Real?" Heider mocked, finally turning to face him. "What happened between us was nothing more than a carnal misstep – one that I thank God every day for saving me from."

Pierre-Antoine resisted the urge to scoff, his chest tightening with indignation. "My feelings for you were real, John. They still are."

"Feelings?" John spat the word as if it were venom. "Our dalliance was a sin, nothing more."

"Says the man whom I caught flirting with that young aide just this morning."

"Preposterous!" John spat, his cheeks flushed with anger. "You have no right to accuse me of such things!"

"Perhaps not," Pierre-Antoine conceded, "But it seems to me that your image as the perfect Christian family man is merely a mask – one that hides the truth of your closeted inclinations."

"Enough!" Heider roared, his fists clenched in rage. "How dare you?"

"At least I am not the one the Covenant plans to manipulate."

"What figment of your imagination is this?"

"Edward MacCorkindale and his ilk are planning to use your secrets against you, John!" Pierre-Antoine exclaimed, desperation etching across his face. "They know about your clandestine affairs with men, and they won't hesitate to expose them if you don't comply with their plans!"

"Nonsense!" Heider's face contorted with fury. "I will not stand for your lies! I am the Covenant's herald, tasked with bringing this nation back to its moral roots under the guidance of God's principles."

"Open your eyes, John," Pierre-Antoine said. "You've been manipulated by the Covenant all your life. You are nothing but a toy to them, easily replaced or discarded once you have served your purpose."

"Manipulated?" John sneered, his eyes narrowing as he glared at the Frenchman with malice. "No, my dear Pierre-Antoine, it is you who fails to grasp the grand design. Did you think they brought you here for your political acumen? No. You're here to ensure your silence—to keep buried our shared past until after the election."

Shock engulfed the Frenchman like a tidal wave, leaving him breathless and lost.

"Look at you, now," Heider mocked. "Poor little Pierre-Antoine, realising he is nothing but a French poodle on a leash."

The Frenchman stumbled away from John, his mind reeling with feelings of betrayal and disappointment. He quickly fled, weaving his way through the labyrinth of hallways like a crazed individual. Heider's merciless cackling echoing in his mind. He ran until he could run no more, stopping in a state of complete exhaustion, both physically and mentally drained. His thoughts raced as he recalled the countless manipulations by the Covenant, and suddenly understanding that he had been nothing more than a pawn in their intricate game.

After a long pause, the maelstrom of his mind receded and his disillusionment became hanger. Then he began to roam the convention center frantically, like a fierce predator on the prowl, scanning every corner for his prey. He finally caught Robert Kay off guard in a crowded hallway and physically dragged him into an isolated alcove.

"Bob," Pierre-Antoine began, his voice laced with the venom of disillusionment. "Your handiwork is nothing short of Judas's kiss—betrayal hidden behind the guise of divine intervention."

"What's going on with you now, Pierre-Antoine?" asked his former mentor calmly. "You always had a flair for the dramatic. A French trait, I suppose."

"John just informed me of the true reason for my presence here – not for my expertise, but to ensure that I do not accidentally reveal our shared history and keep his deepest secrets hidden. Your act of forgiveness was merely a ploy to keep me on a leash. Is there no end to the lies your deceitful mind can conjure?"

Kay, an edifice of austere faith, stared at him intensely. The lines on his face were like the etchings on ancient stone tablets, each one a testament to years spent in service to a power beyond earthly realms. "Pierre-Antoine," he said, his tone a practised blend of paternal concern and unyielding conviction. "The path of righteousness often winds through the valley of deception. We are protectors of a higher order, and our actions are guided by the Almighty."

"The Almighty?" the Frenchman spat, anger bubbling within him. "Do not hide behind divine providence when it suits you!"

"Every soul has its role," Robert Kay replied, unflinching before Pierre-Antoine's vehemence. "And occasionally, the end justifies the means. Your presence here secures John's ascension, and with it, our vision for a world governed by the laws of the Creator."

"And what about Edward MacCorkindale plotting to puppeteer John once crowned?" Pierre-Antoine retorted, the taste of betrayal bitter upon his tongue. "I overheard him discussing with one of your lackeys about his design to coerce him with threats of exposure, to twist his arm until it breaks. Is this also part of your *vision for a world governed by the laws of the Creator?*"

"Again, you are overexaggerating the facts, my dear Mr Lascombes. Edward indeed has his shortcomings, but—"

"Shortcomings? the Frenchman exclaimed in disbelief. That man is nothing but a fanatic, the worst kind I've seen in my years on the political arena! His ideas are so archaic and backwards that they sound like something spewed from the mouth of a delusional preacher, not a potential vice president.

I can't help but feel like the catastrophic event of 2024 is happening all over again right before my eyes. Haven't you learned your lesson from it?"

"We have," Bob replied composedly. "That is why he was only chosen as our VP nominee. He appeals to a particular fringe of our electorate, while John's more moderate views reassure the moderate voters. You know as well as I do that it's the middle ground that wins elections. Incumbent President Thomas has been slipping in the polls lately, in addition to having lost the majority in the House. We must capitalise on the undecided moderate electorate. The Covenant is perfectly in control of the narrative."

"And what if your creature becomes insubordinate once in power, or if John…"

"John is a healthy young man, Pierre-Antoine," Kay replied with a tinge of irritation. "And Edward's zealotry is well within the folds of our strategy. Fear not, for even the most fervent flames are contained within the hearth of our purpose."

"You are treading on dangerous ground, Robert, and one misstep could lead to catastrophic consequences for us all."

"And this is why the Covenant still needs your expertise in world affairs, my friend."

"I won't be swayed by your smooth talks anymore, Bob," Pierre-Antoine said distrustfully. Save them for some gullible person."

"Despite all we have to offer you in return?"

"You are hopeless!" the Frenchman scoffed. "No, I'm done with your countless lies and will leave this place by this evening. Nothing you can say will change my mind."

"Stay and your silence will be richly rewarded," Kay whispered, his voice dripping with honeyed temptation. "The Covenant will harness all its power and influence to support your future bid for the presidency of France."

Pierre-Antoine's breath caught in his throat as he struggled to process the devil's bargain laid abruptly before him. He was a pawn in this game of domination, but one whose silence could secure him a kingdom. First, the unexpected proposal weighed heavily on his conscience with a nauseous taste. Yet, the lure of power promptly sang its seductive siren's song deep within his heart.

"Think carefully, my friend," Robert murmured, his eyes never leaving the younger man's face. "Fortune favours the bold."

Pierre-Antoine stood alone in the shadowed alcove, away from the fervent spectacle that unfolded just beyond the heavy curtains of the convention stage. His mind, a maelstrom of thoughts and emotions, churned with the weight of revelation and deceit. He could feel the weight of Robert Kay's offer pressing down upon him. The Covenant had ensnared him in a web spun from shadows and whispered oaths, offering a throne in exchange for silence—a silence that would let falsehood fester and grow beneath the guise of sanctity.

"Is it not written," he murmured to himself, recalling the biblical tales of old, "that all kingdoms of the world and their splendour can be offered in temptation?" Robert Kay, much like that ancient tempter, promised dominion, yet at what cost?

Could he, like those pillars of faith, resist the lure of temporal power?

A sigh escaped him as he contemplated the grail of presidency dangled before him. The Covenant's machinations were a chalice from which he knew he should abstain, yet the nectar within was sweetened with the honey of potential and laced with the bitterness of betrayal. To expose them would be to stand against a tide that sought to sweep all before it; to join them was to sacrifice a part of his soul upon the altar of expediency. Pierre-Antoine closed his eyes, to better contemplate the crossroads of his destiny. And in that moment of self-reckoning, he felt the inexorable pull of gravity towards the path of least resistance.

"Fortune favours the bold," he whispered, his voice lost amidst the rising crescendo of acclamation from the arena. Yet, even as the adage left his lips, he wondered if true boldness lay in conquest or in the courage to unveil the truth. But the die was cast, and with the solemnity of one who walks willingly into the lion's den, Pierre-Antoine stepped back into the light, his decision sealed within the silent chambers of his heart. He chose to put on the mask of deceit, to play the part scripted for him by the grand architect of the Covenant's design. He chose power over providence.

"*Heider President! Heider President!*" The chant was a clarion call, heralding the dawn of a new era—an era in which Pierre-Antoine would ascend, though the ascent came tethered to a hidden price. In the end, it was the intoxicating allure of influence that bound his tongue, combined with the bittersweet feeling of revenge for past injustices. As the throng's voices swelled to a fever pitch, echoing the triumphs and tragedies of ages past, Pierre-Antoine stood transfixed, a man betwixt damnation and deliverance, while the arena thundered with the sound of destiny unfolding.

12

The Grand Hall of Charleston Convention Center hummed with a nervous energy, the grand Exhibit Hall packed with supporters of John Heider's presidential campaign. Red, white and blue balloons bobbed above the sea of "Make America Godly Again" hats as all eyes fixated on the massive video screens suspended from the ceiling. With bated breath, the crowd watched as the news anchors methodically declared each state, cheers erupting when a state turned red for Heider, boos cascading when one flipped blue for the Democrats. The electoral map gradually filled in like a stained-glass window, a mosaic of the nation's divide.

In a private lounge tucked away from the fervour, an air of trepidation hung heavy. John Heider paced the plush carpet, his eyes fixed on the flickering numbers that would determine his fate. Beside him, Edward MacCorkindale leaned against the wall, arms crossed, eyes narrowed at the mosaic of screens. Their wives sat stiffly on the leather couch, hands clasped in silent prayers, while their children fidgeted restlessly. Campaign advisors and managers typed furiously on laptops and spoke in hushed, urgent tones on their phones. Robert Kay, the evangelist puppet master of the Covenant, stood by the window, his weathered face an inscrutable mask.

Florida goes red! The anchor's voice boomed through the hall, unleashing a tempest of cheers and waving banners.

John allowed himself a small smile, but his stomach churned with an anxiety he dared not show. He turned to his campaign manager, whispering, "What are the chances in our path now?"

Before an answer could come, the screens flashed again. *New Hampshire to the Democrats.*

John's gaze swept the room, taking in the worried eyes of his inner circle. His wife, Sarah, clutched their youngest child to her chest, her smile strained, while MacCorkindale paced like a caged lion, muttering calculations under his breath.

"The race is tight, just as we predicted," Robert intoned, his voice cutting through the tension like a knife. "But fear not, for the Lord favours those who walk in His light. The polls were clear after the second debate - John is the anointed one, destined to lead this nation back to righteousness."

"Polls aren't votes, Bob," John interrupted, harsher than he intended. He softened his tone. "But you're right, we're still in this fight."

In the corner, Pierre-Antoine observed the scene with a detached fascination, an outsider peering into the inner sanctum of power. He studied John, noting the tautness of his shoulders, the flicker of uncertainty in his piercing blue eyes. For a man who exuded such confidence on the campaign trail, who rallied the faithful with fiery condemnations of the 'deep state' and vows to restore America's moral backbone, John seemed uncharacteristically vulnerable at this moment. A sliver of doubt wormed its way into Pierre-Antoine's mind - could it be that the Covenant's chosen vessel, their modern-day David, might fall short of slaying the Democratic Goliath?

"Ohio goes to Heider!" a campaign manager exclaimed, prompting a round of relieved sighs and muttered hallelujahs. But the reprieve was short-lived as the anchor of a news network announced, *'California, with its 54 electoral votes, is called for incumbent President Thomas'.*

John slumped into a chair, his head in his hands. His wife rubbed his back soothingly, whispering scriptures to bolster his resolve. Edward poured himself a whiskey, downing it in one harsh gulp. Robert, stepping aside, remained stoic, his gaze never wavering from the screens.

Heider's gaze drifted to Pierre-Antoine's solitary figure, his hazel eyes inscrutable as they met his. For a moment, he felt stripped bare, all his carefully constructed facades crumbling under that knowing look. *What if we lose?* The thought creeped through John's mind, unbidden and terrifying. He pushed the doubts away, steeling himself for the long night ahead.

The tension in the lounge reached a crescendo as CNN's main anchor, her voice resonating with the gravity of the moment, announced the latest development.

'It is 7:30 am EST, and let's have a look at the current situation. With all states reporting except for Maine's second congressional district, the electoral vote count stands at 269 for President Julius T. Thomas and 268 for Governor John F. Heider. If the Democrats secure Maine's second district, they will reach the 270 electoral votes needed to win the presidency. However, should the Republicans take it, we'll have a tie at 269 each. In that scenario, with Republicans now holding the majority in the House, the Governor. Heider would likely become our next president.'

Inside the lounge, a flurry of activity erupted as advisors frantically dialled their contacts in the House, seeking assurances of unwavering support in case of a tie[15]. Robert Kay's hand landed heavily on his protégé's shoulder. "Fear not, John," he said, his voice brimming with misplaced confidence. "Maine's second district will be ours, and with it, the keys to the White House. The Lord has ordained it."

John nodded, but couldn't shake the dread coiling in his gut. He glanced at Pierre-Antoine, still observing from his corner. The man's face was a mask of stoic resignation, and the American found himself envying that calm.

The hours crawled by, each passing moment a test of faith and fortitude. At 11:30 am, as fatigue and uncertainty reached

---

[15]In the US presidential election, if neither candidate gets a majority of the 538 electoral votes after the Electors meet, the election for President is decided in the House of Representatives, with each state delegation having one vote. A majority of states (26) is needed to win. Senators would elect the Vice-President, with each Senator having a vote. A majority of Senators (51) is needed to win. The procedure is called contingent election and happened three times in US history: 1801, 1825 and 1837.

their zenith, the news finally broke. The anchors, their voices tinged with a mix of exhaustion and excitement, delivered the verdict: *After three recounts, CNN can now project that President Julius T. Thomas has won Maine's second congressional district by a margin of 588 votes. This gives him the 270 electoral votes needed to secure a second term as President of the United States.*

In the lounge, a stunned silence gave way to a chorus of disbelief and outrage Edward MacCorkindale's voice, sharp and insistent, cut through the din.

"John, you can't let this stand. You need to contest these results immediately. Five hundred and eighty-eight votes? That's nothing. We can easily overturn this in Maine."

Heider, his expression a battleground of conflicting emotions, shook his head. "No, Ed. We can't go down that path at the risk of repeating what happened in 2020. Our country is already deeply divided. Challenging the outcome, even for such a small margin of 170 votes, would only further weaken our already fragile institutions. I won't be responsible for—"

"Responsible?" Edward snarled, stepping closer. "You'll be responsible for throwing away everything we've worked for if you don't fight this." He glared at Kay. "I warned you his shoulders weren't broad enough!" Then turning back to his running mate, MacCorkindale's eyes narrowed, his voice dropping to a menacing whisper. "You'll do as you're told, John. Unless you want your little secrets splashed across every front page from here to San Francisco. The Covenant didn't invest all this time and resources in you just to watch you throw it away over a misguided sense of nobility."

Heider felt the blood drain from his face. "I..." he began, his voice faltering.

Pierre-Antoine observed the scene with a growing sense of unease and pity for the man he once knew. In the harsh light of defeat, the true nature of the Covenant's grip on John Heider became starkly apparent. Like a marionette tangled in its own strings, the once Republican saviour seemed to deflate before his eyes, the weight of his role as the Covenant's puppet finally sinking in.

The chaos that erupted within the Charleston Convention Center following the announcement of John Heider's defeat was palpable, a living entity that pulsed through the gathered crowd like an electric current. Shock, disbelief, and simmering anger rippled through the sea of faces, their dreams of victory shattered by a mere 170 votes in a distant corner of the nation.

Amidst the tumult, John Heider strode onto the stage, his presence commanding an instant hush. Eyes blazing with a fervour that bordered on the messianic, he gripped the podium, his knuckles white against the dark wood.

"My fellow Americans," he began, his voice booming through the cavernous space, "we stand at a crossroads in our nation's history. The forces of corruption and deceit have conspired to steal this election from us, to silence the voice of the true American people."

The defeated crowd suddenly erupted with renewed energy, their roars echoing throughout the Grand Hall in a deafening wave of approval.

"My team and I have come to the firm conclusion that this election was rigged, manipulated by the very establishment we sought to overthrow!" John continued, his fist pounding the air. "All the polls were showing a clear lead in my favour in several key-states. This is evidence the deep state is actively working against us, against the American people!" His words were met with outbursts of fury and animosity. "But we will not be cheated. I stand before you today to declare that we will petition the Maine Supreme Judicial Court for a full recount. Believe me when I say we will not rest until every single valid ballot has been accounted for, no matter how many times it takes, until the truth is revealed!"

As the audience erupted into a frenzy of cheers and chants of '*Heider President! Heider President!*', Pierre-Antoine watched from the wings, his heart heavy with foreboding. He had witnessed this passion before during his ministerial tenure, in the determined gazes of multitudes uniting to overthrow an unjust government. But here, in the heart of American democracy, that same passion threatened to tear the very fabric of the nation into pieces.

***

The weeks that followed saw the nation plunged into a maelstrom of discord. Every news channel, every social media platform became a battleground of heated debates and accusations. Pierre-Antoine spent most of his time in his hotel room, observing the escalating chaos every day as the tension reached its zenith, culminating in the Maine Supreme Judicial Court's unanimous decision to uphold the election results.

The response was swift and violent. Far-right groups and Republican supporters flooded the streets of major cities, their protests devolving into riots that raged like wildfires across the urban landscape. John Heider appeared on every news channel, his face a mask of righteous indignation as he railed against the 'activist judges' and 'Democrat conspirators' who sought to undermine the will of the people. In his continuing refusal to accept defeat, he would now take his case to the Supreme Court in pursuit of justice.

When will this end? Unable to remain silent any longer, the Frenchman reached for his phone, his fingers trembling as he dialled Robert Kay's number.

"Bob, it's Pierre-Antoine. We must put an end to this madness before it's too late," he pleaded. "Can't you see the damage that's being done? To the country? To the world?"

But Kay's voice was cool and unperturbed, a stark contrast to the chaos engulfing the nation. "My friend, you worry too much. Everything is under control. The Covenant has a plan, and we will see it through to the end. Once John is confirmed as the new president, all of this foolishness will finally come to an end. Trust in the will of God, and all will be well."

As the call ended, Pierre-Antoine sank back against the pillows, his mind reeling with the implications of Kay's words. *A plan?* The thought sent a jolt of terror down his spine. To what extent would the Covenant go to in order to see their vision realised?

Meanwhile, in the dimly lit confines of the Covenant House, Robert Kay addressed the assembly of prominent members, his usual confidence wavering slightly.

"Gentlemen, I won't mince words. The Supreme Court is a lost cause," Kay admitted, his voice heavy with resignation. "Perhaps it's time we considered conceding the election, regroup and plan for the next—"

"No!" MacCorkindale's chair scraped harshly against the floor as he stood, his face flushed with anger. "Concede? After everything we've accomplished? Never. We've come too far to back down now. There's still one last resort, one final play that will ensure our victory."

As the assembled members leaned forward, their eyes glittering with anticipation, the Louisianan smiled, a cold, predatory grin which sent a chill through even Kay's seasoned mind. "Gentlemen," he said, his voice barely above a whisper, "let me tell you about our next course of action…"

And in the lengthening shadows of the Covenant's inner sanctum, the fate of a nation - and perhaps the world - hung in the balance, poised on the knife's edge between salvation and damnation.

13

The bitter wind of New Year's Day whipped across Charleston, West Virginia, as a sea of humanity gathered before the imposing façade of the State Capitol. Flags bearing the visage of John Heider fluttered in the wind, a testament to the unwavering devotion of his followers. Pierre-Antoine stood at the edge of the stage, his breath misting in the frigid air as he watched John approach the podium. The man's aura was undeniable, his charismatic smile belying the fire that smouldered within his soul.

"My fellow Americans," he began, his voice resonating through the air like the clarion call of a prophet, "today, we stand at the precipice of destiny, poised to reclaim what is rightfully ours!"

The crowd erupted in a deafening roar, their voices rising in a cacophonous symphony of defiance and rebellion. John raised his hands, drinking in their adulation like a man parched for validation.

"They sought to silence us, to bury the truth beneath a mountain of lies and deceit," he thundered, his eyes blazing with righteous fury. "But we will not be silenced! We will not be denied! Just two more days until SCOTUS delivers its ruling and the truth is exposed to the world. My friends, stay steadfast in your belief. I will be declared the rightful winner of this election!"

The Frenchman watched as John wove his spell, his words ensnaring the hearts and minds of his followers. Yet even as he marvelled at the American's oratorical prowess, a sense of unease coiled in the pit of his stomach, a serpentine whisper of the calamity to come. As Heider's speech reached its crescendo, the crowd surged forward, their hands outstretched in a desperate bid to touch their saviour. John descended from the stage, wading into the sea of humanity with the confidence of a messiah, shaking hands and offering platitudes to the adoring masses.

"We're going to win this, folks," John reassured a group of supporters, his voice carrying over the din. "The courts will see the truth. Have faith!"

Pierre-Antoine trailed in his wake, his mind spinning with the implications of Heider's words. How long, he wondered, could this charade continue? How long before the façade crumbled, revealing the rot that festered at the heart of the Covenant's grand design? Lost in his thoughts, he barely registered the sudden commotion that rippled through the crowd. It wasn't until the sharp cracks of gunfire rent the air that he snapped back to reality, his eyes widening in horror as he saw

John crumple to the ground, blood blossoming across his crisp white shirt.

Chaos erupted, screams mingling with the stampede of panicked feet as security personnel swarmed the shooter, tackling him to the ground with brutal efficiency. But it was too late. Pierre-Antoine stood frozen, his mind refusing to process the scene before him. John Heider, the man who had captivated millions, lay motionless on the cold ground, his life seeping away into the indifferent dust of the West Virginia State Capitol grounds. Then, pulling himself together, he rushed to John's side, his heart shattering with each faltering step. "John!" he cried, his voice lost in the cacophony of screams and chaos. "Someone helps! We need a doctor!" But no one came, not even his security too busy, it seemed, dealing with the perpetrator. Finally, Pierre-Antoine managed to grab one of his aides amidst the chaotic scene, her face contorting in shock as she saw the gruesome sight. "Get help, quick!" he commanded. "There may still be a chance to save him."

The aide hesitated for a moment before rushing off to get assistance. Heider's eyes, once blazing with charisma and conviction, now fluttered weakly.

"Pierre-Antoine," he gasped, his voice barely audible above the din.

"I'm here, John," the Frenchman whispered, fighting back tears. "Hold on, please. Help is coming."

"Pierre-Antoine," the American whispered, his voice weakening, "forgive me… for everything…" His hand grasped weakly at his former lover's sleeve. "I was … a fool … I … loved … you and … I never… stopped loving you," he confessed, each word a struggle. "Forgive me... for betraying you. Forgive me ... my love."

Pierre-Antoine's heart clenched, years of pain and longing crashing over him like a tidal wave. "I forgive you, John," he choked out, tears now flowing freely. "Just stay with me. The paramedics are on their way."

John's eyes seemed to clear for a moment, a flicker of his old intensity returning. "The Covenant," he wheezed, urgency in his tone. "They... they sacrificed me ... For the cause."

The Frenchman leaned closer, straining to hear. "What do you mean? John, what are you saying?"

But Heider's strength was fading rapidly. His grip on Pierre-Antoine's arm loosened, his gaze becoming unfocused. With his last breath, he whispered, "Beware... the Covenant... Don't let ... them win ... Promise me..."

As John's eyes closed for the final time, Pierre-Antoine felt a piece of himself die along with the man he had once loved. The crowd's panic swelled around them, a tide of fear and confusion that threatened to sweep everything away. In that moment, cradling John's lifeless body, he realised that this was more than just an assassination. It was the death of an era, and the birth of something far more terrifying. The warnings about the Covenant echoed in his mind, a sinister portent of the darkness to come.

***

A sombre sea of black engulfed the streets of Charleston as tens of thousands gathered to bid their final farewell to John

Heider, the man they believed was destined to lead the nation to greatness and religious renaissance. The air hung heavy with a palpable mix of grief and anger, the collective heartbeat of the crowd pulsing with a shared sense of loss and betrayal.

Amidst the sea of mourners, accompanied by John's widow and orphans, Edward MacCorkindale took to the stage, his eyes blazing with a fervour that bordered on the fanatical.

"My fellow Americans," he began, his voice booming across the hushed crowd, "we gather here today not just to mourn the loss of a great man, but to bear witness to the insidious forces that conspired to silence him." The crowd murmured in assent, their whispers growing louder as MacCorkindale continued, his words dripping with venom. "John was more than a candidate, he was my running mate, my friend, our friend" he declared, his hands grasping the lectern tightly. "He was ... He was the true voice of the people. A voice ... brutally silenced by the very deep state that feared his ascension!"

Pierre-Antoine, standing at the edge of the stage, felt a chill run down his spine. John's final words echoed in his mind, *Beware ... the Covenant*. He watched MacCorkindale with growing unease, recognising the calculated ruthlessness in the man's eyes.

"In their arrogance and corruption, those despicable people who claim to be our representatives saw fit to remove the one man who dared to stand against them, the one man who symbolised America's renaissance." As his accusations grew more inflammatory, the crowd's anger swelled, their shouts of agreement punctuating his every word. "The so-called 'lone gunman' was no more than a puppet," MacCorkindale carried on, his voice rising. "A far-left extremist, manipulated by shadowy forces that would deny us our rightful victory!"

The crowd howled its approval, like a pack of wolves preparing for their next hunt. Pierre-Antoine's gaze darted to the small contingent of Democratic representatives, their faces pale with apprehension.

"My friends, make no mistake: John Heider's ignominious death is proof that he was the rightful winner of the Presidential election," MacCorkindale declared, his voice rising to a crescendo. "And yet, the authorities continue to cover up the truth, to silence those who dare to question their lies. But we will not be silenced. We will not be cowed. As one, we will stand and as one, we will fight. Together, we will honour the legacy of John Heider and fiercely defend the values that have forged our great nation!"

The mourners erupted in a frenzy of cheers and chants, their voices echoing through the streets of Charleston like a clarion call to arms. The Democratic representatives, fearing for their lives, fled the scene, barely escaping the clutches of the enraged mob. As the chaos unfolded before him, Pierre-Antoine felt a sinking realisation. This was more than a funeral; it was the birth of a movement, one that threatened to tear the very fabric of the nation apart.

In the days that followed Edward's speech, the country seemed to be on the brink of collapse. Riots erupted in major cities, with protestors clashing in the streets and law enforcement struggling to maintain order. In the Republican strongholds of the South and Midwest, angry citizens took to the streets, fuelled by MacCorkindale's words and convinced of their own righteousness. They demanded justice for John Heider, the fallen hero who had become a symbol of their cause, and denounced the supposed corruption and power-grabbing of the Democratic establishment.

In the Democrat-led states, counter-protests emerged, with citizens calling for an end to the violence and a return to the principles of unity and democracy. They mourned the loss of John Heider, but also condemned the dangerous rhetoric that had led to his death. And as the unrest spread from city to city, from coast to coast, it became clear that America's future was hanging in the balance. The country was divided, and it seemed that no one knew how to bridge the growing chasm.

As the situation escalated, President Thomas was forced to address the nation. In a sombre speech, he pleaded for calm and called for unity. He offered condolences to the family of John Heider on behalf of the nation and condemned the violence that had erupted in his name. He also denounced MacCorkindale's inflammatory speech and urged the country to reject his divisive message. But Edward was not backing down. In response to Thomas' speech, he called for a nationwide strike, urging his followers to stand together against what he saw as an oppressive government. The country held its breath, unsure of what would come next.

14

Amidst a chilling wind on 20 January 2053, at noon, President Thomas stood upon the Capitol steps with his hand resting on a worn Bible. The weight of the moment hung heavy in the air as he repeated the oath of office, each word laden with the gravity of the crisis facing the nation.

"I do solemnly swear that I will faithfully execute the Office of President of the United States, …"

Pierre-Antoine, watching from afar, couldn't help but wonder if this solemn ritual would be enough to hold together a country teetering on the brink of chaos. As Thomas finished his oath, the applause was muted, overshadowed by the tension that crackled through the air like static electricity before a storm. Then the newly re-inaugurated President stepped to the podium, his face etched with determination.

"My fellow Americans," he began, his voice steady despite the enormity of the challenges before him. "On this important day, symbolising the strength of our democratic institutions, we stand at a crossroads. For the second time in its history, our nation is facing a threat like no other - the threat of division."

The President paused, his piercing dark eyes scanning the crowd before him. He could sense the tension and unease in the air, but he refused to let it shake him.

"You are afraid. I am afraid. The future feels uncertain, and it seems like the fate of our Republic hangs in the hands of uncontrollable forces that could unravel everything we hold dear."

Time stood still as Thomas took a deep breath, his words hanging heavy in the air like a thick fog. The hushed crowd stood frozen, consumed by the deafening howls of the frigid winds and the haunting caws of the ravens circling above like harbingers of doom.

"But I have faith in the resilience and unity of the American people," he continued, his voice growing stronger. "We have faced similar challenges before and always emerged stronger, and we will do so again. On this day, we must remember that we are all Americans, bound by the ideals of freedom, equality, and justice for all. This is why we shouldn't fear because no matter what obstacles may come our way, we have the strength and determination to overcome them!"

After a moment of uncertainty, the crowd erupted into applause, and the President could feel their energy and renewed sense of determination. He continued, his words ringing out like a call to arms.

"We will rise above these challenges. We will come out stronger, more united, more resilient. We are a nation of fighters, and we will not back down!"

The applause grew louder, and Thomas' heart swelled with pride and hope. As he stepped away from the podium, he knew that his words had touched the souls of those gathered. They were ready to face whatever came their way, together.

At midnight on the same day, the news hit like a swift and unexpected blow. The states of Alabama, Arkansas, Kansas, Kentucky, Louisiana, Mississippi, Missouri, Oklahoma, Tennessee and West Virginia, under the leadership of Texas, declared their secession from the Union to form the United Confederation of America with Edward MacCorkindale as their president.

***

The Texas State Capitol in Austin buzzed with a feverish energy, its majestic dome seeming to pulse with the fervour of the large crowd gathered below. Edward MacCorkindale, escorted by the members of his newly appointed cabinet, strode onto the balcony, his eyes gleaming with a mixture of triumph and defiance. The roar of the assembled masses swelled as he raised his hands, a conqueror acknowledging his loyal subjects.

"My fellow patriots," his voice boomed, carrying the weight of history, "today, we reclaim our sovereignty!" The assembly erupted, their cheers echoing off the surrounding buildings like claps of thunder. "The great state of Texas, along with our brethren in Alabama, Arkansas, Kansas, Kentucky, Louisiana, Mississippi, Missouri, Oklahoma, Tennessee and West Virginia, hereby declare our secession from the corrupt Union!"

Cheers of excitement erupted across the Texas Confederate Memorial Lawn, rippling out into the surrounding streets of Austin. "The tyranny of Washington has gone unchecked for too long, and we will no longer bend to their will. And so," MacCorkindale's voice crescendoed, "I humbly accept the mantle of leadership as the first President of the United Confederation of America!"

The crowd's reaction was deafening, a cacophony of jubilation and righteous anger. As a group of individuals attempted to voice their disapproval and denounce the declaration, they were immediately met with physical aggression from those around them and apprehended by nearby law enforcement officers with force. Paying no attention to the brawl, the newly designated president continued his speech with unwavering determination.

"Moments ago, illegitimate President Thomas has declared a state of federal martial law, backed by his corrupted Congress. He now threatens with a full blockade unless we immediately stop, I quote, *all acts of rebellion against the rightful government of the United States of America*. The furious crowd erupted in a deafening roar of anger and cries of defiance. MacCorkindale raised his arms, silencing them with a commanding voice. "To President Thomas, I say this: we will not yield to your murderous regime! As my first act as president, I hereby order the federalisation of all our national guards and regiments. And I call upon every able-bodied citizen to join our forces in defence of our nation. Let it be known that we will respond with force if met with any violent threats towards our confederation!"

At those words, the assembly erupted into a frenzy of cheers and chants of '*U-C-A! U-C-A!*' With a cold, calculating gaze, MacCorkindale surveyed the lively celebration before him. Everything had unfolded exactly as he had planned. While he may not have achieved his ultimate goal of becoming President of the United States, he had successfully wrestled control of crucial states from the grasp of those despicable liberals. Under God's divine rule, the Confederation would be a shining example of righteousness in a decaying world. Before long, other states will rally their cause, realising the errors of their ways, and then the Covenant would be ready for the next phase of their master plan. MacCorkindale couldn't help but smile at the thought of their impending victory and the final realisation of their vision.

***

Pierre-Antoine's footsteps echoed through the marbled halls of the new Covenant's headquarters in Dallas, his heart heavy with the weight of the impending confrontation. He pushed open the ornate wooden doors to Robert Kay's office, finding the evangelist seated behind his desk, his eyes fixed on the multiple screens displaying the unfolding chaos.

"How could you let this happen, Robert?" the Frenchman's voice trembled with barely suppressed rage. "John is dead, the country is tearing itself apart, and you sit here like some detached puppeteer, pulling strings from the shadows."

Kay looked up, his gaze steely and unapologetic. "Pierre-Antoine, my dear friend, you fail to see the bigger picture. This is all part of God's plan, a necessary step towards the establishment of His kingdom on Earth."

"God's plan?" the Frenchman scoffed, his hands clenching into fists. "Just admit it, Bob. You've lost control. Your ambition and pride have blinded you to the suffering you've unleashed. The Covenant has blood on its hands, and John's death is a stain that will never wash away."

"Lost control?" Kay replied, a dismissive sneer playing on his lips. "The birth of a new world order is never without pain, my friend. What is that French expression? ... Oh, yes: *on ne fait pas d'omelette sans casser des oeufs*[16]. His lips curled into a thin smile. "John's sacrifice was regrettable but necessary. And now, with MacCorkindale at the helm of our new Confederation, we stand on the brink of true change. We will preserve what's left of this planet from the foolishness of men, by hook or by crook, if we must. Soon, our cause will prevail, and all shall bow before the righteous might of the Covenant."

As Kay spoke, Pierre-Antoine felt a chill run down his spine. He thought of John's last words, the warning about the Covenant. It all made a terrible, sickening sense now.

"You're insane," he whispered, his voice barely audible. "All of you."

Bob's expression hardened. "Insanity is continuing to believe in a system that has failed us time and time again. What we offer is salvation." He paused, studying Pierre-Antoine's face. "But I can see you're not ready to embrace this truth. For

---

[16] You don't make an omelette without braking eggs.

your own safety, and ours, I think it's time you take another extended vacation."

Before Pierre-Antoine could protest, the door opened, and two suited men entered. Kay nodded to them. "Please escort Mr. Lascombes to the airfield. Ensure he's comfortable on his journey."

For the second time in his existence, the Frenchman found himself surrounded by a team of bodyguards, being forcefully removed from the very people he had faithfully dedicated himself to serving.

"One more thing before you leave," Kay said, stopping the watchdogs a moment. "Remember, Pierre-Antoine, the Covenant's reach is vast, and you cannot escape your destiny. We made a pact with you and when the time comes, we intend to honour it."

"I'd rather meet my death than ever have to deal with you," the Frenchman retorted venomously.

"We shall see... Now, take him away," he commanded with a dismissive wave of his hand.

As Pierre-Antoine was led out, his mind reeled. He barely registered the drive to the private airstrip, the boarding of the sleek jet, or the take-off. It wasn't until they were airborne that reality began to sink in. He gazed out the window at the familiar patchwork landscape below, his reflection ghostly in the glass. Then, the image of Edward MacCorkindale, the self-proclaimed President of the United Confederation of America, appeared standing at a podium, his voice ringing with righteous fury.

"Today, in response to their aggressive actions, we hereby declare war against the tyranny of the so-called federal government of the United States," he proclaimed, his words igniting a fervour among the assembled crowd. "We will not bow to the oppressors who seek to strip us of our God-given rights. The United Confederation of America will rise, and we will fight until our last breath to preserve our way of life."

While the jet ascended, Pierre-Antoine watched the news footage of Confederate troops mobilizing, their faces set with grim determination. The once-united nation was again a battlefield, brother against brother, ideology against ideology. Looking through the window, he knew that the escalating conflict would bring dire consequences not only for the divided nation but also for the rest of the world, as they faced the potential collapse of US hegemony. In the distance, thunder rumbled ominously, a harbinger of the storm that was about to be unleashed upon them all.

SECOND INTERLUDE

Year 2069

15

The aisle was narrow and cramped, but Father Luca Calleja and Brother Willem de Vries managed to squeeze their way off the plane at last. As they emerged into the bustling terminal of Ben Gurion International Airport, Father Calleja took a deep breath, savouring the feeling of solid ground beneath his feet once more. Beside him, Brother de Vries stumbled slightly, his gangly limbs still unaccustomed to the sensation after hours of being folded into an aeroplane seat.

"Careful there, Brother," Father Calleja cautioned with a wry smile. "We can't have you face-planting before our holy mission even begins."

Brother de Vries shot him a mock glare, straightening his rumpled robes.

"Very amusing, Father. I'll have you know my sense of balance is second only to my unshakable faith."

Father Calleja chuckled, clapping the younger man on the shoulder as they made their way through the throng of travellers. All around them, a cacophony of voices rose and fell in a dozen different languages, punctuated by the occasional announcement over the loudspeaker. Wheeled suitcases clattered across the polished floor, and the acrid scent of jet fuel mingled with the aroma of strong coffee wafting from a nearby café.

As they navigated the winding corridors, Father Calleja felt a growing sense of anticipation building in his chest. For weeks, they scoured the internet and social media for any hints or leads that could potentially point them towards the whereabouts of Akhenaten's artifact. But, apart from the video released at the time of its discovery, their efforts were fruitless. Running out of options, the two priests received permission from the Vatican to explore the site where it was last seen and inquire about any potential eyewitness accounts that could provide clues about the stela's location.

Brother de Vries seemed to sense his companion's train of thought, for he leaned in conspiratorially as they walked.

"Do you really think we'll find it, Father?" he asked, his voice barely above a whisper. "The Relic, I mean."

Father Calleja paused, his brow furrowing in contemplation. In truth, he had his doubts — the memory of the night of the bombing and President Lascombes' announcement that he had secured the artefact still haunted him. The bigger question was whether it was still concealed in Jerusalem, or if it had been moved somewhere else, and if so, where?

"I have faith, Brother," he said at last, his tone solemn. "Faith in our mission, and in the guidance of a higher power. Whatever challenges lie ahead, we must trust in the path that has been laid before us. Let's take solace in the fact that we won't encounter the same troubles we faced during our last visit.

Brother de Vries nodded, his eyes shining with a fervent light.

"Amen to that, Father. Amen to that."

And so, they pressed on, two small figures in a sea of humanity, their hearts filled with a sense of purpose that transcended the mundane world around them.

The bustling streets of Tel Aviv rapidly gave way to the arid landscapes of the Judean hills. Father Calleja found himself lost in contemplation, wandering back to the sacred texts that told the stories of the prominent figures from the Bible who had shaped the Holy Land, such as Joshua, David, Solomon, and Jesus. Beside him, Brother de Vries sat in silence, his gaze fixed on the horizon as their vehicle wound its way along the winding roads.

As they drew closer to Jerusalem, however, the mood in the car began to shift. The vibrant energy of the coastal cities had given way to an eerie stillness, a palpable sense of unease that seemed to hang in the air like a miasma. Calleja felt a shiver run down his spine as they passed through the checkpoint to enter the Free City of Jerusalem, the heavily armed soldiers eyeing them with suspicious glares.

And then, as they crested a final hill, the Old City came into view, and Calleja felt his breath catch in his throat. Where once had stood a glittering jewel of civilization, a testament to the enduring spirit of human faith and ingenuity, in its centre now lay a shattered ruin, its ancient walls crumbling, and its sacred sites reduced to rubble. The Jesuit priest closed his eyes, feeling a wave of grief wash over him at the sight. He had known, of course, about the devastation — recalling the sudden burst of blinding light that pierced through the darkness —, had seen the news reports and the satellite images. But nothing could have prepared him for the reality of it, the sheer scale of the destruction that had been unleashed upon this holy place.

Beside him, de Vries let out a low whistle, his voice tinged with horror.

"My God," he breathed. "It's even worse than I imagined."

As they approached the exclusion zone, the sense of oppression grew even stronger. The air seemed to shimmer with an unholy heat, and Calleja could feel the hairs on the back of his neck standing on end. It was as if the very stones themselves were crying out in anguish, their ancient spirits yearning for a peace that had been so cruelly denied them.

And yet, even amidst the unholy destruction, there were signs of life. In the distance, the cleric could see the glint of sunlight on metal, the telltale sign of the massive construction cranes that towered over the ruined cityscape.

"The cleaning and rebuilding efforts," de Vries murmured, following his gaze. "Even in the face of such devastation, they press on."

Calleja nodded, feeling a swell of pride in his chest. It was a testament to the resilience of the human spirit, he thought, that even in the darkest of times, there were those who refused to give in to despair, who clung to hope with a tenacity that bordered on the miraculous.

As Father Calleja and Brother de Vries stepped out of the vehicle, they were immediately confronted by the grim reality of the exclusion zone. Workers clad in bulky radiation suits moved methodically through the debris, their movements slow and deliberate as they cleared away the remnants of the once-thriving city. The suits, a stark white against the ashen landscape, seemed to glow with an otherworldly luminescence, a constant reminder of the invisible danger that lurked in every particle of dust.

Calleja felt a deep ache in his heart as he surveyed the scene before him. The devastation was total, the once-proud buildings reduced to little more than piles of rubble and twisted metal. And yet, even amidst the chaos, there was a strange sort of beauty to it all, a testament to the impermanence of all things earthly.

"It's hard to believe that this was once the beating heart of the Holy Land," Brother de Vries murmured, his voice tinged with awe and sorrow. "To see it reduced to this…"

His colleague nodded, his eyes fixed on the workers as they toiled amidst the ruins. "Do you see these great buildings? There will not be left here one stone upon another that will not be thrown down," he said, quoting Mark 13:1-2. "And yet, even in the face of such destruction, life persists. Look at them, Brother. They labour on, even in the face of impossible odds."

Brother de Vries frowned, his brow furrowing with concern.

"But at what cost, Father? The radiation alone…"

"It is a small price to pay for the chance to rebuild what was lost," Calleja finished, his voice firm with conviction. "They are the guardians of this sacred place, the keepers of its memory. Without them, all of this would be lost to the sands of time."

Carefully, they approached the entrance to the exclusion zone, taking in the desolation that surrounded them. A member of the religious police stopped them, asking about their purpose.

"We have been sent on a special mission from the Vatican," Father Calleja explained. "We are searching for some religious artefacts within the site. Here are our documents," he added, displaying the papers to the officer.

The guard examined them sceptically.

"I apologise, Father," he said. "While your papers seem legitimate, I cannot grant access without authorisation from the High Council."

"How come?" Brother de Vries exclaimed in frustration. "The building was destroyed in the attack."

"The High Council has been relocated to the former Knesset building," the guard informed them. "That is where you can obtain your authorisation."

"I see," replied Calleja, deep in thought. "Thank you for your assistance, officer. We will head there immediately." "You are most welcome, Father."

The priest felt a surge of frustration well up within him. They had come so far, had braved so much, only to be thwarted by the very bureaucracy that was meant to protect the city and its people.

"Let's not wait any time, Willem. Call a taxi, will you?"

And with that, they turned away from the exclusion zone, their hearts heavy with the weight of their mission, their minds fixed on the trials that lay ahead.

***

The High Council loomed before them, a bastion of solemnity amidst the bustling modern neighbourhood of the Free City. Father Calleja and Brother de Vries made their way into the former Israeli parliament building, their footsteps echoing against the marble floors. As soon as they entered the foyer, A priest hurried over to greet them with a smile.

"Greetings, Fathers. May I ask the purpose of your visit?"

"We are on a mission from the Vatican to search the ruins of the Old City," said Calleja. "We were sent here to obtain an authorisation to access the exclusion zone. Here are our credentials."

The priest carefully inspected the documents, reading each page thoroughly.

"I see," he finally said. "This is a matter that must be addressed directly with the members of the High Council. I believe you are already expected. Please, follow me."

"Wait a minute," exclaimed Brother de Vries in surprise. "How could we be expected? No one is aware of our mission."

"Please, follow me, Fathers," replied the priest simply.

He led the two men through an intricate maze of corridors and stairs until they stood before a massive mahogany door, adorned with the crest of the High Council. The priest ushered the two Jesuits inside, before shutting the door behind them.

Father Calleja's heart raced as he spotted the five religious leaders gathered around a mysterious figure at the centre of the room, engaged in an intense discussion. There was an aura of power that radiated from the man, a force that seemed to command the attention of all who stood in his presence.

"Forgive the intrusion, Your Eminences," Calleja began, his voice ringing out in the stillness of the chamber. "I am Father Luca Calleja, and this is Brother Willem de Vries. We come seeking your aid in a matter of utmost importance."

The ecclesiastics turned to face them, their expressions inscrutable. Then, one of the ecclesiastics spoke, his voice filled with happiness.

"Father Calleja!", he exclaimed with surprise. "I almost didn't recognize you. It's so good to see you again, my friend!", he continued, warmly shaking the hand of the startled priest.

"Cardinal Chehab?[17] Your Eminence, it's wonderful to see you as well! And I'm sure you remember Brother de Vries."

""Of course, of course!", the cardinal replied, immediately reaching out to shake Willem's hand. "We have been eagerly awaiting your arrival. But first, allow me to introduce you to the other esteemed members of our council. I'm afraid, I'm the last remnant of the governing body you once knew. My former colleagues having been 'permanently retired'."

The two Jesuits were presented in turn to the Greek Orthodox Patriarch, the Metropolitan Archbishop, the Chief Rabbi and the Grand Mufti of Jerusalem. Then the Cardinal turned to the mysterious figure waiting in the shadows.

"And here is the person who informed us of your imminent arrival: Mr Robert Key from the Covenant Foundation.

---

[17] See *The Servant of the Light*, Stephan Cooper, 2021

As the figure emerged from the dark, Father Calleja found himself staring into the piercing blue of the enigmatic chairman of the Covenant. A wave of surprise and unease washed over the priest, his heart pounding in his chest as he stood in the presence of the man who had the ear of the Holy Father. He immediately noticed that the ministers surrounding Kay seemed to retreat into their seats, their reverence for the man palpable in the air.

"Father Calleja," Kay acknowledged, his voice smooth and measured. "We meet at last. I've heard so much about you."

"Mr. Kay," Calleja replied, his voice steady despite the turmoil within. "I could say the same. I was unaware that the Covenant had any interest in the affairs of Jerusalem."

The evangelist smiled, a thin, mirthless expression that did little to ease the Jesuit's discomfort. "The Covenant has many interests, Father. And when it comes to matters of faith and power, there is little that escapes our notice."

The Jesuit could feel the tension in the room rising, the air thick with unspoken secrets and hidden agendas. If the rumours about the man were right, he knew that he would have to tread carefully, to choose his words with the utmost precision if he hoped to navigate the treacherous waters ahead.

"I see," he said, his mind working furiously to piece together the implications of Kay's presence. "May I enquire what brings you here?"

"Like you, my organisation is curious about the whereabouts of Akhenaten's stela." Kay coolly replied, his gaze sharp and calculating like a serpent sizing up its next target before making a move.

"And what, if I may ask, is the Covenant's interest in this relic?"

Kay stepped back a little, his eyes never leaving Father Calleja's face.

"That, my dear Father, is a question with many answers. Answers that I suspect you are not yet ready to hear."

"I'll be the judge of that," Calleja replied boldly. Then the Jesuit priest turned towards the five clergymen sitting in their chairs with unchanging expressions.

"Honourable members of the Council," he began. "I have come before you at the request of our Holy Father seeking your authorisation to search the ruins of the Old City."

Kay leaned forward, his gaze intense as he locked eyes with the Jesuit priest.

"My men have already scoured the rubbles, Father. Every stone has been overturned, every crevice explored. And yet, traces of the artefact remain elusive, its location a mystery that continues to evade us."

Father Calleja's brow furrowed, a sense of unease growing within him.

"But surely, with all the resources at your disposal, you must have found some clue, some hint as to its whereabouts?"

Robert Kay smiled, a smile that held no warmth.

"Ah, but that is where things become… interesting. You see, Father, we have reason to believe that the key to unlocking this mystery lies not within the ruins themselves, but rather in the hands of an unsuspected Covenant's connection."

Calleja's heart quickened, his mind racing with possibilities.

"A connection? Who do you speak of?"

"Cardinal Paolo del Pietro[18]," Kay replied, his words measured and deliberate.

"That's impossible. Cardinal del Pietro died tragically years ago. There's no way he could have—"

"It appears that the Vatican's investigation, in its haste to close the incident, overlooked some crucial details surrounding the events leading up to his tragic end," the Chairman of the Covenant interjected sharply interrupted. "Details my organisation was able to retrieve in questioning two of the surviving witnesses who were present at the time: Chief Rabbi Yitzchak Eliyahu and Grand Mufti Suleiman Amin al-Sabri. It appears that the good Cardinal, just before passing away, had identified a specific object, an artefact that may hold the answers we seek."

Father Calleja's eyes widened, his breath catching in his throat.

"An object? What kind of object?"

"That, I'm afraid, is where our information becomes... fragmented," Kay admitted, his fingers steepled before him. "Our witnesses have experienced... how to say this? 'A lapse in their cognitive abilities'. A ring, or maybe a necklace. All we know is that this object is currently in the possession of the Prophet Shenouda."

---

[18] See The Servant of the Light, Stephan Cooper, 2021

Calleja gasped in surprise. The very same man the Church was actively trying to neutralise held the key to locating the stela.

"And what is it that you propose, Mr. Kay?" the Jesuit asked, his voice steady despite the turmoil within. "How do you suggest we recover that elusive object?"

Robert Kay leaned back, his eyes glinting with a hint of amusement.

"Why, Father, I thought you'd never ask. The Covenant has a plan, a strategy that will allow us to… persuade Prophet Shenouda to cooperate with our efforts."

"I'm curious to hear how you intend to achieve this," the Jesuit priest mocked. "The Prophet is under constant surveillance and protection. Approaching him directly would be a monumental challenge, one that could jeopardise our entire mission."

Brother de Vries nodded in agreement, his eyes darting between the Jesuit priest and the chairman of the Covenant.

"Father Calleja is right. We cannot risk exposing ourselves or our intentions. Surely, there must be another way to obtain the information we seek."

Kay's lips curled into an enigmatic smile, his pale grey eyes glinting with a hint of mischief.

"Gentlemen, gentlemen," he said, his voice smooth as silk. "You underestimate the reach and resources of the Covenant. We have ways of obtaining what we need, even from the most well-guarded of individuals. Rest assured," he continued, his tone measured and confident, "that my organisation will handle the details. You need not concern yourselves with the specifics. Just trust that we will secure the information we require, by any means necessary."

The room fell silent, the weight of Kay's words hanging heavy in the air. Father Calleja exchanged a glance with Brother de Vries, a silent communication passing between them. They both knew that they were treading on dangerous ground, but they also understood the gravity of their mission. *May God guide us*, Calleja prayed silently, his heart heavy with the burden of his responsibility. *And may He forgive us for the choices we must make in the name of preserving His truth.*

PART THREE

Deception

Year 2054

16

Amidst the echoing grandeur of the Palais des Congrès in Paris, a symphony of applause and cheers reverberated through the vast space, resounding against the ornate columns that stood as silent witnesses to the unfolding historic moment. The clock had barely struck midnight on the 26 April 2054, when Pierre-Antoine Lascombes' campaign team erupted in a triumphant cacophony, their exuberance a living testament to their leader's stunning success. Les Républicains Progressistes[19], with Pierre-Antoine as their candidate, had secured a decisive lead with 32% of the votes, propelling him to the lead in this first round of the French presidential race. As the final results poured in, it became evident that Charles Le

---

[19] The Progressist Republicans.

Guen from Les Patriotes[20] snagged the second position with 28% of the votes. The narrow-margined result cast a long shadow over the festivities, a harbinger of the ideological clash that awaited. Pierre-Antoine's lips tightened almost imperceptibly. So, it would be the candidate of the far-right facing him in the second round on May 10th. A contest between progress and populism, between the light of reason and the spectre of extremism.

From his vantage point on the balcony overlooking the grand hall, he surveyed the jubilant crowd of supporters below. Their ecstatic chants of '*Lascombes President!*' reverberated through the cavernous space, igniting a fire within him. His eyes flickered towards the media screens displaying the polls for the second round — a narrowed-margin win seemed likely. But in this game of political chess, certainty was as elusive as a mirage.

The television screen then shifted to the sombre faces of the two defeated left-wing candidates, standing together in solidarity. "We call upon our supporters," they intoned gravely, "to vote for Pierre-Antoine Lascombes in the second round. The very survival of our Republic and its democratic values hangs in the balance. A vote for Lascombes is a vote to halt the march of fascism in our beloved nation."

Their impassioned entreaty, however, was met with a tempest of bitterness from their base. A chorus of boos and jeers punctuated the air, the sound of disillusionment and

---

[20] The Patriots.

betrayal. The candidates raised their voices to be heard above the din. "Our personal political beliefs must yield to the greater imperative. France must not fall into the hands of those who would trample on our liberties and cast us back into the dark ages of intolerance and oppression."

Pierre-Antoine watched, his face an inscrutable mask. The irony was not lost on him - these were the very opponents who had once branded him a threat to democracy. Now, they hailed him as its saviour. At that moment, the weight of history seemed to press upon his shoulders, the ghosts of France's tumultuous past whispering in his ear. Richelieu and Bonaparte, De Gaulle and Mitterrand - all had stood at such crossroads, their choices shaping the destiny of the nation. Now it was his turn to take up the mantle, to lead France forward into a new era of enlightenment.

Standing in splendid isolation above the revelry, Pierre-Antoine surveyed not just the jubilant present but also the sinuous path that had led him here—a path that began more than a year ago on American soil, amidst turmoil and tumult. The solace of his solitude allowed a rare introspection. As he peered into the heart of his own odyssey, the exodus from America's chaos emerged as a pivotal genesis, a baptismal departure from a land mired in strife to one steeped in the promise of revolutionary renewal. What he had since achieved, this dizzying ascent to the precipice of power, was nothing short of a Herculean feat, an edifice erected without the dark counsel of the Covenant or the Machiavellian machinations of Robert Kay—the man whose shadow he had escaped, whose influence he now repudiated with every fibre of his being. This victory was entirely his own, a testament to his unyielding will and singular vision—a narrative untainted by the fingerprints of puppeteers or prophets.

His reverie was interrupted by the insistent buzz of his secured phone. The name on the screen brought a genuine smile to his face: Monika Richter.

"Monika, to what I owe the pleasure of this call?" he asked with a hint of mischief.

"Come on, Pierre-Antoine, don't be daft", she replied. "My heartfelt congratulations," she then intoned, her words suffused with warmth and sincerity. "May your triumph today be but a prelude to victory in the coming fortnight."

"Your support means the world, Monika. But tell me, I sense there's more to this call?"

A soft chuckle. "Perceptive as always, but I guessed you heard the rumour. The CDU has officially chosen me to lead them into the September general elections," she proudly declared. "It seems we may both be shaping Europe's future very soon."

Pierre-Antoine's eyes lit up. "Monika, that's wonderful news! You'll make an exceptional Chancellor. Together, our nations can reshape the Union, sculpt it into a confederation that honours our shared values and diverse heritage, not bureaucracy and division."

"Indeed. My apologies, I need to shorten our call as duties await. Congratulation again."

"No worries, Monika. Congratulation to you, too. Speak soon."

No sooner had he ended the call than his phone buzzed again, his half-brother Jorge Sanchez[21].

"Hermanito![22]" Jorge's rich baritone filled the line. "I just heard the news. Felicidades![23] You've made us all proud, Pierre-Antoine."

"Gracias, Jorge. But save your congratulations for after the second round. The real fight is just beginning."

"You will win, Pierre-Antoine. I know it. The winds of change are blowing across Europe."

"Indeed, Jorge. And I hear you're doing quite well yourself as the leader of the Unión Democrática Española[24]. I have no doubt that you'll win a majority in the upcoming Spanish general elections."

"Your faith in me is much appreciated," his half-brother said, his voice touched with genuine affection. "Alright, I'm not going to take much more of your time on this busy night. Congratulations again and talk soon. Adiós![25]"

As the call ended, Pierre-Antoine gazed out over the celebrating crowd once more. The pieces were falling into place, a grand chessboard of European politics with him at its centre. A new dawn was breaking, and Pierre-Antoine Lascombes stood ready to usher in an era of unprecedented unity and strength for the continent he loved.

---

[21] See Book 1, *The Servant of the Light*.
[22] Little brother!
[23] Congratulations!
[24] The Spanish Democratic Union
[25] Bye!

"We have finalised your speech, Monsieur Lascombes," his personal aide whispered, pressing a folder into his hands.

Pierre-Antoine took several minutes to go through the document. Every sentence was a work of precision, with each word meticulously selected for maximum impact. The writing was concise yet eloquent. The verdict was immediate.

"Excellent work, Maurice. As usual. What would I do without you?"

"I'm only doing my job."

"As Confucius said, he who speaks without modesty will find difficult to make his words good. Very well, I guess it's showtime then."

Pierre-Antoine stepped into the embrace of the multitude assembled at the Palais des Congrès. A cavalcade of applause surged to meet him, the air electric with the scent of victory. The throng of supporters morphed into a sea of jubilation, waves of elation crashing against the shore of his consciousness. As he prepared to address his supporters, the large screens behind him flickered to life, revealing the grinning face of Charles Le Guen. The far-right candidate's face was alight with a triumphant grin, his eyes gleaming with a feverish intensity.

"My fellow citizens," Le Guen declared, his voice ringing with conviction. "Tonight, we stand on the precipice of a great victory. In two weeks, we will reclaim France for the true patriots, and together, we will take back our country from the corrupt elites who have betrayed us!"

The crowd before him erupted into a frenzy, their cheers and chants filling the air like the howls of a pack of wolves. Le

Guen basked in their adulation, his arms raised in a gesture of defiance.

"But there is a serpent in our midst," he continued, his tone turning venomous. "Pierre-Antoine Lascombes, the man who claims to be the saviour of our nation, is nothing more than a puppet, dancing to the tune of a foreign master. In the coming days, I will unveil the undeniable proof of his corruption, and the world will see him for the traitor he truly is."

A wave of astonishment rippled through the hall. Eyes widened in disbelief, mouths agape in shock. The accusation hung in the air like a noxious cloud, suffocating in its intensity. Pierre-Antoine felt a chill run down his spine, a sense of foreboding that settled in the pit of his stomach. He knew Le Guen was capable of many things, but this? This was a new low, even for him. But he couldn't let it show. He couldn't let the doubts take root and the whispers of uncertainty spread like wildfire. He had to act, and act quickly.

With a determined stride, he made his way to the podium, his face a mask of righteous indignation. The cameras flashed, the reporters clamoured, but he paid them no heed. Putting his scripted speech aside, Pierre-Antoine focused solely on the words he was about to speak, the message he needed to convey.

"Mes chers compatriotes,[26]" he began, his voice steady despite the turmoil brewing within him. "Charles Le Guen's accusations are nothing more than the desperate ravings of a demagogue, willing to burn the very fabric of our democracy

---

[26] My fellow citizens.

to slake his thirst for power. These are the tactics of fascists and tyrants, not of those who truly love France."

He paused, letting the weight of his words sink in. The room was silent, hanging on his every syllable.

"I categorically reject these baseless allegations. They are lies, conjured from the fevered imagination of a man who would see our great nation fall into darkness. But we will not be swayed. We will not be intimidated. His voice rose, his passion building with each passing moment. "I call upon all those who believe in the values of our Republic, who believe in the power of truth and justice. Let's unite against this beast of totalitarianism that threatens to devour all we hold dear. Together, we shall overcome this challenge and emerge stronger, more united than ever before."

The crowd erupted in applause, their cheers drowning out the lingering doubts. Pierre-Antoine basked in their support, his heart swelling with pride and determination.

But as he returned to his headquarters, the weight of Le Guen's accusation settled upon his shoulders once more. The previous assurance of his team has now transformed into chaos. The rumour of his potential corruption was spreading quickly through social media, like a toxic substance. Distancing himself from the commotion, Pierre-Antoine couldn't shake the feeling of unease, the nagging sense that something was amiss. But he pushed it aside, burying it deep within the recesses of his mind. He had a fight to win, a country to lead. And he would not rest until the truth was revealed, until the forces of darkness were vanquished once and for all. The die was cast, the gauntlet thrown. And he would meet it head-on, with all the strength and conviction of a man born to lead.

17

Two days later, Pierre-Antoine stood before a wall of screens in his campaign headquarters, his tall frame rigid with anticipation. The largest display flickered to life, revealing the face of his rival, Charles Le Guen, addressing a hastily called press conference. The atmosphere was electric, charged with anticipation and dread.

"Patriots of France, members of the press," he began, his voice booming through the microphone. "Today, I stand before you not as a candidate, but as a messenger of truth. A truth that will shake the very foundations of our rotten democracy." He paused, letting his words sink in. The room was silent, the only sound the clicking of cameras and the scratching of pens on paper. "I have in my possession irrefutable evidence of corruption at the highest levels among our representatives. Evidence that implicates my opponent, Pierre-Antoine Lascombes, in a scheme to sell out our nation to foreign interests."

A murmur rippled through the crowd, a mixture of shock and disbelief. Le Guen held up a hand, silencing them.

"Yes, you heard me correctly," he stated firmly. Pierre-Antoine Lascombes, the darling of the establishment, the epitome of our modern diplomacy, is nothing but a crooked politician willing to betray his country for personal gain." The murmurs among the press grew louder as they began to bombard him with questions, quickly silenced by the Patriots' leader. "Behold," he roared, gesturing to a large screen behind him. "The truth lays bare."

The screen flickered to life, and the image of Maurice Léger, Lascombes' personal aide, filled the frame. He was seated at a table, across from a man in a dark suit that Pierre-Antoine instantly recognised as Leonid Shafirov, the Russian Ambassador to France.

"Do we have an agreement?" the ambassador asked, his voice tinged with a Russian accent.

"Yes," Léger replied.

Then Shafirov placed a dark leather briefcase onto the table, promptly opened by the aide, revealing a significant amount of money in stacks of 500 euros banknotes.

"Mon Dieu," Pierre-Antoine whispered, his mind racing. "What treachery is this?"

"You can count, it's all there," the ambassador declared.

"I trust you," Léger declared, his face a mask of greed. "The Russian government's generous contribution to Monsieur Lascombes' campaign is greatly appreciated."

The Russian leaned forward, his eyes glinting with malice. "And in return?"

"Once Monsieur Lascombes is elected, he will change France's stance on Russia and will use his influence to sway the European Union from its support for the Ukrainian government. You have his word."

"Voilà!" Le Guen exclaimed triumphantly as the video concluded, his smile wide and predatory. "The man who seeks to lead our nation is but a marionette, dancing on strings held by foreign puppeteers!"

The room erupted in chaos. Journalists shouted questions, cameras flashed, and the air crackled with tension.

The leader of the Patriots waited for the tumult to subside, then spoke again, his face a mask of disgust.

"I call upon Pierre-Antoine Lascombes to withdraw from this race immediately. To spare our nation the shame of his corruption, and to allow a true patriot to take his place."

At the same time, chaos erupted in Les Républicains Progressistes' campaign office. Phones rang incessantly, and staffers rushed about in a panic. Pierre-Antoine remained motionless, his thoughts a maelstrom of disbelief and betrayal. Was it possible that Maurice Léger, whom he trusted implicitly, could have betrayed him so thoroughly? Would the people he had dedicated his life to serving now turn their backs on him? He turned to his personal aide, who stood motionless in his seat, his face livid.

"Maurice...?" Pierre-Antoine muttered.

"I am innocent, I swear!", the aide replied, before bursting into tears. "This was not me ... I'd never... I don't understand."

The campaign manager, a young woman named Camille, placed a hand on his shoulder.

"We have to respond," she said, her voice urgent. "We have to deny these charges, to fight back."

Lascombes nodded, his mind racing. He knew what he had to do, knew the words he had to say. But even as he prepared to face the cameras, to proclaim his innocence to the world, he couldn't shake the feeling that the ground was shifting beneath his feet.

Within hours, the polls, once so promising, began to collapse. The media, once so enamoured of Lascombes' charisma and vision, turned on him with a vengeance. Editorials denounced him as a traitor, a puppet of foreign powers. Social media buzzed with rumours and innuendo, each post a nail in the coffin of his candidacy.

And through it all, Charles Le Guen smiled, a Cheshire grin that seemed to mock Lascombes' every move. He had played his hand masterfully, had struck at the heart of his opponent's credibility.

In the wake of chaos, the centrist and left-wing factions, once divided by ideology, coalesced into a Democratic Alliance, unified in their singular purpose—to thwart the ascent of the far-right. Their clarion call was for withdrawal, urging Pierre-Antoine to cede his place at the vanguard of the election to Gérard Belkacem, the Socialist candidate whose third position at the first round now placed him as a saviour to rally behind.

"Pour l'avenir de la République,[27]" they intoned, their voices laced with solemnity and urgency, imploring the Les Républicains Progressistes' candidate to sacrifice his ambition upon the altar of democracy.

As the narrative unfolded across national media, the social networks too were ablaze with fervour and speculation. The collective digital consciousness buzzed with approval at the prospect of Belkacem's ascension, their algorithms churning out predictions of his inevitable victory should he stand in the final round.

But Pierre-Antoine would not go quietly into the night. He would fight, would claw his way back from the brink. For the sake of his vision, for the sake of the nation he loved, he would not surrender. However, deep in his heart, a seed of doubt had taken root. A nagging whisper that perhaps, just perhaps, the darkness was too deep, the corruption too entrenched. And as he stood before the cameras, his voice ringing out in defiance, he couldn't escape the feeling that he was fighting a losing battle. That the die had been cast, and the outcome already written in the stars.

***

The clacking of keyboards filled the war room, a cacophony of desperation as Pierre-Antoine's campaign team scrambled to salvage the wreckage of his candidacy. Phones trilled

---

[27] For the future of the Republic.

incessantly, each unanswered ring a harbinger of doom. In the eye of the storm, Maurice Léger stood, his face a mask of righteous indignation. The prominent members of Les Républicains Progressistes' political bureau had gathered for an emergency meeting and were eyeing the man with suspicion.

"I am innocent," he declared, his voice rising above the din. "This video is a fabrication, a vile attempt to smear my name and destroy our campaign."

"Maurice," gently said Myriam Laval, the Secretary General, "it's still time to confess and redeem yourself. Think of the party, of Pierre-Antoine. The earlier you do it, the quicker we can salvage his chances for election."

"I swear on my life," the aide pleaded, his voice cracking, "I've never met with the Russian ambassador. This is a lie, a monstrous fabrication!"

"Oh, come on, man!" snarled Henri Drumond, the Vice-President, "the evidence is damning. You have brought shame upon us all."

Pierre-Antoine watched the scene unfold, his heart heavy with conflicting emotions. Despite the damning video evidence, he could not bring himself to believe that Maurice, whom he had trusted for years, could have betrayed him so heedlessly. And yet, he knew that the political tide had turned against them – against him – and that, at one point, sacrifices would have to be made. But he could not bring himself to throw him to the wolves.

"I believe you, Maurice," he said softly.

"Are you out of your mind, Pierre-Antoine?" exploded Drumond in disbelief. "Do you realise the shit our campaign is in right now? Do you want to sink it even further?" The Vice-President had been a long-term rival to Pierre-Antoine and never fully accepted his defeat in the primaries several months before. He pointed an accusing finger at the other members of the bureau, directing his anger towards them. "I warned you that he didn't have the courage to follow through. But no one listened. And now, here we are, in this mess. You all have a hand in this disaster."

"Henri, let's not give in to our anger," Laval objected. "Now is not the time to let your bitterness take over."

"No, I won't calm down. We need to pick up the pieces and make things right." Drumond's eyes bore into Pierre-Antoine with a determined look. "You have to step up as the leader you were meant to be. Sack Maurice!"

"If I do that, I'll look just as guilty as he does."

"Then we have no choice. The bureau must vote on a motion to remove Maurice for betraying our party's values and clear our candidate of any wrongdoing."

"But that would make us appear like fools," objected Myriam. "Why not suggest that Pierre-Antoine resign and hand Le Guen the presidency on a silver platter, while you're at it?"

At her words, the members of the bureau erupted into chaos, arguing with each other tumultuously.

"Stop it. I'll resign!" suddenly shouted a voice among the uproar. They all stopped arguing, looking with astonishment at Maurice standing straight up with determination. "I'll resign and take the blame," he said calmly."

"Maurice, you can't— "

"Pierre-Antoine, I hate to admit it, but Henri is right," Léger's expression was one of defeat. "For you to have even the slightest chance at winning, I will have to take responsibility and confess that I used my position to deceive the Russian ambassador. It's the only option."

Pierre-Antoine felt the weight of the world upon his shoulders, the burden of leadership crushing his spirit. He reluctantly accepted Maurice Léger's resignation, forced by the pressure from his own party members, while still harbouring doubts about the man's guilt. He could only pray that this brutal sacrifice would not be in vain and truly turn the tide of his predicaments.

18

As the days passed, Pierre-Antoine threw himself into the campaign, his every waking moment consumed by the fight. He spoke to the crowds with a passion that bordered on the divine, his words a clarion call to the forces of democracy.

But even as he rallied the faithful, doubt gnawed at his soul. Despite Maurice Léger's brave decision to take responsibility for the scandal, the polls were a grim testament to his fading hopes, each new number a nail in the coffin of his candidacy.

As the week came to a close, he retreated to his office in an attempt to find some peace. Despite his best attempts, the situation had not improved and there seemed to be no glimmer of hope on the horizon. For the first time in his career, he was faced with the harsh reality of defeat and the looming possibility of giving way to Gérard Belkacem who had a better chance to win. It felt like a betrayal, a surrender of everything he had worked for. But as he stared at the papers scattered on his desk, each one a reminder of his failed attempts, he knew that his options were running out. No matter how hard he tried, his prospects seemed to be slipping further and further away from him. And for a man who had prided himself on his determination and resilience, this realisation was almost too much to bear. As the hours ticked by, he sat in that stuffy office, lost in his thoughts and struggling with his emotions.

A soft tapping at the door interrupted his sombre thoughts. Isabelle Veyre, his loyal assistant who had stood by him through thick and thin, appeared.

"Pierre-Antoine?" she called softly.

"Yes Isabelle?"

"Tristan is here and needs to speak with you. He says it's urgent."

"Tristan?" Pierre-Antoine furrowed his brow, trying to place the name.

"The head of our communications department."

"Of course. Let him in. I could use some distraction, anyway."

The sound of Tristan's footsteps echoed in the spacious room as he approached Pierre-Antoine's desk, bringing with him an air of urgency and importance.

"Tristan, please take a seat. What is so urgent that it requires my immediate attention amidst all of my current misfortunes?"

"Well—"

"Wait. Let me guess. We got an anonymous tip revealing that Le Guen's allegations are a scam," Pierre-Antoine said sarcastically.

Tristan's face showed shock, as if he had been caught off guard.

"How... how did you know, Sir?"

"What do you mean, how did I know?" Now it was Pierre-Antoine who looked surprised.

"The tip, Sir. We indeed received one two hours ago, sent anonymously to my office.

"You're kidding, right?"

"I assure you, Sir. Two hours ago, the mail was delivered and among it was a brown envelope with my name on it. Upon opening it, I found a single USB key inside. Nothing else. I had our IT team check for any malicious software, but they confirmed that it was clean. So, I decided to see what was on the USB. And, Sir, you won't believe what it contains..."

Pierre-Antoine's campaign team worked through the night, meticulously verifying the evidence before strategizing their next move. The digital contents revealed irrefutable evidence that the video implicating Maurice Léger had been an incredibly realistic deep fake created by Russia's Foreign Intelligence Service – the SVR. The plot ran even deeper: the fake video had been intended to interfere with the French elections and destabilise the country politically, all to ensure that Charles Le Guen – who was ironically the favoured candidate of Russia's ignominious President, Grigory Alexeyev – would emerge victorious.

As dawn broke, Pierre-Antoine couldn't wait any longer and hurried out of his office towards the group congregated around a large table. Tristan greeted him with a satisfied smile.

"Tell me," he pleaded, unable to contain his anxiety any longer.

"It's all real, Sir. Each and every piece of evidence has been verified and certified. It's... it's unbelievable. Whoever sent this—"

"We'll address that later," Pierre-Antoine interjected. We have less than a week until the second round, we must focus on outsmarting Le Guen at his own tactics. We just need the right moment."

***

The opportunity presented itself sooner than expected. Charles Le Guen, riding high on his newfound lead, had called a press conference, no doubt to gloat over his impending victory. Pierre-Antoine's team moved swiftly, alerting the media to a bombshell revelation. As Le Guen took the stage, his smile wide and his words dripping with disdain, they struck. The screen behind Les Patriots' leader flickered to life, first displaying the video staging Maurice speaking to the Russian Ambassador. The recording briefly glitched before shifting to another image, this time showing Le Guen sitting in the same spot where Léger had been just moments before. The presidential candidate stared in disbelief at the unexpected footage, causing chaos to erupt in the room. Reporters shouted questions and cameras flashed as Le Guen tried to regain control. He quickly straightened himself up, his face displaying anger.

"These are treacherous tactics!" he yelled. "This is a despicable ploy to sabotage my campaign using underhanded methods. Whoever is responsible for this deception will face the full force of justice. I refuse to let my name and reputation be tarnished by some—"

He was cut off by another flicker of the screen, now displaying Pierre-Antoine surrounded by his team inside the headquarters of Les Républicains Progressistes.

"Mes chers compatriotes," he began with confidence. "After being subjected to a week-long smear campaign, the truth has finally come to light. Undoubtedly, my opponent will try to discredit the images you have just witnessed as fake. But I hold in my hands undeniable evidence of his deceit," he declared, gesturing towards a stack of papers. "Do not be fooled, there is only one betrayer here — one who claims to be a patriot while conspiring with our enemies. Shame on you, Le Guen! You may call for justice now, but true justice will be served by the French people when they vote on Sunday."

Le Guen's face turned ashen, his words stumbling as he tried to maintain his composure. But it was too late. The truth, like a searing light, had illuminated the darkness of his lies.

As the media frenzy erupted, Pierre-Antoine felt a surge of hope. He thought of Monika and Jorge, of their shared vision for a stronger Europe. This wasn't just about clearing his name; it was about preserving the very foundations of democracy. Outside, he could hear chants growing: "Lascombes President! Lascombes President!" The tide was finally turning.

In the days that followed, his campaign surged, riding a wave of public outrage and renewed hope. The Democratic Alliance, once his fiercest critics, now rallied behind him, their call for unity a clarion cry against the spectre of foreign interference.

Pierre-Antoine took to the campaign trail with a renewed vigour, his speeches a tapestry of soaring rhetoric and heartfelt conviction. He spoke of a France united, a France strong in its values and resolute in its defence of democracy. And the people responded, their voices rising in a crescendo of support. But even as hope swelled within him, Pierre-Antoine couldn't shake the feeling that the hardest battle was yet to come. That the forces of darkness, once defeated, would not rest until they had extracted their revenge. He steeled himself for the fight ahead, drawing strength from the unwavering support of Monika and Jorge, from the resilience of the French people. Come what may, he would stand tall, a beacon of hope in a world beset by shadows. For he was Pierre-Antoine Lascombes, and he would not be broken.

***

The sun rose over Paris on the 10th of May 2054, casting a warm golden light upon the city as it awakened to the dawn of a new era. Pierre-Antoine Lascombes, surrounded by a swarm of journalists, kept at a distance by his security team, stood in line at his local polling station, his heart pounding with anticipation as he prepared to cast his vote. The weight of the moment settled upon his shoulders.

"Bonjour, Monsieur," the polling official greeted him with a polite nod. "Votre carte d'identité, s'il vous plaît.[28]"

"Voici[29]," he replied, handling over his identification card. A slight tremor in his hand revealed the anxiety pulsing through his body. He made his way towards the voting booth, feeling the gravity of this moment set upon him like a heavy cloak. As he stood alone in the quiet enclosure, Pierre-Antoine took a deep breath and paused before choosing his ballot. With eyes closed, he silently prayed for guidance and wisdom as he prepared to take on the responsibility he had long sought after. With a deep breath, he sealed his envelope before stepping out of the booth with a determined stance, before walking to the see-through urn ready to receive his vote.

"Monsieur Pierre-Antoine, Louis, Marie, Lascombes, né le 5 septembre 2010 à Pibrac, département de Haute-Garonne[30]," announced the president of the polling station.

Pierre-Antoine firmly pushed the envelope through the narrow slot.

"A voté![31]" declared the president as he handed back the ID card. "September 5th? You share a birthday with Louis XIV."

"Indeed," Pierre-Antoine responded with a playful grin.

"Perhaps it's fate."

"Anything is possible," Pierre-Antoine replied, shrugging his shoulders.

---

[28] Your ID card, please.

[29] There you are.

[30] Mr Pierre-Antoine, Louis, Marie, Lascombes, born 5 September 2007 in Pibrac, Department of Haute-Garonne.

[31] Has voted.

As he stepped out onto the bustling Parisian street, a cacophony of voices and clicking cameras engulfed him. Reporters jostled for position, their questions overlapping in a frenetic chorus.

"Monsieur Lascombes! Your thoughts on today's election? Are you confident you can win?"

Pierre-Antoine raised a hand, his voice cutting through the clamour with practised ease.

"Today, the people of France will make their voices heard. I have faith in our democracy and in the wisdom of our citizens."

"Is it true that the leaders of the German CDU and of the Spanish Democratic Union are here with you today? asked another one. "Does this signify changes in store for the European Union? Should other members of the Union be concerned about this potential alliance?"

"Ms Richter is here as a very close friend, nothing more. As for Mr Sanchez, it's no secret that he is my half-brother. I have no further comments on the matter. Now, if you'll excuse me, I need to return to my campaign headquarters, and I'll see you all tonight for the election results."

***

As the hours ticked by, tension mounted, the air electric with anticipation. In the campaign headquarters at the Palais des Congrès, supporters and campaign workers alike huddled around screens, watching the news coverage with bated breath. Pierre-Antoine found himself pacing the room, unable to shake the nagging fear that gnawed at the edges of his composure. Monika Richter and Jorge Sanchez stood by his side, their presence a bulwark against the rising tide of uncertainty.

"Have faith, hermanito," Jorge urged, placing a supportive hand on his half-brother's shoulder. "You have fought for this moment, and the people will see the truth."

Pierre-Antoine nodded, drawing strength from their bond. "You're right, Jorge. We must trust in the wisdom of the electorate – and in our shared vision for a better future."

"I just received news from Germany," Monika said while turning off her phone. "You're heading to an undeniable victory."

"Humph!" Pierre-Antoine huffed with frustration. "Monika, remind me, once in power, to request that the EU Commission bans the release of polls in other member states on election day."

"Stop being so grouchy," she retorted. "What are you worried about? Le Guen's chances have plummeted since the announcement on Tuesday. There is absolutely no way you can lose."

"You know I don't trust polls, and I can't forget what happened in the US."

"Leave the US to their fate, at least for now. What happened there is the result of fifty years of allowing bigotry, illiberality and partisanship to thrive freely. This is Europe!"

"Still. I can't shake this feeling that something will happen right at the end, with the Covenant cloaked in the shadows, ready to strike when we least expect it."

"They've been silent for almost a year," his half-brother replied. "Surely, they have bigger problems to deal with in America than to meddle in French affairs."

"Don't underestimate the reach of their vile influence, Jorge."

As the clock ticked closer to the designated time, a hush fell like a sacred shroud over the assembly. A digital display appeared on the screen, counting down the final seconds with a dramatic soundtrack. And at exactly 8pm, Pierre-Antoine's image materialized, revealing a score of 73.5%.

"Mesdames et Messieurs, il est vingt heures,[32]" the voice of one announcer rose, imbued with the gravitas of history. "As you can see from our exit poll, we forecast that Pierre-Antoine Lascombes has been elected as your new President of the Republic with an overwhelming majority!"

A thunderous roar erupted, a cathartic release of pent-up emotion, as jubilation swept through the throngs of supporters. Confetti rained down like manna from heaven, and the chant, '*Lascombes Président!*' resounded, a psalm of victory for the ages. Pierre-Antoine raised his arms, an embodiment of triumph, while the future of France shimmered before him like a mirage made manifest.

Monika's eyes met his, alight with the reflection of shared dreams; they had weathered the storm and emerged into the promise of a new dawn. Jorge embraced his brother, their

---

[32] Ladies and gentlemen, it is 8pm.

bond transcending blood and ideology—a confluence of purpose and passion.

"You've done it, hermano. You've done it!" he exclaimed with pure joy. "Madre's going to be so proud."

"We will both make her proud, Jorge. It will be your turn next months. Then yours, Monika," Pierre-Antoine continued, turning to Monika who sat calmly but with tears of joy in her eyes. "And together, we will reshape the old word to a bright future. A future for all."

"Go to your supporters, Pierre-Antoine," she simply replied. "It's their victory as much as yours. Go and celebrate with them. It is your moment. Ours will come soon enough."

As he stepped out to address the jubilant crowd, the air thick with hope and celebration, Pierre-Antoine felt the weight of his responsibility settle upon him like a mantle. The cheers of '*Vive la France! Vive Lascombes!*' washed over him in waves.

"Thank you," he called out, raising his hands to silence the crowd. "Thank you all for your unwavering support and dedication. Together, we have achieved something truly remarkable. Tonight, we celebrate not only a victory for our campaign, but a triumph for democracy and the future of our great nation."

By midnight, the official results were announced, cementing his undeniable victory. As the celebrations continued into the night, the streets of Paris came alive with the sound of revelry, a symphony of hope echoing through the ancient city. A new chapter had begun, and though the challenges ahead were vast and daunting, one thing was certain: under the leadership of Pierre-Antoine Lascombes, France would face them united, standing tall as a beacon of hope and progress for all of Europe.

19

Ten days later, on the 20th of May 2054, Pierre-Antoine stood at the entrance of the Elysée Palace, his tall frame cladded in an impeccably tailored suit, poised to be inaugurated as the thirteenth President of the Fifth Republic. His heart pounded with a mixture of pride and responsibility as he entered the Cour d'honneur, flanked by a detachment of the Republican Guard. Their immaculate uniforms and disciplined demeanour served as a testament to the solemnity of the occasion.

Inside the palace, Pierre-Antoine met with his predecessor, Charles Cavaignac who, several months before, had decided not to seek re-election after serving one term. The two men shook hands, a symbolic passing of the torch. "Congratulations, Mr. Lascombes," Cavaignac said, his tone warm yet tinged with the weariness of a man relieved of a great burden. "The hopes of France now rest upon your shoulders."

Pierre-Antoine nodded solemnly. "Thank you, Mister President. Your service to our nation will not be forgotten. I stand ready to bear the responsibility placed upon my shoulders and will not let our nation down."

The two men spent the next thirty minutes in a private conversation, discussing the various important matters that the new administration would have to address. Then Pierre-Antoine escorted the departing president to the entrance with all the pomp and circumstance of befitting a monarch. The sound of his footsteps lingered for a moment before fading into the annals of history. Pierre-Antoine watched as the limousine disappeared into the bustling streets of Paris before taking a deep breath and prepared himself for the investiture ceremony.

The Salle des Fêtes of the Elysée Palace was adorned in regal splendour, its grand chandeliers casting a warm glow upon the dignitaries and esteemed guests in attendance. As the Chamber Orchestra of the Republican Guard played a solemn march, Pierre-Antoine strode into the hall, accompanied by the Prime Minister, the President of the Senate, and the President of the National Assembly. The gravity of the moment weighed heavily upon him; a reminder of the trust placed in him by the citizens he now vowed to serve.

The President of the Constitutional Council read the proclamation of the election results, his voice steady and resolute. Pierre-Antoine signed the investiture report, each stroke of his pen a commitment to his people. He then received the insignia of the Grand Cross of the Legion of Honour from the hands of the Grand Chancellor, who also presented him with the collar of Grand Master of the Order.

Stepping up to the podium, Pierre-Antoine gazed out at the sea of faces before him, a tapestry woven from the diverse threads of the French nation.

"Mes chers compatriotes," he began, his voice echoing through the hall, "I stand before you today humbled by the trust you have placed in me. I promise to be a President for all of France, to listen to your hopes and fears, and to work tirelessly in service of our great nation." As he spoke, Pierre-Antoine's thoughts wandered to the obstacles that awaited him—the political divides that could potentially tear apart French society, the upcoming general elections, the economic insecurities looming in sight, and the threat of international crises with the decline of American dominance. Yet, even in the face of these trials, he felt a surge of determination, a resolve to lead his country towards a brighter future. "Together," he declared, his voice rising with the fervour of conviction, "we will forge a new path for France and for Europe. We will face the challenges of our time with courage and unity, guided by the timeless values that have made our nation a beacon of liberty and justice for the world."

As the invited dignitaries stepped forward to offer their congratulations, Pierre-Antoine felt a sense of destiny, a conviction that he had been called to this role for a purpose greater than himself.

The ceremony continued as he stepped out on the terrace overlooking the gardens, Pierre-Antoine stood side by side with the Prime Minister and the presidents of the two assemblies. The Republican Guard snapped to attention, their uniforms a sea of crisp blue and gold. As the strains of the Marseillaise filled the air, Pierre-Antoine placed his hand over his heart, the words of the national anthem a sacred vow upon his lips. As the final notes of the anthem faded into the spring breeze, a 21-gun salute thundered across the city, heralding a new era for France.

In that moment, with the eyes of the world upon him, Pierre-Antoine Lascombes knew that he had reached the pinnacle of his political career. He had clawed his way to the top through sheer determination and the force of his own will, unbeholden to any man or entity. The Presidency was his, and his alone, a testament to his unwavering resilience in the face of adversity.

***

As the night descended upon the Elysée Palace, the Salle des Fêtes flared with magnificence, a dazzling display of opulence and power. Crystal chandeliers cast a warm glow upon the assembled dignitaries and guests, their faces a kaleidoscope of admiration and envy as they gathered to celebrate the inauguration of the newly invested president. The grand reception was in full swing, and the air buzzed with excitement, laughter, and the clink of champagne glasses. Pierre-Antoine, elegant in a tailored suit, moved effortlessly through the crowd, engaging in conversation with various dignitaries and political figures.

As he spoke to the dean of the diplomatic corps, a crisp voice cut through the air like a flag snapping in the wind. It was Lieutenant-Colonel Denis Ferrand, head of the Security Group of the Presidency of the Republic, standing before him with his back straight as a bayonet.

"Monsieur le Président," he said, his voice low and urgent. "May I introduce you to Lieutenant Barnabé Sainte-Rose, who has been assigned to oversee your personal security."

Pierre-Antoine extended a warm hand to the young lieutenant, his eyes meeting Sainte-Rose's in a firm and reassuring gaze.

"Welcome, Lieutenant. I trust your experience and judgment will keep us all safe."

"Thank you, Mr. President," replied Sainte-Rose, holding Pierre-Antoine's gaze with equal intensity. "I am thankful to have been chosen for this responsibility, and I will make sure to provide discreet but diligent protection for your person."

"We are grateful, Lieutenant. But tell me, Sainte-Rose? That's from the Caribbean, isn't it? Guadeloupe?"

"No Sir, Martinique."

"Indeed. A beautiful island, with such vibrant…"

As they exchanged a few more words, a brilliant burst of light flooded the room. Pierre-Antoine turned to see fireworks erupting over the gardens, painting the night sky in a kaleidoscope of colours. The assembled guests gasped in delight, moving outside for a better view.

In that moment of distraction, a familiar voice whispered near his ear, "Quite the spectacle, isn't it, Pierre-Antoine?"

The President's blood ran cold. His heart raced as he turned, only to find Robert Kay standing before him like a ghostly apparition from his past. The American evangelist's grey hair seemed to glow in the pulsing light of the fireworks, his pale skin accentuating the intensity of his gaze.

"Robert," Pierre-Antoine managed, his voice tight. "I wasn't aware you were on the guest list."

The Covenant chairman's thin lips curved into a smile that didn't reach his eyes. "Oh, I have my ways. Shall we find somewhere more... private to talk?"

Ignoring any potential objections from Pierre-Antoine, Kay steered him towards a secluded lounge. As the door closed behind them, muffling the sounds of celebration, tension crackled in the air like static electricity.

"I guess congratulations are in order, Mr. President," Kay began, his voice dripping with insincerity. "Quite the achievement, wouldn't you agree?"

Pierre-Antoine's jaw clenched.

"Thank you. It was a hard-fought campaign."

"Indeed, it was," Kay nodded, his eyes glinting. "Especially—" An insistent knock on the door interrupted him.

"Is everything alright, Mr President?"

"Yes, everything's fine, Lieutenant. Pierre-Antoine answered impassively. "I just need a few minutes alone."

"Understood, sir. I'll be right outside if you need me."

"Thank you, Lieutenant." Pierre-Antoine's eyes narrowed as he struggled to maintain his composure. "What do you want, Robert?"

"Ah, straight to business," Kay replied, a wicked grin spreading across his face. "As I was about to say, a striking victory. Especially after that nasty business with the video. It's fortunate that the truth came to light just in time, isn't it?"

A chill ran down Pierre-Antoine's spine.

"What are you saying, Robert?"

Kay's smile widened.

"I'm saying that the Covenant always keeps its promises. We said we'd help you become President, and here you are."

The implications of Kay's words hit Pierre-Antoine like a physical blow. He stumbled back, gripping the edge of a nearby table for support.

"You... you were behind the evidence that cleared my name?"

"Let's just say I have some influence with President Alexeyev," Robert replied, his tone casual, as if discussing the weather. "It was a simple matter to persuade him to reveal the truth about the SVR's involvement."

As the severity of the revelation settled upon him, Pierre-Antoine felt the room closing in, the weight of Kay's machinations crushing his spirit. Fury and despair warred within him, his mind racing to process the depth of the deception.

"Of course, Mr. President," Robert continued smoothly, "I expect something in return for saving your presidential bid."

A wave of shock and dismay wash over Pierre-Antoine, his mind reeling at the implications of the Covenant chairman's words. He had always known that the evangelist was a dangerous man, but he had never imagined the depths of his duplicity.

"What do you want from me?" he asked, his voice barely more than a whisper.

"You'll simply ensure for the time being that France stands on neutral grounds and tempers Europe's ire should Ukraine face Russia's wrath."

"That's... that's impossible," Lascombes sputtered. "It goes against everything I worked for, everything France stands for!"

"Here are the terms of the Covenant and the will of Jesus."

"Blackmail, then? Wrapped in piety?" Pierre-Antoine's words were daggers concealed in velvet. "And what if I refuse?" he challenged, defiant.

"We will unleash a social media campaign so devastating that it will ruin your presidency before it even begins," Kay declared with a sinister smile. "And keep in mind, you still need to secure a majority in the upcoming general elections."

A cold shiver ran down Pierre-Antoine's spine as he knew that a threat from the Covenant was not to be taken lightly. He could not afford to defy the evangelist, not now. Not when the fate of his Presidency hung in the balance, with the lingering shadow of the recent scandal still fresh in everyone's minds.

"Consider it, Pierre-Antoine. I'm certain you'll find our arrangement to be a small price to pay for all of this." Kay sneered, gesturing towards the opulence surrounding them. "Let's look at the positives. The Covenant has no desire to interfere with your plan for reforming the EU into a confederation of nations instead of pushing for further integration. In fact, having Europe kept divided aligns with our interests even more than you realise. So, you are still helping our cause, even if unintentionally," Kay boasted arrogantly. Pierre-Antoine remained speechless, unable to find words to respond. "Well, I'll leave you to your thoughts. Go back to your guest, Mr President; enjoy the party! It is your night, after all." With a final nod, he vanished as quietly as he had appeared.

Left alone, Pierre-Antoine felt the gravity of his office transform into a crucible. The intoxicating nectar of victory soured upon his lips, replaced by the bitter draught of moral quandary. Here he stood, where countless had before, at the nexus of glory and righteousness, while trapped in a prison of his own making, with no clear path to escape.

***

A month later, the air in Madrid was electric, thick with the exultation of triumph as Jorge Sanchez stood before a sea of supporters, their cheers reverberating off the facades of the historic Plaza Mayor. The ancient stones bore silent witness to his ascent, the Unión Democrática Española sweeping an absolute majority in the Cortes like a tide commandeering the shore.

Sanchez's voice, robust and clear, cut through the cacophony of celebration like a bell tolling the dawn of a new era. He spoke of unity, of strength drawn from diversity. It was a victory not just for him or his party, but for the grand design he shared with Pierre-Antoine—reforming the European Union into a more tightly bound confederation of nations.

"Viva España! Viva Europa![33]" Sanchez's words resounded, igniting a surge of pride and hope in the hearts of his listeners. He promised a future where each nation was a vital and vibrant thread in the broader weave of continental solidarity. And in that moment, the plaza seemed to glow with the promise of a better tomorrow, a testament to the power of words and the vision they could inspire.

***

Three months hence, under skies that seemed to hold their breath, Berlin responded in kind. Monika Richter, embodying the resilience of her nation, emerged victorious. The Christian Three months hence, under skies that seemed to hold their breath, Berlin responded in kind. Monika Richter, embodying the resilience of her nation, emerged victorious. The Christian Democratic Union, under her stewardship, had claimed the chancellery with a mandate that resonated with Pierre-Antoine's continental ambitions. Her victory speech was a masterclass in poise and passion, delivered from the steps of the Reichstag where history's shadow loomed both heavy and hallowed.

"Wir stehen zusammen, als ein Europa[34]," Monika proclaimed, her voice imbued with the gravitas of Germanic lore. Her blue eyes, reminiscent of the tranquil waters of the Rhine, held a flicker of St. Elmo's fire, a harbinger of the tempest of change she intended to usher in. She spoke of cooperation and

---

[33] Long live Spain! Long live Europe!
[34] We stand together, as one Europe.

interdependence, invoking the spirit of Charlemagne and the dream of a united realm, not by conquest but by consensus.

The crowd gathered before her, a sea of faces as diverse as the European continent itself, hung onto her every word, their hearts swelling with pride and hope.

Pierre-Antoine, watching from a nearby balcony, felt a lump form in his throat as he listened to Monika's words. He had always believed in the power of unity, but seeing it embodied in the form of this strong, determined woman, he felt a renewed sense of purpose and determination. As the cheers and applause rose around him, he couldn't help but think that this was just the beginning of a new era for Europe. And he was honoured to be a part of it.

***

A week later, the recently appointed Chancellor descended the grand staircase of the Bundeskanzleramt[35] to greet Pierre-Antoine and Jorge, whom she had invited to discuss the future of Europe. Dressed in a sharp, yet stylish royal blue suit, Monika exuded an aura of confidence and happiness. After warmly hugging her best friend and his half-brother, they posed together for the customary photo, symbolizing the emergence of a new generation in European politics.

Then, the three newly elected leaders retreated to the Office of the Federal Chancellor on the seventh floor. There, away from prying eyes, they would draw plans to reforming the EU

---

[35] The German Chancery.

institutions. Across the continent, time seemed to stand still as governments and citizens held their breath, anxiously awaiting to see what decisions this new political alliance would make.

THIRD INTERLUDE

Year 2069

20

Yekaterina Alexandreyevna's office in the Kremlin, bathed in the golden glow of a setting sun, seemed to echo her frustrations. The shadows cast by the towering bookshelves danced along the walls as she paced back and forth, her heels clicking sharply against the polished marble floor. Her hands clenched tightly at her sides, betraying the storm of emotions that raged beneath her furrowed brow. The Russian president and her Minister of Foreign Affairs, Ivan Kozyrev were locked in a verbal duel, their discourse as sharp as the edge of a Cossack's sabre.

"Your obstinacy blinds you, Ivan," Yekaterina's voice resonated with a timbre that commanded attention, each word articulating her discontent with the legacy left by her father. Her hands, those of a woman who cradled both power and despair, gestured emphatically as she delineated the breadth of her disillusionment. "The grandiose dream of a Greater Russia has crumbled to ashes, leaving nought but the bitter taste of irony upon our tongues."

Ivan remained impassive; his countenance etched with the lines of many hard-fought political battles. "Yekaterina, you must understand—" he began, only to be cut off by her incisive interjection.

"Understand?" Yekaterina's voice crescendoed, her gaze unflinching as she bore into him with the intensity of one who had seen visions of empire rise and fall. "I understand all too well the consequences of hubris. My father's vainglorious quest has bound us to an odyssey of penury and ignominy."

She moved toward the window, the panorama of Moscow's skyline a stark reminder of a nation's tarnished glory. The once-proud spires now seemed to bow in collective shame, the city's heartbeat a murmur of lost greatness.

"Behold the fruits of his labour," she continued, her arm sweeping towards the view beyond the glass. "A country diminished; its people cloaked in the drab garb of disillusionment. Where is the renaissance he promised? We are pariahs in the eyes of the world, Yvan. Our economy languishes under the weight of sanctions and debts, our influence dwindles like the last rays of sun upon the winter solstice."

The question hung in the air like the thick scent of incense in a cathedral, its tendrils curling around Yekaterina's thoughts and entwining themselves with the memories of her father's legacy. She could feel the echoes of his ambition reverberating through the very foundations of Russia, the same ambition that had led them down this treacherous path.

Her words carried the weight of prophetic lamentation, echoing through the chamber with the resonance of St Basil's bells. It was more than disappointment—it was the mourning of a daughter for a father's squandered dream, for a nation adrift in the relentless currents of history.

"Tell me, Ivan," she said, her voice laced with bitterness, "do you ever wonder if there is a limit to what one should sacrifice for the sake of power? For the glory of one's nation?"

Ivan studied her for a moment, his eyes searching hers for the source of her anguish. He considered her words, weighing them against the backdrop of their shared experiences – the trials they had faced, the victories they had achieved.

"Power, Yekaterina, is a double-edged sword," he said at last. "It can be wielded to protect and preserve, or to conquer and destroy. Your father's intentions were noble, even if the consequences have been... severe. However, don't disregard the milestones he achieved. Under his rule, Russia expanded its dominion, securing territories that had long eluded our grasp. These UN sanctions are not the indictment of his policies but rather the machinations of foreign powers, envious of our sovereignty and success. They wish to stifle our ascent by weaving a tapestry of restrictions, each thread an attempt to unravel the fabric of our nation's strength.

"Expanded its dominion?" Yekaterina's retort was a sharp crack in the hushed atmosphere of the office, like the first thunderclap of a tempest long foretold. "Territories gained at what cost? Those lands are barren trophies won in Pyrrhic victory. The world views us with wary eyes, Ivan. We have become Icarus, soaring on wings of hubris, only to plummet for our folly." She resumed pacing the room, her steps measured and deliberate.

"Look beyond the veil of immediate triumphs, and you will see the desolation wrought by short-sighted ambition. My father's legacy is akin to a desert mirage—beguiling in promise, yet upon approach, nothing more than shifting sands of disillusionment. At what point do we acknowledge that the price of ambition is too steep? My father has bartered away our future for ephemeral gains. And now, as the gilded facade erodes, we stand exposed before a tribunal of nations—our coffers emptied, our pride shattered, and our heritage auctioned off to the highest bidder. And now, with the Federation of Europe growing ever stronger under Pierre-Antoine Lascombes and Monika Richter, our position becomes more precarious by the day.

"True, the European Federation poses a significant challenge," Ivan conceded, an undercurrent of unease threading its way through his words. "But if we remain steadfast and adapt to the shifting sands of global politics, we can overcome this obstacle and emerge stronger than ever before."

"Perhaps," she mused aloud, her gaze distant as she pondered the tangled web of political intrigue and religious tradition that had led them to this moment in history. As the sun dipped below the horizon, casting long shadows across the room, Yekaterina found herself caught between the darkness of doubt and the flickering light of hope.

In the dimly lit chamber, the Russian president stood before a painting by Adam Albrecht depicting Emperor Napoleon Leaving the Kremlin. The French emperor, riding a white horse, was contemplating the Russian capital in flames and the rushed evacuation of his armies. His face was a mixture of sadness and disillusion, mirrored by the anguish of his generals regrouped behind him. "Look at this, Ivan," she whispered, "even he, failed. The empires are forged in blood and fire, yet they all fall to ruin in the end. What makes us any different?" She kept staring at the artwork, a sinister reminder of her possible demise. "Belief alone will not save us," she murmured. "We need more than faith, Ivan. We need a miracle."

The silence that followed was shattered by the sudden click of the door, a subtle yet intrusive sound, revealing a mysterious figure bathed in shadow. Yekaterina and Ivan turned as one toward the unwarranted intrusion, their consternation manifesting in narrowed eyes and furrowed brows. The apparition stepped forward into the dim glow of the lights, his eyes gleaming with a sense of purpose that seemed to pierce through the gloom. His suit was impeccably tailored, the cut modern yet exuding an ageless quality, as if woven from the very fabric of authority itself.

"Perhaps I can be of assistance," he intoned, his voice calm and authoritative, yet tinged with an undercurrent of danger that sent a shiver down Yekaterina's spine.

"Who are you?" she demanded, her heart pounding as she struggled to maintain her composure in the face of this unexpected intrusion. "And how did you get into my private chambers? "

"I am Mr Kay, Associate Director of the Covenant Foundation," he replied, his gaze never wavering as he met her steely stare, "and came at the request of your minister for foreign affairs. We have been watching your plight, Yekaterina Alexandreyevna, and we share your desire to see Russia regain its rightful place on the global stage. Your father's vision," he continued, "though grandiose, faltered under the weight of its own ambition. But where mortals stumble, providence extends a hand." He paused, allowing the gravity of his words to sink into the soil of her mind. "The Covenant is well apprised of Mother Russia's plight. We stand ready to offer assistance, to aid in restoring the splendour of your great nation and its rightful place upon the world's stage."

His assurance was the soothing balm to the burn of Yekaterina's earlier fervour. Here stood a harbinger of potential salvation—or so he proclaimed. The Covenant, a name whispered in corridors of power, now offered a lifeline amidst the turbulent seas that threatened to engulf her homeland. However, Yekaterina's initial solace at Mr. Kay's sudden appearance slowly gave way to a simmering scepticism, her eyes narrowing as she assessed the implications of his words.

"I remember, you know. Your organisation," she said cautiously, her voice laced with doubt and suspicion, "was behind my father's decision to invade Ukraine. You played a part in leading Russia down this path of isolation and decline. Forgive me if I don't immediately trust your intentions."

"Please excuse our president's candidness, Mr Kay," Ivan interjected, his gaze never straying from the enigmatic figure before them. "Understandably, we have seen the fruits of your so-called assistance, and they have left a bitter taste in our mouths. What makes you think Yekaterina would be willing to risk further catastrophe by accepting aid from those who helped bring us low?"

Mr. Kay regarded them both with an inscrutable expression, gauging the depth of their resolve.

"Times change, Mr Kozyrev," he replied softly, his words echoing through the chamber like a ghostly whisper. "And with them, the landscape of power shifts and evolves. Our role in Russia's past was born of necessity – a necessary sacrifice to bring about a greater good. But now, the time has come for a new alliance, one that will restore your nation to its former glory and set it on the path to a brighter future."

"A new alliance?" exclaimed the Russian President, mistrust etched into her features like cracks upon a weathered statue. "On what terms? Russia is no beggar at the table of opportunists."

"Terms, Ms. Alexandreyevna, are the concern of merchants and peddlers," the man replied with an enigmatic smile. "We deal in covenants, in oaths bound by higher callings than mere commerce. Just as the Ark found safe harbour on Ararat's bosom after the deluge, so too shall Russia find refuge within our fold."

Yekaterina's gaze, sharp as a shard of Siberian ice, pierced the mysterious man who stood before her. She leaned back against the leather chair, its creases groaning under the shifting weight of her scepticism.

"Your words are honeyed," she began, her voice steady but edged with the frost of doubt, "but what proof can you offer that The Covenant possesses the means to lift Russia from this quagmire? We do not need platitudes; we need a bulwark against the tide that threatens to engulf us."

The mysterious man's smile did not waver, nor did the gleam in his eyes dim. He moved with deliberation; each step measured as if he trod upon hallowed ground. "Madame President," he intoned, his voice a resonant baritone that seemed to carry the echoes of ancient choirs, "The Covenant is the shepherd that guides lost flocks through valleys shadowed by death. Our reach extends beyond the mere physical; our resources are not confined to ledgers and coins." He paused, allowing his words to settle like dust upon the relics of bygone eras. "We are the keepers of secrets that have shaped the world since time immemorial. The influence we wield is carved into the bedrock of civilizations, as enduring as the Sphinx's silent vigil or the unyielding stones of Jerusalem. Consider us like the oasis of Siwa", he continued, his voice in a soothing cadence. "It witnessed Alexander the Great's quest for the wisdom of the oracle and could once again predict the genesis of a new Russian destiny. As Nefertiti gazed upon a vision that outlasted her reign, so too might you behold a future where Russia rises, Pharaoh-like, from its ashes."

Yekaterina's eyes narrowed, but the seed of curiosity had been sown in the fertile soil of her resolve. She could not deny the allure of such enigmatic declarations, nor could she ignore the ember of hope that flickered within her—a hope for Russia's resurgence, for a legacy that would eclipse the tarnished dream her father had left behind.

"Spare us your mystical words and speak plainly, Mr Kay" she demanded, her voice imbued with the steel of command befitting her lineage. "I'm asking you again: what tangible aid can The Covenant provide? We stand on the precipice, and words will not halt our fall."

The faint glow of a dying ember illuminated Mr. Kay's face as he leaned in closer, his voice lowered to a conspiratorial whisper. "My organisation," he went on, "is an ancient and powerful organisation that has shaped the course of history since its inception. Our reach extends into the highest echelons of political power, our influence a subtle yet potent force that guides nations toward our ultimate vision."

Yekaterina studied the mysterious man, her eyes narrowing as she attempted to discern truth from deception. Ivan, on the other hand, remained cautiously silent, willing to hear more before passing any judgment.

"Consider," Mr. Kay continued, "the rise and fall of empires, the delicate balance of global order – all orchestrated by The Covenant's unseen hand. We have intervened in times of crisis, our wisdom and resources preventing cataclysmic consequences on countless occasions."

At the sound of Mr Kay's words, the Russian president looked instinctively at the painting hanging behind her desk. *He lost, we won,* she thought. *What went through his mind when he realised it was all over?* As the eloquent man painted a picture of The Covenant's vast network and resources, Yekaterina stared back at him. *And you? Which role did your organisation play at the time? How long has it been pulling the strings from the shadows? Are you really the hidden puppeteer you claim to be, or just another garrulous con artist trying to exploit our current impediment?*

"Think upon this," Mr. Kay intoned, his voice echoing with biblical gravity. "We have allies and agents embedded within every major government, including your own. Our connections run deep and wide."

"Yet you speak of them as if they were mere pawns," Yekaterina interjected, her curiosity warring with her distrust. "What assurance do we have that you will not simply manipulate us as well?"

"An astute observation," Mr. Kay conceded, his gaze steady and unyielding. "But it is not control we seek, but rather cooperation. Our goals align, Yekaterina Alexandreyevna – the prosperity of Russia and the stabilisation of global politics. Like you, we are becoming increasingly worried about President Lascombes' real intentions and the growing influence of the European Federation globally. With the collapse of the United States as a superpower, the balance of the world has been jeopardised and needs to be restored. In the eyes of my organisation, Russia is our best contender to achieve this goal. We are, in a sense, kindred spirits."

"You seem to forget one key element in your appraisal, Mr Kay," Yekaterina declared with gravity. "Thanks to my father's foolish ambitions, Russia is highly indebted to China, to a point where our economy is completely dependent on their goodwill. Quite a bad start for the upcoming challenger of the European Federation's influence, don't you think? Maybe China would be a better candidate for your secret endeavours."

"A mere hitch, Madame President," replied the man with assurance. "China's ambitions have never been global dominance, except perhaps commercially. Despite their best efforts, the country's institutions are and will always be undermined by their intrinsic dispositions to corruption and greed. China has replaced England as a nation of shopkeepers, to use the expression used by the gentleman hanging behind your desk. My organisation will use its influence to alleviate the burden your creditor holds on to your finances, should you accept our assistance."

The air in the room grew heavy with anticipation as Yekaterina's scepticism began to crumble beneath the weight of Mr. Kay's words. The vision of a Russia unburdened by sanctions and political strife, standing tall and proud once more on the world stage, suddenly popped into her mind. She exchanged a look of cautious optimism with Ivan Kozyrev, their shared dreams for their nation beginning to take shape in the space between them.

"You... you have the power to do this?" she then asked Mr Kay, disclosing her last notes of incredulity.

"Consider it as a token of the Covenant's good will and intentions," the man replied placidly.

"Such an alliance would not come without risks," Yekaterina mused, her thoughts drifting to the legacy she hoped to leave for future generations. "But if The Covenant can help us navigate these treacherous waters, we may yet find our way back to solid ground."

"Indeed," Mr. Kay agreed, his eyes gleaming with purpose. "Together, we can chart a course through the labyrinth of international politics, steering Russia toward a brighter future." The shadowed corners of Yekaterina's office seemed to hum with a silent agreement as Mr Kay leaned forward, his voice a low murmur that echoed with the gravity of unspoken promises. "Our assistance will be concrete, measurable, and swift," he assured them, the firelight dancing in his eyes, casting an otherworldly glow upon his face. "You have my word."

Yekaterina's gaze fell upon the antique chess set displayed on a nearby table, its pieces locked in eternal battle – a tableau of geopolitical manoeuvring frozen in time. She pondered the weight of Mr. Kay's pledge, her heart heavy with the responsibility she bore for her people and their future. The potential alliance with The Covenant was a gambit fraught with risk, but perhaps it was the bold move Russia needed to regain its footing on the world stage.

"Your word carries great power," Ivan acknowledged, his voice tinged with both reverence and trepidation. He regarded the mysterious man before him, wondering what secrets lay hidden behind his enigmatic smile. "But what is your organisation's interest in assisting us and what will be the price of our cooperation?"

"Patience, my friend," Mr. Kay replied, his eyes narrowing ever so slightly. "All will be revealed in due course. "Consider what I have said," he intoned, casting his gaze outwards as though envisioning the city's transformation, "but do not keep us waiting too long. This is a one-time opportunity, and our offer will not last long."

With these last words, he strode to the door, pausing only to bestow upon them a final, penetrating glance—one that left a trail of anticipation mingling with the dust motes dancing in the slanted light. "Hope," he murmured, almost reverently, "is the star that guides us through the darkest night. Await our signal, and prepare for the dawn."

And with that, he departed, leaving Yekaterina and Ivan ensnared in the web of prophecy and promise. A silence settled over the room, thick with the essence of nascent schemes and concealed revelations.

PART FOUR

Fool's games

Years 2054 - 2056

21

The Oval Office was bathed in an eerie silence, the weight of a nation's fate pressing down upon its occupants. President Julius Theodore Thomas sat behind the Resolute desk[36], his fingers steepled, his brow furrowed with the lines of a thousand sleepless nights. Gathered before him were the pillars of his administration: Elizabeth Doyle, the Secretary of State; Gerald White, the National Security Advisor; and General William Fitzpatrick, the Chairman of the Joint Chiefs of Staff.

"Mr. President, I'm afraid the news from the front is grim," General Fitzpatrick began, his voice grave as a tolling bell. "Our intelligence suggests that the Confederate forces are on

---

[36] Name given to the large desk that American presidents frequently use at the White House in the Oval Office. This piece of furniture was a gift from Queen Victoria to American President Rutherford B. Hayes in 1880

the verge of a decisive breakthrough in Richmond. The fighting has been... intense."

President Thomas closed his eyes, the weight of the words settling upon his shoulders like a leaden cloak. "How long can our troops hold out?"

"Not long, sir," the General replied, his gaze unwavering. "We're running dangerously low on ammunition, and morale is... well, it's not good."

The President looked to the General with a bewildered expression.

"How is it possible that we are running low on ammunition?" he asked in disbelief. "Surely, our factories should be able to keep up with the demand and resupply our troops."

"Sir," said the general, "I feel it is my duty to remind you that our primary ammunition plants are located in territories controlled by the Confederacy. While we have begun converting other sites, such as those in Michigan and Indiana, it is a time-consuming process. Additionally, we are facing rising costs of raw materials. By the time we are able to produce at full capacity, it may be too late."

Gerald White leaned forward; his hawkish features etched with urgency.

"Mr President let's be realistic. We need to find another way to resupply our forces, and fast. If Richmond falls..."

"I know," the President interjected, his voice heavy with the burden of leadership. "If Richmond falls, it's only a matter of time before they march on Washington."

Elizabeth Doyle, who had been listening intently, chose this moment to speak.

"Mr. President, I know this may seem like a long shot, but... what about the European Union? Its members were our allies once, part of NATO. Perhaps they could be persuaded to lend us aid in our hour of need."

The Commander in Chief looked up, a flicker of hope dancing in his dark eyes.

"You think they would help us?"

"It's worth a try," Doyle replied, her voice steady with conviction, "at least until we become self-sufficient again. The ties that bind us are deep. They've stood by us in the past, and we've stood by them. It's time to call upon those bonds of friendship and shared history."

President Thomas nodded slowly, the gears of his mind turning.

"We used to be the top supplier of weapons globally. And now, here we are, desperately begging for assistance," he said with bitterness in his voice. He paused for an instant, his mind fast-wandering the illustrious past of a once proud nation. Then, returning to the present, his face displayed a resolute look. "Elizabeth, you're right. It's time to ask for help. I want you to embark on a diplomatic mission to Europe. Meet with their leaders, especially those of France, Germany, and Spain. Plead our case, remind them of our shared values and the stakes we all face. We need their help, now more than ever."

The Secretary of State rose from her seat, her posture radiating determination.

"I'll leave immediately, Mr. President. I won't rest until I've secured their support."

As she turned to leave, President Thomas called after her.

"Godspeed, Elizabeth. The fate of our nation may well rest in your hands."

***

The halls of the Bundeskanzleramt in Berlin echoed with the click of Elizabeth Doyle's heels as she strode towards the conference room. Flanked by Pierre-Antoine, President of France; Monika Richter, the German Chancellor; and Jorge Sanchez, Prime Minister of Spain, she felt a flicker of hope amidst the gathering darkness.

As they took their seats around the polished oak table, Elizabeth wasted no time in launching into her appeal.

"President Lascombes, Chancellor Richter, Prime Minister Sanchez. I come to you today not just as a representative of the Union of the Democratic States[37], but as a friend in dire need." She paused, letting the weight of her words settle upon the room. "Our nation is torn asunder, locked in a civil war that threatens to consume us all. I come the bearer of dire news. The Confederate forces are on the march, and without immediate military aid, I fear that our cause may be lost."

Elizabeth turned to Pierre-Antoine, her eyes shining with the intensity of her conviction.

"President Lascombes, France and America share a bond that stretches back to the very birth of our nation. Your

---

[37] After the secession of the southern states, the remaining part of the United States was temporarily renamed the Union of the Democratic States.

country stood with us in our fight for independence, and we have stood together through two world wars. I ask you now, in the name of that sacred bond, to stand with us once more."

Pierre-Antoine leaned forward, his expression sombre.

"Madame Secretary, your words stir the very heart of France. We have indeed shared much, and the thought of America falling to the forces of division and hate... it is a prospect too terrible to contemplate." He glanced at Monika and Jorge, a silent communication passing between them. "And yet, the decision to intervene militarily... it is not one that we can make lightly, nor alone. This is a matter that concerns all of Europe, and as such, it must be brought before the European Council."

Monika nodded, her voice soft yet firm.

"Elizabeth, please know that we hear your plea, and we feel your anguish as if it were our own. But as President Lascombes says, this is a decision that requires the input and consensus of all EU member states."

Jorge Sanchez spoke up, his tone reassuring.

"We will call for an emergency meeting of the European Council, and there, we will present your case with all the force and passion it deserves. You have our word on that."

The Secretary of State felt a wave of emotion wash over her, a mix of gratitude and trepidation. She knew that the road ahead would be long and fraught with uncertainty, but in this moment, in the company of these steadfast allies, she allowed herself a glimmer of hope.

"Thank you," she whispered, her voice thick with the weight of a nation's fate. "Thank you for hearing me, for standing with us, even if only in spirit for now. The United States will not forget this kindness, nor the bonds that bind us."

As the meeting drew to a close, Elizabeth Doyle found herself wandering the streets of Berlin, her mind a whirl with thoughts of war and peace, of alliances forged and broken. She paused before the Brandenburg Gate, its stately columns a silent testament to the enduring power of unity in the face of adversity.

"E pluribus unum," she murmured, the Latin phrase falling from her lips like a prayer. "Out of many, one."

It was a truth that had guided her nation since its inception, a truth that she clung to now, in this darkest of hours. For if the United States was to weather this storm, if it were to emerge from the crucible of civil war unbroken, it would need more than weapons and armies. It would need the strength of its ideals, the power of its alliances, and the unwavering conviction that even in the face of division and strife, there was still hope for a brighter tomorrow.

"Madam Secretary, is everything alright?" asked her assistant, interrupting her thoughts.

"Yes, Sam. Take me back to the hotel. I need to talk to the President.

22

The sounds of mortar fire and artillery shells echoed through the command centre in Richmond, a cacophonous symphony that sent tremors through the walls and floor. General William Fitzpatrick stood stoically amidst the frenzy of activity; his steely gaze fixed on the large digital map that dominated the room. Red and blue dots danced across the screen, a macabre ballet representing the ebb and flow of battle raging just miles away.

Staff officers rushed about, shouting orders into headsets and relaying urgent reports from the front lines. The tension was palpable, a living entity that coiled around each person like a serpent, constricting tighter with each passing minute. Worry lined the faces of even the most battle-hardened soldiers as the sounds of Confederate artillery drew ever closer, an ominous drumbeat that heralded impending doom.

A young private, barely out of his teens, approached Fitzpatrick with a dispatch clutched in his trembling hand. The general took the paper, his eyes scanning the hastily scrawled message. His blood ran cold as he read the dire news - Confederate forces had breached the southern defensive line and were now pouring into Richmond, engaging the Union troops in brutal street-to-street urban warfare. The general's mind raced, weighing the impossible choice before him, like a modern-day Abraham agonizing over the sacrifice of Isaac. He could order his men to stand their ground and fight to the last, a noble but futile gesture that would result in catastrophic casualties. Or he could sound the retreat, pulling back to Fredericksburg to regroup and fight another day, abandoning Richmond to the enemy.

He stared at the dispatch for a long moment, the weight of command heavy on his broad shoulders. How many times had great leaders faced such a decision throughout history? Caesar at the Rubicon, Napoleon at Waterloo, Lee at Gettysburg. Now it was his turn to decide the fate of his army. With a heavy sigh, he turned to his staff.

"Send out the order. All units are to disengage and fall back to Fredericksburg immediately. We'll make our stand there."

A murmur of surprise rippled through the room, quickly replaced by grim determination as the staff set about relaying the general's commands. The radio crackled to life as units checked in, acknowledging the retreat order. But then a gruff voice broke through the static.

"Negative, command. This is Able Company holding the line. We've got those rebel bastards on the run. We're not giving up an inch of ground, not today."

Fitzpatrick snatched the radio handset, his voice booming with the authority of God Himself.

"Able Company, this is General Fitzpatrick. You are hereby ordered to fall back to the rendezvous point outside the city immediately. Acknowledge!"

"With all due respect, Sir," the voice replied, "we're not going anywhere. Richmond is our home. We'll defend her to the last man if we have to."

"Who am I talking to? Over."

"This is Reserve Sergeant Will MacKay, General. My men and I are holding the Powhite Parkway. ... We have blown up the bridge, Confederate troops cannot cross there anymore. They have withdrawn—"

"They have withdrawn because Confederate troops have taken the Nickel Bridge. If you maintain your position, you'll be caught from behind in no time."

"Our position his secured, those bastards will—"

Fitzpatrick's voice boomed through the room.

"Listen carefully, Reserve Sergeant MacKay," he bellowed. "I need capable soldiers to protect the capital, not dead heroes. So, swallow your pride and follow orders to regroup in Fredericksburg!"

The general slammed down the handset in frustration. Insubordination, no matter how well-intentioned, could not be tolerated. Not now, with so much at stake.

Miles away, a scene of utter chaos unfolded as Confederate troops stormed into Richmond, overwhelming the last pockets of Union resistance. Soldiers in combat gears kicked down doors, tossing grenades into buildings and raking the rubble-strewn streets with assault weapons' fire. Screams of the wounded and dying mingled with the roar of burning vehicles, a hellish din that rose to the smoke-choked heavens.

Some soldiers, drunk on the thrill of victory, began to loot abandoned shops and homes, stuffing their packs with whatever valuables they could carry. Others rounded up the battered remnants of Union prisoners, herding them like cattle to an uncertain fate.

Suddenly, a heavily armoured personnel carrier roared down the cratered avenue, crushing debris beneath its tracks. It ground to a halt and the rear hatch swung open, disgorging a towering figure in an immaculate grey uniform.

Major General Thomas Houston Wallace strode forward, his icy blue eyes surveying the destruction with a mix of satisfaction and disdain. He was a living legend among the Confederate ranks, a brilliant tactician whose ruthless strategies had delivered victory after victory. Men both respected and feared him, in equal measure.

"What is the meaning of this?" he roared, his voice cutting through the din like a whip crack. "I gave strict orders - no looting, no reprisals! We are soldiers, not savages. Any man caught disobeying will face summary execution. Am I understood?"

A chorus of "Yes, sir!" rang out as the chastened troops quickly fell into line.

"Now Regroup and resupply," he ordered. Houston Wallace allowed himself a small smile of triumph as he gazed upon the burning ruins of Richmond, a jewel of the Old Dominion now firmly in Confederate hands. But there was no time to savour the moment - the road to Washington lay open, and he meant to march down it.

***

An anxious hush fell over the Europa building in Brussels as the leaders of the European nations arrived to attend the emergency meeting, the clack of their polished dress shoes striking the marble floors echoing through the cavernous lobby. Monika Richter, Pierre-Antoine Lascombes and Jorge Sanchez strode in side by side, their expressions stoic masks concealing the weight of the monumental decision resting on their shoulders. The cameras flashed incessantly, and reporters shouted in a frenzy, their questions bouncing off the walls of glass and steel. Despite the chaos, the three leaders remained composed, nodding politely and exchanging handshakes with their counterparts while refusing to reveal any information to satisfy the insatiable media. After posing for a few more pictures, they all proceeded to the meeting hall, where they would be deliberating America's fate.

For the next two days, Elizabeth Doyle walked nervously back and forth along the shiny corridors, her high heels leaving a mark on the already worn-out floor. On any occasion, she would eagerly grab the arm of every aide and assistant who passed by, her grey eyes pleading for any scrap of news, any whisper of the ongoing discussions. But they would merely shake their heads before scurrying away. Finally, overcome with exhaustion both physically and mentally, the Secretary of State leaned against the window, gazing out at the bleak Brussels sky as if the answer lay hidden in the clouds. How had it come to this - the fate of her country, her people, decided behind closed doors an ocean away? She felt as helpless as a leaf caught in a whirlwind, tossed around without control, at the mercy of the surrounding forces.

At the end of the second day, the President of the European Council and President of the Commission finally emerged, ascending the podium in the press room side by side, a united front. Cameras clicked and flashed, a cacophony of shutters and shouted questions threatening to drown out their words.

"After a long deliberation, it is with heavy hearts that we must refuse the Union of Democratic States' request for military assistance in America's internal conflict," the Council President intoned solemnly. "The European Union cannot in all conscience choose sides or provide weapons in this issue, which it considers to be an internal affair of the country. We will, however, offer every available humanitarian aid to assist all civilians affected by the ongoing hostilities."

The room erupted in a frenzy, reporters leaping to their feet and shouting over one another.

But the Secretary of State heard none of it, the pronouncement striking her like a physical blow. She staggered back, steadying herself against the wall as despair crashed over her in a suffocating wave. After all the shared history, the alliances and pacts and promises, her nation was deserted. Left alone against the gathering darkness.

A gentle touch on her elbow jolted Elizabeth Doyle back to the present. An aide pressed a folded note into her hand. It bore a simple message: *Chancellor Richter requests you meet her in the Schuman Lounge.*

Elizabeth found Monika standing by the window, bathed in wan grey light, her shoulders slumped beneath an invisible burden. The German Chancellor turned as she entered, sorrow etched across her elegant features.

"Elizabeth, I am so sorry," Monika said softly, reaching out to clasp the other woman's hands. "Believe me, this was not a decision we made lightly. But the majority of the Council members are reluctant to provide any military assistance to the Union. They fear angering Russia or China and potentially being dragged into a worldwide conflict."

"You're leaving us to fend for ourselves," Elizabeth replied bitterly, pulling away. "Whatever happened to NATO, to our 'special relationship?'"

"I wish we could do more," Monika insisted, her eyes glistening with unshed tears. "But we have our own peoples to think of. Given the current situation, we can only provide humanitarian aid, as stated in the official declaration. I am truly sorry."

She squeezed Elizabeth's hands once more before turning and walking out, leaving the Secretary of State alone with the crushing realisation that settled over her like a shroud. For the first time in its history, America stood utterly alone against the oncoming storm.

23

The sun hung low in the sky, casting its rays upon the blood-soaked fields surrounding Fredericksburg. The once-verdant landscape had been transformed into a hellscape of churned mud and shattered bodies, testament to the ferocity of the battle that raged between Union and Confederate forces. Then, the thunder of artillery shattered the morning stillness, reverberating through the streets of the scarred city like the fury of an angry god.

In his field command centre, General William Fitzpatrick pored over tactical digital maps streaked with red and blue lines, coordinating troop movements as reports flooded in from all sectors.

"Sir, the 14th regiment is requesting reinforcements on the western flank," an aide called out. "They're being hammered by Rebel artillery."

Fitzpatrick's jaw tightened, grief and anger swirling inside him. Too many brave soldiers had already lost their lives on this once-peaceful Virginia land, just as they had on this very spot over a hundred years ago. He would not condemn more to perish needlessly.

"We can't spare any more men. Tell Colonel Pritchard to hold the line at all costs!" Fitzpatrick ordered. "We must preserve our strength for the next assault."

Miles away, Confederate General Thomas Houston Wallace surveyed the battlefield through binoculars, a cruel smile playing on his lips as Union defences buckled. Ruthless and cunning, Houston Wallace cared nothing for the human cost, only total victory at any price. With a commanding stance, he paid no mind to the chaos of Couriers delivering reports from his battlefield commanders.

"General, the Union defence line is thinning in the centre," a major reported breathlessly. "If we commit the reserves now, we can punch through and cut it in half."

A wolfish grin spread across Houston Wallace's craggy face.

"Then that's precisely what we'll do. Send in the 7th infantry with support from the 3rd artillery and 2nd assault helicopter battalion. Smash their defences and show no quarter. We'll drown those bastards in their own blood."

As the Confederate reserves surged forward in a determined assault, the Union centre buckled and then shattered under the onslaught. Soldiers turned and fled as secessionist troops poured through the gap.

"Send in the 1st and the 5th battalion," Houston Wallace barked to his aide. "Crush their right flank once and for all. Let none survive."

Panic-stricken voices crackled across the radio in the Union's command post. "They've broken through! We can't hold them, we're being overrun!"

Fitzpatrick gripped the edge of the table, his knuckles white. He could visualize the Confederate flags fluttering victoriously over the field among the screams of the dying. In that moment, he knew the awful truth in his bones - he was outmatched by Houston Wallace's ruthless cunning and willingness to sacrifice human lives for victory.

"Signal the retreat," Fitzpatrick commanded hoarsely to his aides, defeat bitter as wormwood on his tongue. "Fall back to defensive positions around Washington. We'll make our stand there. May God have mercy on us all."

***

As the battered remnants of the Union forces limped back towards Washington in a grim procession, a palpable sense of despair settled over the capital. Soldiers erected makeshift barricades in the streets as civilians huddled fearfully in their homes.

President Julius Thomas paced back and forth in the Oval Office of the White House, his complexion turning pale as he listened to General Fitzpatrick's grim voice coming through the speakerphone.

"Fredericksburg has fallen, Mr. President. We couldn't hold our ground against their cunning tactics. The confederates are on the march straight for Washington."

Thomas felt an icy dread grip his heart. The Second Civil War he had desperately tried to prevent was now reaching its bloody denouement in what felt like a replay of the events of December 1862. Except this time, the Union forces were in disarray. As if answering his darkest thoughts, the phone rang again. It was Elizabeth Doyle, the Secretary of States, her voice strained.

"Mr. President, I'm afraid our allies will not intervene. They refuse to take side fearing a reaction from Russia and China. There will be no military assistance forthcoming. We stand alone against the darkness."

Thomas slowly set the receiver down, feeling the last flicker of hope gutter out within him like a dying candle. They were alone. All his efforts, all the lives lost, had been for nothing. An oppressive weight settled on his shoulders, smothering and heavy.

"Mr. President, we have to consider all options, no matter how distasteful." The grave voice of his National Security Advisor intruded on the bleakness of his ruminations. "A targeted nuclear strike on the approaching Confederate forces may be our only chance to turn the tide."

Thomas spun to face him, eyes wide with disbelief.

"You can't be serious! Unleash nuclear weapons on our own soil? On American citizens?"

"These rebels are traitors, sir, not citizens. Thousands more will die if we don't act decisively now."

For a sickening moment, President Thomas felt the temptation of it — the power to destroy his enemies utterly, to visit radioactive retribution on those who sought to tear the Union asunder. It would be a most terrible salvation. He imagined the blinding flashes erupting across the Virginia countryside, the towering mushroom clouds staining the sky. Followed by the screams of civilians scoured to bone and ash in the atomic inferno. And in the aftermath, a lifeless wasteland sinking into poisoned desolation. But from the depths of his despair, the President summoned a reservoir of strength, a fierce determination to do what was right for his nation, even in the face of such overwhelming odds.

"No. If we unleash that evil, we are no better than the wickedness we oppose. I will not have history remember me as the man who rained fire on his own people. May God forgive us all, but we must find another way." He turned to his ashen-faced Chief of Staff. "Give the order for the government and Congress to evacuate to Philadelphia. We'll regroup there and determine our next move."

As his aides hastened to relay his commands, Thomas cast one final look around the Oval Office. The iconic room had been occupied by icons and giants - Lincoln, Roosevelt, Kennedy. Leaders who had faced down secession, depression, and nuclear armageddon. And now it was his turn to join their hallowed yet burdensome ranks - Julius T. Thomas, the President who lost Washington. Tears stung his eyes as he took in the familiar trappings of power and history for the last time. The elegant curtains, the storied desk, the oil paintings of his predecessors gazing down in silent judgment.

Power was an illusion, Thomas realised, as ephemeral as the mortal men who temporarily wielded it in this very chamber. All that pomp and tradition and ancient ritual - it was ultimately meaningless in the face of raw military might and merciless force of arms. With a final, almost reverent nod to the American flag standing sentinel in the corner, the president walked out into the waiting darkness, leaving behind the smouldering ruins of his tainted legacy.

***

Edward MacCorkindale sat behind his mahogany desk in the stately office of the Confederate President in Austin, his steely eyes scrutinizing the stack of military dispatches strewn before him. Each report told of resounding victories, of Union forces in retreat, of the inexorable march of Confederate boots trampling the once hallowed ground of the North.

A wicked smile played at his thin lips as he savoured the taste of long-awaited triumph. He leaned back in his leather chair, relishing the weight of destiny settling upon his shoulders like a sacred mantle. At last, the depraved Babylon that once was the United States would fall, turned to ashes and dust by the righteous armies of the South, just as the prophets of old had foretold.

Suddenly, the heavy oak doors burst open, and a young aide rushed in, his face flushed with excitement.

"Mr. President! News from Fredericksburg!"

MacCorkindale rose to his feet, anticipation crackling in the air like a gathering storm.

"Come on, speak up!" he demanded impatiently.

"A great victory, Sir! The Union troops are in full rout. General Houston Wallace sends word that the road to Washington lies wide open before us, ripe for the taking!"

A laugh of pure, unadulterated joy burst from MacCorkindale's throat. He threw his arms wide, as if to embrace the very hand of Providence itself.

"Hallelujah!" he declared, his voice booming with righteous fervour. "Once again, the Lord has delivered our enemies into our hands!"

He turned to the ornate phone on his desk, the Gilded receiver glinting in the afternoon sun. With a steady hand, he dialled the private line to his top general.

"Mr President, it's an honour," the supreme commander said.

"Houston Wallace, you magnificent bastard!" MacCorkindale boomed. "Like David before Goliath, you have struck a mortal blow against our foes. Truly, the Almighty smiled upon you this day."

"The men fought like lions, sir," Houston Wallace replied, his voice crackling with static and barely restrained elation. "The Union dogs turned tail and ran. Washington is ours for the taking. What are your orders?"

MacCorkindale paused, a beatific glow suffusing his rugged features as he envisioned himself striding through the vanquished streets of the country's once-proud centre of power. At last, the reins of the nation would be firmly in the grasp of the righteous. No more would the depraved old order hold sway.

"Secure the city, General," the President instructed, his voice hardening with steely resolve. "Then, reduce all its monuments to ashes. The Capitol, the White House, every vestige of their vaunted government — raze it to the ground!" he hissed, his voice dripping with venom. "Let it be a purifying flame, scouring the earth of Babylon the Great, the Mother of Harlots and Abominations."

Silence crackled over the line for a long moment.

"Sir..." Wallace began uncertainly. "Are you certain? The city could be a valuable prize..."

"It is a cancer!" MacCorkindale snapped, slamming a fist on his desk. "A modern Gomorrah, seething with wickedness and corruption! It must be excised, root and stem! Let it be reduced to ruins and bitter memory, a testament to the folly of those who defy the will of the Almighty!"

"...Understood, Mr. President," Wallace replied grimly. "It will be done as you order."

As the line went dead, MacCorkindale sank back into his chair, a fevered light burning in his eyes. The ecstasy of vindication coursed through his veins, sweeter than the finest Kentucky bourbon.

"The old order crumbles," he whispered, a beatific smile on his face. "And from its ashes, a new Jerusalem shall arise, with the Southern Cross ascendant over all. Praise be to God, who has made me His instrument of divine retribution!"

His laughter rang through the halls of power, exultant and mad, as the first wisps of smoke began to rise over the distant Capitol dome.

24

Chaos consumed Washington, D.C. as the once-proud capital erupted into pandemonium. Union soldiers, defeated and demoralized, staggered through the streets in a disorderly retreat. Government workers hastily shredded and incinerated sensitive documents, desperate to keep precious secrets from falling into Confederate hands. Civilians, their faces etched with sheer terror, threw whatever belongings they could gather into overloaded cars before fleeing the doomed city.

From the window of his armoured presidential limousine, President Julius Thomas watched the apocalyptic scene unfold with a profound sense of despair and regret. The defeats at Richmond and Fredericksburg had been decisive blows, shattering the Union army's ability to defend the city. Now, the evacuation to Philadelphia was their only hope of regrouping and launching a counterattack.

As the motorcade sped down Pennsylvania Avenue, it passed mobs of looters smashing store windows, armed thugs brawling in the streets. The capital of the free world had descended into a Hobbesian state of nature — solitary, poor, nasty, brutish and short. Thomas saw in the mayhem a premonition of the bleak destiny that awaited the nation if the Confederates prevailed.

"My God, what is to become of our republic?" he murmured under his breath, the words of the Gettysburg Address echoing in his mind. "Shall government of the people, by the people, for the people perish from the Earth?"

In the distance, the dome of the U.S. Capitol building was wreathed in flames, its neoclassical splendour crumbling into ash and smoke. The sight pierced President Thomas' heart like a dagger to the chest. That shining citadel on a hill, that temple of liberty and democracy, was being reduced to ruins before his eyes.

As the motorcade reached the outskirts of the city, it passed convoys of Humvees packed with grim-faced soldiers, Abrams tanks rumbling down the highway, helicopters whirring overhead — the last remaining Union forces streaming north in a full-scale retreat. Thomas knew their fight was far from over. They would regroup, resupply, and return to retake what was theirs. The Union would be preserved, at whatever the cost.

Hours later, an eerie silence descended upon the abandoned capital, its streets deserted except for blowing rubbish and mangled debris. Then, an ominous rumble, distant at first but growing steadily louder. The heavy tread of boots. The clanking of tanks. The whirr of helicopter blades. Like a plague of locusts, the Confederate forces swarmed into the city, an endless procession of troops and armoured vehicles. Soldiers marched in perfect unison, bayoneted rifles held at the ready, eyes gleaming with zealous fervour beneath their helmets. Attack choppers buzzed overhead, casting menacing shadows. The very earth seemed to tremble before their might.

At the head of this conquering army rode Major General Thomas Houston Wallace, towering atop his command Humvee like a modern-day Hannibal surveying a fallen Rome. Immaculately pressed uniform adorned with medals, firm jaw set in smug satisfaction, he emanated an aura of supreme confidence and vindication. As a man of deep faith, Houston Wallace saw himself as an instrument of divine justice, the David anointed by God to topple the Goliath of Northern aggression and perversion. He relished the glory of this triumphal entry, the culmination of all his cunning strategies and brilliant manoeuvres.

"What are your orders, sir?" asked Colonel Jefferson, his second-in-command. "Shall we secure the perimeter or pursue the routed enemy?"

Houston Wallace pondered for a moment before replying.

"Send out patrols to subdue any lingering resistance and assert our control. But our primary task lies ahead. We shall purify this den of iniquity with holy fire. Every vestige of its defiance against the Almighty must be demolished without mercy."

"Sir?" Jefferson looked puzzled. "Burn the city? But…surely—"

"Are you questioning a direct command from our Commander in Chief, Colonel?" Houston Wallace interrupted sharply. "These monuments glorify a heretical government that spat upon the Lord's natural order. President MacCorkindale has deemed that these affronts to God must be razed to ash. You would do well to obey His anointed without hesitation."

Jefferson swallowed hard and nodded. "Understood, General. I'll relay the order at once."

Soon, great gouts of flame roared upwards from the Capitol, the White House, the hallowed memorials and museums - all the cherished symbols of the once-great republic. Fire hungrily consumed wood and stone, marble and metal, erasing centuries of history in a frenzied blaze. As the conflagration painted the dusky skies an infernal orange and filled the air with heat and soot, Houston Wallace whispered a prayer, exulting in the destruction of a sinful empire.

***

Hundreds of miles away, in the heart of the Confederate capital of Austin, the capitol of the Confederation gleamed under the Texas sun, its neoclassical dome and colonnades pristinely white against a flawless blue sky. Upon its grand balcony stood President Edward MacCorkindale, arms outspread as he basked in the ecstatic cheers of the adoring crowd packing the square below. They gazed upon him with nothing short of worshipful awe, their rightful ruler leading them towards salvation. Rapturous chants of *'Glory be to God!'* and *'The South is risen!'* filled the air.

MacCorkindale drank deep of their veneration, a beatific smile spreading across his craggy features. He felt the presence of the Lord Almighty flowing through him, the power and the righteousness. He was the instrument of divine providence, called to cleanse America of its sins and forge a new covenant that will enlighten all nations across the globe. Raising his hands for silence, the throng immediately hushed in reverent anticipation.

"Brothers and sisters in Christ," he intoned, voice booming. "Today, the Lord has granted us a most wondrous victory! The depraved hordes of the Union have been routed at Fredericksburg, scattered before our noble warriors like chaff before the wind! Even now, our gallant armies occupy their decadent capital, that foul Babylon on the Potomac!"

The jubilant masses erupted at this revelation, many sinking to their knees and ecstatically praising Jesus for delivering them dominion over their enemies. The president allowed the celebrations to continue for a minute before gesturing for quiet again.

"Yet, conquest alone will not suffice to build the sanctified republic the Almighty demands of us. No, we must scour the legacy of the old, sinful Union from the very earth, erase all traces of their perversions. And so, I have commanded the obliteration of Washington, that festering swamp of sodomy and socialism. Let it be reduced to cinders, its memory cast into oblivion! Only then may we raise a new, godly civilization in its place!"

The crowd exploded into hysterical exultation at this declaration, many speaking in tongues or writhing on the ground as they were overcome with religious fervour. MacCorkindale raised his eyes and arms heavenward, tears of joy streaming down his face.

"We shall build a new America, one purified of vice and sin. An America that bows to God alone as His supreme ruler. A new age dawns, my children!" he cried. "The Kingdom of God is at hand, and we, the chosen faithful, shall be its builders! Hallelujah!"

Basking in their worship a few moments more, he finally turned and strode into the capitol, the crowds still chanting hosannas behind him. As the door shut, he allowed himself a small, private smile, knowing that his work was not yet done. He had led his people to the threshold of the Promised Land, but one more trial awaited before they could claim their inheritance. Entering his office, he sat at his sanctified desk, overcome with exhaustion and exultation. The Confederate flag hung prominently on the wall, its crimson cross and starry saltire an emblem of the pure Christian republic he had sworn to create. Opposite it was a painting depicting the Prophet Elijah calling down fire from heaven to consume the pagan altar. To MacCorkindale, it was a biblical allegory for his sacred duty to annihilate the Union's capital of sin.

"Dear Lord," he whispered. "You have led us to the very cusp of glory. Grant me strength now to take the final step. Let Your will be done."

As if on cue, the phone rang just as MacCorkindale concluded the prayer. He picked it up.

"Mr. President, this is Major General Houston Wallace," came the voice on the line. "Washington is secured. We await your next orders."

MacCorkindale smiled serenely, sensing the Lord's guiding hand at work. The day of judgment was finally at hand.

"Thank you, General," he replied. "You have done well, as have all our anointed warriors. Withdraw now to a 20 miles distance. And let the unbelievers and apostates know the terrible swift sword of the Almighty's wrath!"

"Could you please say that again, Mr. President? I'm afraid I didn't quite catch your last statement," the general said with a concerned tone.

"You heard me perfectly well, General. Withdraw our troops 20 miles from the city and contact me once this is done."

"As you order, Mr. President," Houston Wallace said solemnly before hanging up.

A couple of hours later, the phone rang again.

"Mr President, all troops have retreated to a distance of twenty miles from the city., as ordered. I await your next instructions."

"Pray, General. Pray as God is coming."

As the line went dead, MacCorkindale leaned back and smiled, eyes gleaming with the light of fanatical resolve. The abomination of Washington, seat of the heathen Union, would soon be wiped from existence like Sodom and Gomorrah.

From its ashes would rise the New Jerusalem, with the Confederation as the one true Zion. His holy crusade was nearing its inevitable climax.

Pressing a special button on his desk, he uttered a few words into the secure channel, sealing the fate of millions:

"Admiral, initiate Isaiah Protocol."

***

In the halls of power across Europe, shockwaves reverberated as news of Washington's atomic annihilation reached the continent's capitals. Diplomats and leaders alike were gripped by a visceral horror, the likes of which had not been seen since the darkest days of the Second World War. The world stood frozen, eyes wide and mouths agape, as televisions and phones lit up with images of a mushroom cloud rising over the once-proud capital. The unthinkable had become real.

In Paris, an emergency meeting of the European triumvirate was hastily convened. Pierre-Antoine, his face ashen, paced the room like a caged lion. Jorge and Monika sat in stunned silence, their minds struggling to process the enormity of what had transpired.

"My God, what have they done?" the French President finally spoke, his voice barely above a whisper. "An American city...wiped off the map by its own people. It's...it's inconceivable."

Monika, ever the voice of reason even in the most trying of times, tried to steer the conversation towards pragmatism.

"We must consider our response carefully," she said, her words measured but tinged with an unmistakable tremor. "This is no longer just an American affair. The repercussions will be felt across the globe."

"She's right," Jorge approved grimly. "We were fools to think we could remain neutral in this conflict. If nothing is done, this madness will soon reach our very doorstep."

Pierre-Antoine stopped his pacing and turned to face his colleagues, a flicker of doubt crossing his handsome features.

"Perhaps...perhaps we should have intervened sooner. Supported the legitimate government against these...these zealots."

Monika shook her head sadly.

"We cannot change the past, mon ami[38]. But we can shape the future. Europe must stand united now more than ever. We must be a beacon of stability in a world gone mad."

As the three leaders deliberated, their minds heavy with the weight of history, President Julius Thomas sat alone in his makeshift office in Philadelphia's City Hall. The room felt cavernous, empty—a far cry from the warm familiarity of the now-evaporated White House.

Thomas stared at the executive order on his desk, the words blurring before his eyes. With a trembling hand, he signed the document declaring Washington, D.C. a no man's land—a haunted monument to the nation's grievous wound — and

---

[38] My friend.

warning the Confederation that any further use of nuclear weapons would result in retaliation.

"How did it come to this?" he whispered, his voice cracking. "My God, what have we done?"

Miles away, in the heart of Austin, President Edward MacCorkindale met with his generals and advisors, an air of smug satisfaction suffusing the room. The destruction of Washington had been a master stroke—a righteous blow against the infidel Union. Now, the final phase of their holy crusade beckoned.

"Gentlemen," he began, his eyes alight with zealous fervour, "the Lord has blessed our cause. But our work is not yet done. We must press on, bring the entire nation under the dominion of God's chosen."

The assembled men nodded, their faces hard with resolve. Plans were made, strategies plotted. The Confederate war machine would roll on, an inexorable tide, until every last corner of America knelt before the Almighty.

And through it all, MacCorkindale smiled, secure in his delusions of divine mandate. He was the anointed one, the holy warrior of God. And like Joshua at Jericho, he would see the walls of the wicked brought tumbling down.

25

Pierre-Antoine leaned forward, his hands clasped tightly as he regarded Monika and Jorge across the polished mahogany table. The weight of his words hung heavy in the air, like gathering storm clouds foreshadowing a tempest.

"We must face the truth, the situation in America is deteriorating rapidly," he said, his voice grave. "The global consequences could be catastrophic if we don't act swiftly."

Monika's brow furrowed, a flicker of concern in her blue eyes.

"What are you proposing, Pierre-Antoine?"

He took a deep breath, bracing himself.

"Realistically? We need a more unified Europe. A federal Europe, to protect our security and interests in the face of America's decline."

Jorge shifted uneasily in his seat, a frown etched on his face.

"Pierre-Antoine, this isn't the platform we were elected on. The people expect us to maintain the status quo, not radically reshape the very foundations of Europe."

The French president shook his head vehemently.

"The status quo is no longer an option, Jorge. The fall of the American hegemony leaves us exposed, vulnerable. We must adapt quickly, or risk being swept away by the tides of change."

Monika's gaze drifted to the window, the soft light of the Parisian afternoon filtering through the curtains. In her mind's eye, she saw the ghosts of history - the rise and fall of empires, the ebb and flow of power. She knew, deep in her bones, that Pierre-Antoine was right. Europe could no longer sustain its divisions, not now, not with the world order crumbling around them.

"I agree with Pierre-Antoine," she said softly, her voice carrying the weight of conviction. "We have to act, even if it means challenging the very beliefs that brought us to power."

Jorge sighed heavily, the burden of leadership etched in the lines of his face. He thought of his family, of the future he wanted for his children. A future of stability, of security. And in that moment, he knew that future could only be achieved through unity.

"Very well," he said, his voice resolute. "I'll stand with you, hermanito. Let us forge a new path for Europe, together."

Pierre-Antoine nodded, a glimmer of hope in his eyes. But he knew that convincing Monika and Jorge was only the first step. The real battle lay ahead, in persuading the French political class and the other EU members to embrace his vision.

***

The Congress Hall in Versailles echoed with the hubbub of the French deputies in senators gathered for a special address by the President. Pierre-Antoine slowly climbed to the podium and stood before them, his bearing regal, his voice clear and strong.

"Ms President of the Congress, Mr. President of the Senate, Ms Prime Minister, members of the government, deputies and senators," he began, "I come to you today with a proposition that may seem radical, even unthinkable. But in these uncertain times, we must be bold. We must be visionary."

A ripple of astonishment passed through the gathered politicians, their faces a mix of scepticism and intrigue. Charles Le Guen, leader of Les Patriots, leaned forward, his eyes narrowed.

"And what exactly is this bold vision of yours, President Lascombes?" he shouted.

"The gentleman from the opposition is invited to wait for the President to finish before asking any question," the President of the Congress lectured.

Nonetheless, Pierre-Antoine met his gaze unflinchingly.

"A federal Europe. A Europe united not just in name, but in structure, in purpose, in destiny."

The room erupted in a cacophony of voices, some raised in support, others in vehement opposition. Pierre-Antoine's own party, Les Republicains Progressistes, seemed divided, uncertainty etched on their faces.

"This is madness!" Le Guen declared, his voice rising above the din. "You would upend centuries of history, of national sovereignty, for what? A pipe dream of unity?"

Pierre-Antoine remained steadfast, his conviction unshakeable. He stared at the leader of the Patriots who, despite his setbacks in the presidential election, had still managed to get himself re-elected as a representative.

"It is not a pipe dream, Monsieur Le Guen. It is a necessity. In a world where the old order is crumbling, where the very foundations of our security are threatened, we must adapt. We must evolve. Or we will perish. This morning, I called for an emergency meeting of the European Council to propose a referendum on the creation of a federal Europe."

The room grew quiet, his words hanging heavy in the air as everyone processed their meaning. But soon enough, the noise resumed, and conversations erupted again with chaotic energy. Pierre-Antoine could see the doubt in their eyes, the resistance to change. But he knew, with unwavering certainty, that this was the path they must take. For the sake of Europe, for the sake of the world.

The battle lines were drawn, the stage set for a struggle that would determine the very future of the continent.

***

As the different heads of state and government met for the European Council, the grand chamber filled with the echoes of hushed conversations and the shuffling of papers. Pierre-Antoine solemnly sat at the head of the table, flanked by

Monika and Jorge. The gravity of the moment was not lost on any of them. As the meeting began, the French president rose to his feet, his voice clear and resonant.

"Esteemed members of the Council, I asked you to join me today for this emergency meeting as we stand at a crossroads. The world as we know it is changing, and we must change with it. If our countries and our institutions are to withstand these transformations, the creation of a federal Europe is longer an option; it is an imperative."

He spoke with a passion that seemed to ignite the very air around him, his words painting a vivid picture of a Europe united, strong, and secure.

"Imagine a Europe where our resources are pooled, our strengths combined, our weaknesses mitigated. A Europe that can stand toe-to-toe with any power, any threat."

A low buzz of conversation filled the room as the gathered leaders murmured in a mix of concern and approval.

Monika leaned forward, her voice clear and resolute.

"The French President is right. We cannot afford to be divided, not now. The challenges we face demand unity, cooperation, and a shared vision for the future."

Jorge nodded in agreement, his eyes scanning the room.

"The days of hesitation are over. We made a mistake by rejecting the opportunity to support the democratic forces in America. Our narrow-mindedness has disrupted the global balance and could pose a threat at any moment. We must act, and we must act decisively. A federal Europe is the only way forward."

The room buzzed with a mix of excitement and apprehension as the members of the Council grappled with the magnitude of the proposal. Pierre-Antoine could see the wheels turning in their minds, the calculations being made.

For five long days, the negotiations continued, each member state bringing their own concerns, their own demands to the table. Pierre-Antoine, Angela and Jorge navigated the complex web of diplomacy with a deft hand, his persuasive skills put to the ultimate test.

Finally, on the fifth day, the Council reached a decision. The referendum would go forward, the fate of Europe to be decided by its people. Furthermore, they agreed for the vote to be counted as a whole, preventing any state from vetoing it. Pierre-Antoine felt a surge of elation at this personal victory, tempered by the knowledge of the battle that lay ahead.

***

Back in France, the campaign began in earnest. The opposition wasted no time in mounting their attacks, decrying the very idea of a federal Europe as a threat to national identity, to sovereignty. In the hallowed halls of the French parliament, the debates raged, each faction vying for the upper hand. The far-right and far-left parties were particularly vocal, their arguments steeped in nationalism and fear of liberal capitalism.

"This is an unacceptable betrayal of France's territorial integrity!" Charles Le Guen declared, his voice shaking with outrage. "A knife in the back of those who heroically sacrificed their lives in the First and second World Wars to defend our nation's sovereignty. We will not be subsumed into some European superstate, our identity erased, our traditions trampled. Hear me when I say President Lascombes is a traitor to the very essence of France!"

Pierre-Antoine watched the proceedings with a heavy heart, the weight of the opposition's words pressing down on him. Monika and Jorge, like many of their counterparts, were dealing with similar challenges. The destructive force of nationalism still lingered, he thought. It's going to be a long and bloody battle.

As the first polls began to trickle in from across Europe, the news was grim. Support for the referendum was low, the fear and uncertainty stoked by the opposing side taking hold, with no light at the end of the tunnel.

26

Pierre-Antoine stared into the unforgiving lens of the camera, the harsh studio lights casting sharp shadows across his chiselled features.

"... The No campaign would have you believe that a united Europe is a threat to individual sovereignty, identities," he said, his voice steady and resolute. "But I ask you, what greater threat is there than the spectre of a fractured continent, vulnerable to the will of any outside force seeking to impose their own ideology?" As he spoke, images of the devastation wrought by the First and Second World War played across the screen behind him, a stark reminder of the consequences of division. "We have seen the cost of disunity, the price paid in blood and suffering. And now, as the world trembles on the brink of chaos, we must choose a different path."

Pierre-Antoine's words were met with a smattering of applause from the studio audience, but he could still see doubt in some, the hesitation born of years of ingrained scepticism and mistrust in the mainstream media. Social media was wreaking havoc on the Yes campaign, spreading outlandish and delusional conspiracy theories. He knew that he would need to do more than simply appeal to their sense of history, their fear of the past.

"And with those final words, we will conclude our broadcast for tonight," the host declared. "Mr. President, thank you for joining us and engaging with our viewers. Next week, at the same time, we will welcome Charles Le Guen, leader of the No campaign in France. Until then, have a wonderful night."

After exchanging a few, Pierre-Antoine headed to the studio's exit, closely flanked by Lieutenant Barnabé Sainte-Rose.

"How was I?" asked the French President.

"Flawless, as usual, Mr President."

"Yeah, but was it enough to convince more people?"

"It's not my place to answer, Mr President," Barnabé said, impassible.

"Sometimes, I wish it was," Pierre-Antoine sighed. "So, what's the rest of the program?"

"Well, we are taking you back to the Élysée Palace for the night," the Lieutenant replied, consulting his notes. "Then tomorrow morning, we leave at 10 am for a few days touring the province, starting in Lyon."

"And Isabelle?"

"She'll join us at 9.30, before we leave."

Pierre-Antoine sighed again.

"I am the President of France, and I have spent the last month striding the country and the TV chat shows instead of doing what I was elected for: ruling France. And sometimes, it feels like it will never end."

"It's not my—"

"—place to answer. Yes, I know," the President said, slightly irritated. "Let's go, at least let me have a good night sleep."

In the days that followed, Pierre-Antoine took his message to the streets, speaking at rallies and town halls across France. He met with workers in the bustling ports of Marseille, farmers in the sun-drenched fields of Provence, students in the hallowed halls of the Toulouse.

And everywhere he went, he was met with the same questions, the same doubts. *How can we trust Brussels to represent our interests?* they asked. *How can we be sure that our voices will be heard?*

The President listened patiently, his brow furrowed in concentration. And each time, with the passion of a true believer, he responded the same.

"The European project has always been a work in progress, a dream not yet fully realised. But it is a dream worth fighting for, worth sacrificing for." He spoke of the need for greater transparency, for a more direct connection between the people and their representatives in Brussels. Of a single policy to combat climate change. He described a future in which the diverse voices of Europe could come together in harmony, united by a common purpose and a shared destiny.

But even as his words stirred the hearts of some, Pierre-Antoine could feel the toll that the campaign was taking on him. The long hours, the constant travel, the endless stream of interviews and debates - it was all beginning to wear him down. Late at night, in the solitude of his hotel room, he would stare at his reflection in the mirror, searching for signs of weakness, of doubt. The attacks from his opponents had grown more vicious, more personal, with each passing day. They kept calling him a traitor, a sell-out, a puppet who betrayed its ideals for foreign interests.

And in his darkest moments, Pierre-Antoine began to wonder if they were right. Was he asking too much of the French people, of the European people? Was he leading them down a path from which there could be no return?

But then he would think of Monika and Jorge, of the unwavering faith they had in him, in their shared vision, how they were facing the same hardships with apparent inexhaustible energy. He would remember the sacrifices that so many had made in the name of a united Europe, the lives lost, and the dreams deferred. And he would find the strength to carry on, to keep fighting for the future he believed in. For he knew that the alternative - a Europe divided, a world in chaos - was too terrible to contemplate.

As the campaign progressed, Pierre-Antoine could feel the momentum shifting, the tide slowly turning. The polls were still close, the outcome far from certain. But there was a new energy in the air, a sense of possibility that had been lacking before. And so he pressed on, his voice growing hoarse from the endless speeches, his eyes bloodshot from the long nights spent strategizing with his team. He knew that there would be no rest, no respite, until the final votes were cast, and the future of Europe was decided.

***

As the campaign headed to its final week, Pierre-Antoine stepped onto the stage in the Palais des Congrès in Paris, the bright lights momentarily blinding him as he faced the sea of expectant faces. This was the meeting of the last chance where Monika and Jorge, as well as other European leaders, had congregated with him in a show of unity. The auditorium was packed, the energy palpable as he took his place behind the podium. He could feel the weight of the moment, the significance of the words he was about to speak.

"My fellow Europeans," he began, his voice steady and clear. "Tonight, we stand at a crossroads, a moment of great opportunity and even greater risk. The world around us is changing, the old order crumbling before our very eyes. And in this time of uncertainty, we must ask ourselves: what kind of Europe do we want to be?" He paused, letting the question hang in the air. "Do we want to be a divided Europe, a collection of disparate nations each pursuing their own narrow interests? Or do we want to be a united Europe, a beacon of hope and stability in a troubled world?"

The audience held its breath, thick with anticipation, as if the outcome of this one answer would dictate the future for years to come.

"I believe that we are stronger together," he continued, his voice rising with each word. "That our shared values, our common history, bind us in ways that no border or boundary can ever divide. And that is why I am calling for a new vision of Europe, a Europe that is not just a collection of nations, but a true federation, united in purpose and in spirit."

As he spoke, Pierre-Antoine could feel the energy in the room shifting, the momentum building behind his words. He knew that he was tapping into something deep and powerful, a longing for unity and purpose that had lain dormant for too long.

"In a week time, you will be called to decide on the future you want for our continent. Before casting your vote, think carefully. Your choice will not only affect you, but also generations to come. They will look back and judge us accordingly. Let's ensure that they have the future they deserve — one where our freedoms are protected, our borders are secure, and Europe stands on its own without outside influence or fearing nuclear retaliation. On the 21 March 2055, let's vote yes!"

The crowd erupted in applause, the fervour of their response catching Pierre-Antoine off guard. He could see the passion in their eyes, the yearning for something greater than themselves.

But even as the crowd cheered, he could still sense the opposition lurking in the shadows, the forces of division and nationalism that threatened to tear Europe apart. He knew that they would stop at nothing to undermine his campaign, to sow discord and doubt among the people. Despite his best efforts, the rumours were still spreading more vivid than ever with their whispers of secret deals and hidden agendas.

As the fervour of the rally began to subside, Pierre-Antoine found himself in a quiet moment of introspection. He gazed out at the sea of faces, their expressions a mix of hope, determination, and uncertainty. The weight of their expectations settled heavily upon his shoulders, and for a fleeting instant, he questioned whether he was truly equal to the task at hand.

Sensing his unease, Jorge approached, his eyes filled with concern.

"What troubles you, hermanito?" he asked, his voice low and gentle.

Pierre-Antoine sighed, his gaze distant.

"The polls," he murmured, "they still show a dead heat. After all our efforts, all our speeches and debates, the outcome remains as uncertain as ever."

Jorge nodded, his expression thoughtful.

"True," he acknowledged, "but you must not lose heart. The people have seen our vision, and they will not be swayed by the lies and fearmongering of the No campaign."

Monika joined them, her presence a comforting balm to Pierre-Antoine's troubled soul.

"Jorge is right," she said, her voice filled with quiet conviction. "You have awakened something in the hearts of the people, a longing for unity and purpose that will not be easily extinguished. We must have faith, not only in our cause, but in the wisdom of those we seek to serve."

Pierre-Antoine felt a surge of gratitude for his friends, their unwavering support a beacon in the darkness of his doubts. He thought of the sacrifices they had made, the risks they had taken to stand by his side in this fight for the soul of Europe.

In their eyes, he saw the same fire that burned within his own heart, the unquenchable desire to forge a better future for all. They were right. This was not the time to give up. No matter what fate awaited them in a week, he was determined to fight until the very end.

27

The scorching Texas sun beat down upon the sea of supporters gathered before Austin's capitol. On the balcony stood President MacCorkindale, his eyes aflame with a zealous fervour. He raised his fist to the heavens, his voice booming like thunder.

"Brothers and sisters in Christ, the time has come to strike against the serpent that slithers at our northern borders!" Waving a stack of papers in the air, he proclaimed: "I hold evidence that the Canadian Pharisees are conspiring with the godless heathens of the Union, arming them against our righteous cause. Like the mighty Samson, we shall bring the temple down upon their heads and put an end to their meddling once and for all!"

The crowd erupted in a deafening roar, their voices rising as one in a chorus of rage and bloodlust. After a last salute, Edward MacCorkindale returned to his office with the confidence of the righteous.

"Well, General, I am entrusting the next steps to your capable mind. The Union troops are disorganised and lacking in morale, making it an opportune time for decisive action." The President threw the stack of papers in a bin. "Pathetic fools," he sneered with disdain, "ready to buy any truth."

Among the other members of the war cabinet, Major General Houston Wallace stood silent and pensive, his hawkish gaze sweeping across the room with an air of calculated intensity. The gears of strategy turned in his mind, as inexorable as the mechanisms of war.

"I will deceive the Canadians by appearing to advance towards Alaska by sending two battalions in the direction of Calgary. While they are focused on stopping our advance, I will send three of our best battalions to capture Winnipeg and crush their forces off-guard from behind. Then, we will march east towards Ottawa to—"

"— to trap the Union troops caught in a pincer, killing two birds with one stone by securing the Canadian territories," MacCorkindale finished. "An ingenuous plan, General! Let's now work on the details…"

As the sun dipped below the horizon, painting the sky in hues of blood and fire, the Confederate war machine stirred to life. Tanks tread bits into the parched earth, transports groaned under the weight of men and munitions, and the relentless drumbeat of marching feet echoed across the land. The first cruel notes of the apocalyptic symphony had been struck, and all North America would soon tremble before its dread music.

***

In the secure depths of the Philadelphia City Hall situation room, President Julius Theodore Thomas hunched over a gleaming table, his piercing gaze fixed upon the latest intelligence reports. The flickering screens cast an eerie pall over his chiselled features, etching lines of grave concern across his brow.

"Our intelligence has intercepted orders from the Confederate command, Mr. President," announced a general. "They plan to lure Canadian forces westward while their main battalions march towards Winnipeg, catching them from behind. If they succeed…"

"They'll surround our remaining troops from the north. Then it will be the end of us," said the President, impassible.

Thomas's advisors shifted uneasily, the weight of the moment bearing down upon them like a physical force.

"Mr. President," ventured one, "we must act swiftly. The Canadians must be warned, and our forces mobilised to counter this brazen aggression."

The President nodded grimly, his mind racing with the implications of the looming crisis.

"Get me Prime Minister Tremblay on the line," Thomas commanded. "We must use this intelligence to forge an alliance, a united front against this madness. We must gather and deploy every available resource we have. I will not allow the Confederates to gain even a single inch of free land."

***

In a dimly lit command centre, Canadian and Union military leaders huddle around glowing screens and flickering maps. The air was thick with tension, as rapid-fire conversations crackle over secure communication lines.

"Tremblay has given the order," barked a grizzled Canadian general, his face a mask of grim determination. "We're moving the 1st Armoured and the 3rd Infantry to defensive positions around Winnipeg. And we're deploying drones and satellites to track the Confederate advance."

"Acknowledged," nodded his Union counterpart, a wiry man with piercing blue eyes. "We're mobilizing the 101st Airborne and the 4th Mechanized. They'll link up with your forces and establish a perimeter. And we're tasking every intelligence asset we have to monitor their communications and troop movements."

As the orders went out and the forces begin to move, a palpable sense of urgency grips the room. Men and women, united by a common purpose, worked frantically to position troops, coordinate logistics, and analyse the flood of data pouring in from the front.

In this crucible of crisis, old rivalries and suspicions had melted away, forged into a bond of shared resolve. Canadian and Union, standing shoulder to shoulder against the rising tide of chaos and destruction. They knew that the fate of nations hanged in the balance, that the future will be written in the blood and sweat of the coming battle.

Yet even as they steel themselves for the ordeal ahead, a flicker of hope burns in their hearts. Hope that their united strength will be enough to turn back the Confederate onslaught. Hope that the sacrifices to come will not be in vain. And hope that from the ashes of war, a new and better world may yet arise.

***

The thunder of artillery shattered the pre-dawn stillness, as a hail of shells rained down upon the outskirts of Winnipeg. Columns of Confederate tanks and armoured vehicles surged forward, their engines roaring like the war cries of enraged beasts. The combined Canadian and Union forces, entrenched and determined, returned fire with a fury born of desperation and righteousness.

Major General Houston Wallace surveyed the battlefield from his command post, his brow furrowed in concentration. *How did they know we were coming?* he asked himself, bewildered. *And why are Union troops present as well?* The realisation hit him like a punch in the gut. *Someone had betrayed us!*

"Push forward!" he barked into the radio. "We must breach their defences at all costs!" Around him, staff officers scramble to relay orders and coordinate the assault, their faces etched with grim determination.

As the sun climbs higher in the smoke-choked sky, the battle descended into a brutal slugging match, with each side trading blows and shedding blood for every inch of ground. The once-peaceful suburbs of Winnipeg became a labyrinth of rubble and twisted metal, echoing with the screams of the wounded and the dying.

As the hours drag on and the casualty reports mounted, General Houston Wallace's confidence began to waver.

"Where are our reinforcements?" he demanded, his voice rising in frustration. "We're being slaughtered out here!" The radio crackles with static, the reply lost in the cacophony of battle.

Unbeknownst to Houston Wallace, the tide of the battle has already turned. Canadian snipers, their skills sharpened in the harsh wilderness of the North, picked off Confederate officers and machine gunners with ruthless efficiency. Union drones, their cameras all-seeing and their missiles precise, rained death upon the enemy's supply lines and communications hubs.

As the sun began to set, casting long shadows across the blood-soaked streets, the Confederate advance faltered and then collapsed. Soldiers, their spirits broken, and their ammunition spent, throw down their weapons and fled in panic. General Houston Wallace, his face ashen with disbelief, gave the order to retreat, his dreams of conquest shattered like the stained-glass windows of Winnipeg's cathedral.

In the chaos of the withdrawal, a single shot rang out, piercing the din of battle like the trumpet of an avenging angel. The Confederate supreme commander slumped forward on his armoured car, a crimson stain spreading across his chest. As he fell to the ground, his life ebbing away, he saw a last vision of his beloved Austin, its streets lined with cheering crowds and its buildings draped in the colours of the Confederacy in honour of the Conqueror of Washington.

With a final shuddering breath, Major General Houston Wallace passed from this world, his legacy forever etched in the annals of war and the hearts of those who fought and died beside him on the blood-soaked streets of Winnipeg.

***

In his office of the Philadelphia City Hall, President Julius Theodore Thomas paced before his cabinet, his eyes alight with a newfound hope.

"Gentlemen," he declared, his voice ringing with conviction, "the victory at Winnipeg is a sign from the Almighty himself. I strongly believe it marks a pivotal moment in this fratricidal civil war, a beacon of light guiding us towards the restoration of our great nation."

The cabinet members nodded in agreement, their faces etched with a mix of relief and determination. Secretary of Defence, Marcus Holloway, leaned forward, his brow furrowed.

"Mr. President, while this victory is indeed cause for celebration, we must not let our guard down. The Confederates are seriously wounded, but they are far from defeated."

"You are right, Marcus," President Thomas consented, his gaze distant as if peering into the future. "We must press our advantage, rally our allies, and strike while the iron is hot. The road ahead will be long and fraught with peril, but with God as our shepherd, we shall overcome the forces of division and hatred."

As the cabinet meeting adjourned, the president retired to his private study, his mind heavy with the weight of his responsibilities. He kneeled before the antique crucifix that once belonged to his grandfather, a Baptist preacher who campaigned for the Civil Rights.

"Lord," he whispered, his voice thick with emotion, "grant me the strength and wisdom to lead our nation through this dark night and into the light of a new dawn."

Meanwhile, in the heart of the Confederacy, President Edward MacCorkindale slammed his fist on the mahogany desk, his face contorted with rage.

"Incompetent fools!" he roared, his eyes blazing with fury as he glares at his war cabinet. "That's what you are. Houston Wallace was the finest general in the Confederation, and you let him die on the battlefield like a common foot soldier!"

The cabinet members exchange uneasy glances, their faces pale with fear. General Beauregard Jackson, his voice trembling, ventures a response.

"Mr. President, it's important to note that the Canadian forces, along with Union troops, were unexpectedly waiting for us in Winnipeg. Even Major General Houston Wallace was caught off guard by this development. We need to consider the possibility of betrayal—"

MacCorkindale's nostrils flare, his voice dripping with venom.

"Excuses! I will not tolerate failure, not when the very fate of our nation hangs in the balance. Regardless of any betrayal, the ease with which our top commander was killed is a disaster in its own right. We must redouble our efforts, call upon every able-bodied man to take up arms and fight for the glory of the Confederation!"

As the war cabinet scurried from the room, their tails tucked between their legs, the president sank into his chair, his head in his hands. He reached for the half-empty bottle of bourbon on his desk, seeking solace in the amber liquid.

"Houston Wallace, my friend," he muttered, his voice barely audible, "your sacrifice will not be in vain. I swear on the blood of our fathers, the Confederation will win, and your name will be forever enshrined in the pantheon of heroes." He took a quick swig of the spirit before shouting. "Damn you, Thomas! You may have won this one, but I am not one to be easily defeated. May you rot in hell." He abruptly stopped his tirade as a realisation dawned on him. In a frenzy, he grabbed his phone.

"Margaret?"

"Yes, Mr President?"

"Get me Simons on the line immediately."

***

Days later, in the bustling streets of Philadelphia, the Union capital, joy and relief hanged in the air like a palpable mist. Banners and flags adorned the buildings, and the sound of laughter and cheers echoed through the city. President Thomas, his step lighter and his smile brighter than it has been in months, waved to the adoring crowds from the balcony of the City Hall. The sight of such a display of cheerfulness was a soothing remedy for his soul, instilling a sense of optimism for what lay ahead.

Suddenly, multiple gunshots pierced the air, shattering the festive atmosphere like a hammer through glass. Thomas stumbled, a look of shock and confusion on his face as a crimson stain spread across his chest. Screams of horror and disbelief filled the air as the President, with several members of his cabinet, crumpled to the ground, his life's blood pooling on the cold stone.

In the chaos that followed, a figure was seen fleeing the scene, a smoking gun clutched in his hand. As the authorities gave chase, the assassin was apprehended, his face twisted with hatred and his eyes gleaming with the fervour of a zealot. "For John Frederick Heider!" he screamed, his voice raw with emotion. "The Union must pay for their crimes against the true believers!"

As news of the President's assassination spread like wildfire, the Union plunged into a maelstrom of grief, anger, and uncertainty. There were reports of sporadic protests and riots in various cities, as the people struggled to come to terms with the sudden power vacuum and the uncertain future that awaits them. The dream of a united America, so tantalizingly close just days before, seemed to slip away like sand through an hourglass. In the halls of power, whispers of succession and political manoeuvring began to circulate, even as the nation mourned the loss of a leader, a visionary, and a man of God.

On the day following the slaughter, an emergency meeting of the Union's leadership and representatives convened.

Newly sworn President Caroline Nguyen, her face etched with sorrow and determination, took her place at the head of the assembly, the mantle of leadership thrust upon her shoulders.

"We cannot let this tragedy divide us," she solemnly declared, her voice trembling with emotion. "President Thomas' vision of a united America must endure, even in the face of this heinous act."

But even as she spoke, the cracks in the Union's foundation began to widen, as factions and ideologies clashed. Some called for vengeance against the Confederate rebels, demanding blood for blood, while others urged caution and restraint, fearing that further escalation could lead to the nation's ultimate demise.

Amidst the quarrel, a group of influential figures from the Northeastern states spoke out, their faces grim with resolve. Led by the charismatic Governor of New York, Alexander Holbrooke, they put forward a radical proposal: the formation of a new alliance, a bulwark against the rising tide of violence and extremism.

"We cannot stand idle while our nation tears itself apart and our enemy lurks at our gates," Holbrooke argued, his voice low and urgent. "We must stop deceiving ourselves. Washington is lost for generations to come. We cannot continue to hold on to hope of a return to a gone past. The Union's military and economic state makes it unable to withstand fighting alone, and even our allies across the Atlantic are hesitant to support us." He paused, letting his words sink in. "It is time for us to chart a new course," he then continued, "one that will ensure the survival of our people and our way of life. We must capitalise on the only alliance available to us and strengthen our forces before even considering resuming any fighting. This is our only path forward. E Pluribus Unum. This was once the motto of our great nation, as intended by our founding fathers. But under pressure from religious groups, we have forsaken this ideal. It is time for us to return to our roots and recommit to what our country represents. Therefore, I propose a motion to request a partnership with Canada in forming a joint union."

Following several gruelling hours of heated discussion, a majority of the delegates finally came together to support the motion, enticed by its assurances of stability and protection. However, the representatives from the West Coast states adamantly rejected the outcome of the vote and went their separate ways.

The next day, the Canadian government, extended a hand of friendship and support, recognizing the common threat posed by the Confederation of the Southern States and their extremist ideology. And on March 19th, 2055, the Eastern States Federation was formally established, a powerful alliance of like-minded states committed to the preservation of democracy and the rule of law.

On the same day, across the continent, in the once-verdant valleys of California, a new power rose from the ashes of the old world order. Born of the revolutionary fervour that swept through the nation in the wake of President Thomas's assassination, the American Socialist Republic emerged as a beacon of hope for those who dreamed of a more just and equitable society.

Then, on March 20th, 2055, the three belligerents, the American Socialist Republic, the Eastern States Federation, and the Confederation of the Southern States, each battered and bruised by the weight of war, agreed to a temporary cease-fire, a fragile peace born of exhaustion and desperation. As the guns fell silent, and the smoke cleared, a new chapter began in the history of the American experiment. Little did anyone know, this pivotal moment would have far-reaching repercussions for the rest of the world in the years ahead.

28

The glare of the television flickered across Pierre-Antoine's face, casting shadows in the dimly lit room. His eyes were transfixed on the news anchor, her words shattering the tense silence.

"Breaking news from North America — Following President Julius Theodore Thomas assassination, what was left of the United States has fractured, with the formation of the Eastern States Federation and the American Socialist Republic." The anchor continued, sombre tones carrying grim tidings from across the Atlantic. Each word reverberated like a funeral bell, deepening the lines on Pierre-Antoine's brow.

He thought of Thomas, the stalwart Democrat who had carried the torch of democracy against Edward MacCorkindale's onslaught. Now snuffed out, like a candle in the tempest. The American experiment, that shining city upon a hill, had crumbled into warring factions, Babel reborn. What ramifications would this upheaval portend for tomorrow's referendum in Europe? Pierre-Antoine pondered, a tangle of nerves and anticipation in his gut.

The tension in the Yes campaign headquarters was palpable as the clock inched towards 6 PM. Pierre-Antoine, Monika and Jorge stood side by side, their eyes glued to the large TV screen. Supporters milled around them, nervously whispering and checking their phones for updates. This was the moment they had fought for, the dream of a United Federation of Europe hanging in the balance.

The French President clasped his hands tightly, his knuckles turning white. Would this be the hour of reckoning, the final triumph over the forces of division and chaos?

Suddenly, the TV anchor appeared, her face grave.

"It is 6 PM and we can now reveal the first exit poll results throughout Europe..." The room fell deathly silent. Breaths were held, hearts raced. "...In a shocking turn of events, the Yes campaign is predicted to win with 52% of the vote, defying the final polls.

For a long moment, no one moved. It was as if time itself had frozen, unable to comprehend this twist of fate. Then, like a dam bursting, the room erupted in cheers and shouts of joy. Supporters hugged each other, tears streaming down their faces. The impossible had happened.

Pierre-Antoine turned to Monika and Jorge, his eyes wide with disbelief.

"We did it" he whispered hoarsely. "We actually did it."

Monika smiled, her blue eyes shining with triumph.

"This is such a relief," she then sighed. "But, how come? The polls were so tight."

Jorge leaned in, eyes locked on the unfolding numbers.

"The American crisis…it must have swayed the undecided. They saw the consequences of division first-hand, and it tipped the scales in our favour."

As the celebrations continued around them, Pierre-Antoine's mind raced with the implications of this historic moment. A United Federation of Europe, born from the ashes of division and strife, united not by the sword, but by the will of its people, was finally within reach. It was like a phoenix rising, a testament to the indomitable spirit of the European people.

Then the main screen cut to the No campaign headquarters, where the mood was decidedly sombre. Supporters sat in stunned silence, unable to comprehend their defeat. Taking the stage, Charles Le Guen raged against the result, his face red with fury.

"This referendum is a sham, a travesty of democracy!" he bellowed, his voice echoing through the suddenly hushed room. "The deep state, the globalist elites, have manipulated the results to further their own agenda. We will not accept this fraudulent vote!"

Pierre-Antoine felt a surge of anger rising within him. How dare Le Guen seek to undermine this historic moment? He glanced at Monika and Jorge, saw the same outrage mirrored in their eyes.

As the hours ticked by, tension filled the air. The news channels were reporting conflicting exit poll results, some with a margin close to 50%, others with a larger gap. Uncertainty lingered, making the atmosphere tense. On the television sets, members of both the Yes and No campaigns debated fiercely over whether such a narrow margin represented sufficient weight for a clear mandate.

Then, just before midnight, the final result flashed across the screen: 53.98% in favour of the United Federation of Europe. The room exploded again with cheers and shouts, drowning out Le Guen and his followers' desperate objections.

Pierre-Antoine took to the stage to address the ecstatic crowd. The euphoria was intoxicating, a heady mix of relief, joy and determination. He raised his hands, calling for silence.

"My fellow Europeans," he began, his voice ringing out with conviction. "Today, we have made history. We have chosen unity over division, hope over fear. This is not a victory for any one campaign or ideology. It is a victory for the European dream, for the values of democracy, human rights, and the rule of law that bind us together." He paused, letting his words sink in, feeling the weight of destiny upon his shoulders. "Let me be clear: we will not be deterred by baseless accusations or fearmongering. The future United Federation of Europe has been given a mandate, and we will honour it. We will work tirelessly, relentlessly, to build a Europe that is stronger, fairer, and more united than ever before!"

The crowd roared their approval, chanting Pierre-Antoine's name. He raised his fist in solidarity, his eyes blazing with determination.

"Now, the real work begins. We must seize this mandate and move swiftly to build the federal institutions and common policies that will make our Union strong. It will be an uneasy path, but we will not rest until the United Federation of Europe becomes a reality. Vive l'Europe![39]"

As the cheers reached a crescendo, Pierre-Antoine stepped back from the podium, his heart pounding with adrenaline. This was his life's work, the fulfilment of a dream generation in the making. There would be obstacles ahead, powerful forces arrayed against them. But tonight, under the starry skies of a continent reborn, anything seemed possible.

In the middle of the surrounding celebrations, Pierre-Antoine felt a buzz in his pocket. He glanced at his phone, surprised to see a message from Robert Kay. *'We need to meet. Urgently. Europe's future hangs in the balance.'*

He swiftly showed the message to Monika and Jorge, saw their faces darken with suspicion and loathing.

"The Covenant, again," Monika hissed, her voice dripping with contempt. What do they want now?"

Jorge shook his head, his expression grim.

"Nothing good, I suspect. Robert Kay is a snake, a puppetmaster pulling strings behind the scenes.

Pierre-Antoine hesitated, torn between his distrust of Kay and the nagging sense that this meeting could be crucial.

"I share your concerns," he said at last, "but perhaps this is an opportunity we cannot afford to pass up. If we can gain some insight into the Covenant's plans, it may give us an advantage in the battles to come."

---

[39] Long live Europe!

Monika and Jorge exchanged a glance, a silent conversation passing between them. Finally, Monika sighed, her shoulders slumping in resignation.

"You're right, of course. We can't afford to be caught off guard. But Pierre-Antoine...be careful. Don't let him get inside your head."

Pierre-Antoine nodded, his jaw set with determination. As he typed out a reply to Kay, agreeing to the meeting, he felt a chill run down his spine. He was about to come face to face with the man who embodied everything he despised, everything he had sworn to fight against. But for the sake of Europe, for the sake of all they had built, he would do what needed to be done. No matter the cost.

***

Pierre-Antoine stepped through the central portal of the church of Saint-Sulpice in Paris, the ancient stone edifice looming above him like a sentinel. Emblazoned above the entrance were the words *'The French people recognize the Supreme Being and the immortality of the soul,'* a relic of the French Revolution that seemed to mock him now. What supreme being would condone the machinations of men like Robert Kay and the Covenant?

Beside him, Barnabé Sainte-Rose shifted uneasily, his hand resting on the holster of his concealed weapon.

"I don't like this, sir," he murmured, his eyes scanning the shadows that pooled around the church's entrance. "At least, let me accompany you inside."

Pierre-Antoine shook his head, his gaze never leaving the inscription.

"No, Barnabé. The Covenant may be many things, but they won't harm me in a place of worship. Wait here. I will signal if I require assistance."

The lieutenant frowned, his instincts warring with his loyalty.

"As you wish, sir. But I will be watching."

With a nod of acknowledgment, Pierre-Antoine stepped across the threshold, the heavy wooden door swinging shut behind him with a resounding thud. The air inside was cool and musty, tinged with the scent of incense and old stone. He blinked, his eyes adjusting to the dim light filtering through the stained-glass windows.

"I'm glad you could make it, Pierre-Antoine." The voice seemed to come from everywhere and nowhere at once, echoing off the vaulted ceilings.

A figure materialised from the shadows, as if conjured by some otherworldly force. Robert Kay stood before him, a smile playing at the corners of his mouth. He was dressed in a dark suit, his grey hair neatly combed, his pale skin almost luminous in the candlelight.

"Come," Kay said, gesturing toward a small chapel off to the side. "We have much to discuss."

Pierre-Antoine followed, his footsteps echoing on the marble floor. As he entered the Chapel of the Souls of Purgatory, he felt a chill run down his spine. The chapel was dimly lit, the only illumination coming from a few flickering candles and the eerie glow of the stained-glass window. The central motif depicted the Crucifixion, Christ's agonised face staring down at him accusingly. On either side of the chapel were two murals, their images faded with age. To the left, a dying man lay surrounded by his family, the inscription below reading *'Religion encourages Christians to suffer in this life to avoid the pains of purgatory.'* To the right, another scene depicted a group of mourners huddled around a grave, their faces turned towards the heavens, while the soul of the departed passed through the gates of paradise. The words *'Prayer for the dead obtains the deliverance of souls suffering in purgatory'* etched beneath.

Pierre-Antoine's skin crawled as he took in the macabre imagery. Was this some kind of message from Kay and the Covenant? A call for repentance, a warning of the fate that awaited those who defied them?

"You've betrayed us, Pierre-Antoine." Kay's voice was soft, almost conversational, but there was an undercurrent of menace beneath the words. "We had an agreement. Europe was to remain divided, weak. And yet here you are, championing the cause of unity."

Pierre-Antoine bristled, anger rising in his chest.

"You're one to talk of betrayal," he spat. "Your schemes in America have thrown the world into chaos. The Covenant has lost control of its own creation. Edward MacCorkindale is a madman, a loose cannon that threatens us all."

The Covenant chairman's eyes flashed, his smile twisting into a sneer.

"MacCorkindale is a means to an end, nothing more. A tool to be used and discarded when his usefulness has run its course."

"And John?" The French president demanded, his voice rising. "Was he just another pawn in your game, too? If the Covenant hadn't ordered his assassination, the United States might still be existing."

Robert Kay shrugged, seeming unconcerned.

"Sacrifices must be made for the greater good. Heider was an obstacle, a stumbling block on the path to righteousness. His death was regrettable, but necessary."

Pierre-Antoine shook his head in disbelief, his fists clenched at his sides. How could Kay speak so casually of murder, of the destruction of nations? What kind of twisted ideology drove the Covenant and its adherents?

"You're insane," he whispered, his voice hoarse with emotion. "You're playing with fire, Robert. You're jeopardising the balance of the entire world for the sake of your own deluded ambitions."

Kay's smile only widened, his eyes gleaming with a fanatic light.

"The world is already out of balance, Pierre-Antoine. It has been for centuries. Only through the Covenant's guidance, through the coming of a new age, can harmony be restored. And you, my friend, have a part to play in that glorious future…whether you realise it or not." Kay's words hung in the air, heavy with portent. In the shadowy recesses of the chapel, the stained-glass depiction of the Crucifixion seemed to loom larger, the tortured figure of Christ silently bearing witness to the unfolding drama.

"What are you talking about?" Pierre-Antoine demanded, a sinking feeling in the pit of his stomach. "What role could I possibly have in your twisted schemes?"

Kay stepped closer, his voice dropping to a conspiratorial whisper.

"Don't you see, Pierre-Antoine? Everything that has happened, every move we've made, has been leading up to this moment. The partition of the United States, the dividing of power in Europe...it's all part of a greater plan, a divine purpose." He gestured to the murals flanking the chapel, the depictions of suffering and redemption. "The world must be purged, cleansed of its sin and corruption. Only through the fires of conflict, through the crucible of war, can humanity be reborn and prepare for the second coming of Christ and the New Jerusalem. And you, Pierre-Antoine...you are destined to be a catalyst for that glorious transfiguration."

The president stared at Kay, horror and revulsion warring within him. The evangelist's words were those of a madman, a fanatic lost in the throes of religious delusion. And yet, there was a terrifying certainty in his voice, a conviction that chilled him to the bone.

"You're talking about a global war," he said slowly, the realisation dawning on him like a nightmare. "A global conflict that could destroy everything, everyone. Millions would die, entire nations wiped out..."

"A small price to pay for the salvation of humanity," Kay interjected, his voice ringing with fervour. "The Covenant has been working towards this moment for generations, Pierre-Antoine. We have positioned the pieces on the board, set the stage for the final act. And when the dust settles, when the last battle is fought...the faithful will be rewarded, and the wicked will be cast into the pit."

Robert Kay's revelation hung in the air like a miasma, a suffocating blanket of madness and zealotry that threatened to smother Pierre-Antoine's very soul. He had always known that the Covenant's ambitions were grand, that their influence stretched far beyond the realm of religion. But this...this was outside anything he had ever imagined, a vision of apocalyptic horror that defied comprehension. He stared at the American evangelist, his mind reeling, unable to comprehend the sheer scope of the Covenant's insanity.

"You can't be serious," the French president whispered, his voice barely audible above the pounding of his own heart. A heavy hush descended upon the chapel, only broken by the gentle flickering of the candles before Pierre-Antoine continued speaking. "I won't be a part of this," he said, his voice trembling with a mix of fear and revulsion. "I won't help you unleash hell on earth, no matter what you believe. I'm not your pawn, Kay. I'm not a tool to be used and discarded."

Kay's smile faded, his eyes hardening with a cold, implacable resolve.

"You have no choice, Mr President. You are already a part of this. You can either embrace your destiny...or be crushed beneath it."

Pierre-Antoine felt a surge of nausea, his stomach twisting in knots. He had always prided himself on his ambition, his drive to shape the world according to his own vision. But now, faced with the true scope of the Covenant's plans, he felt like a helpless puppet, a mere cog in a vast and terrible machine.

"I said I won't do it," he whispered, his voice first barely audible over the pounding of his own heart, before growing louder and more resolute. "I won't be a part of your insanity. I'll stop you, Kay. I'll find a way to expose the Covenant, to bring your twisted plans to light."

The chairman laughed, a harsh, grating sound that echoed off the chapel walls.

"You can try, Pierre-Antoine. But you will fail. The Covenant is too powerful, too deeply entrenched. It has many allies, some whose wealth is beyond belief. And in the end…you will come to see the truth of our cause, the righteousness of our purpose. It is your destiny, whether you accept it or not."

The French president stared at Robert Kay, his mind reeling with the implications of the American's words. The muted colours of the stained-glass window cast an eerie glow upon the evangelist's face, his features twisted into a mask of zealous conviction.

"Don't you see, Pierre-Antoine?" Kay implored, his voice rising with fervour. "This is the path you were always meant to walk. From the moment you turned away from your parents' godless liberalism, from the moment you embraced the sacred truths of the Covenant, you were set upon this course. It is your destiny to stand at my side as we usher in the Kingdom of God on Earth."

Lascombes shook his head, his throat tightening with a mixture of revulsion and despair.

"No, I won't be a part of this madness. I may have been misguided in my youth, I may have been drawn to the Covenant's promises of order and purpose…but I see now how wrong I was. How wrong we all were." He stepped forward, his eyes blazing with a newfound resolve. "I will not help you plunge the world into chaos and destruction. If that means I must stand against the Covenant, if that means I must become the Antichrist in your twisted mythology…then so be it."

Kay's eyes narrowed, his lips curling into a sneer.

"You fool," he hissed. "You think you can defy the will of God? You think you can stand against the inexorable tide of history? The Covenant's plan is already in motion, the pieces are already in place. There is no stopping it now."

Pierre-Antoine felt a sudden wave of dizziness wash over him, his vision blurring at the edges. He stumbled backward, his hand groping for the solid stone of the chapel wall. In that moment, he saw with terrifying clarity the true depths of his own folly, the arrogance and hubris that had led him to this point.

I was so blind, he thought desperately. *So consumed by my ambition, my desire for power and control. I thought I could shape the world according to my own will…but in the end, I was just a puppet, dancing on the strings of the Covenant.* He looked up at Kay, his eyes burning with a fierce, defiant light.

"I may have been a fool," he said quietly, "but I will not be a monster. I will not help you bring about the end of everything

I hold dear. I will fight you, Kay. I will fight the Covenant with every fibre of my being. And if I must die in the process...then so be it."

Robert Kay stared at him for a long moment, his expression unreadable. Then, with a sudden, swift motion, he turned and strode away, his footsteps echoing hollowly on the marble floor.

"We shall see, Mr President," he called over his shoulder, his voice cold and mocking. "We shall see."

As the evangelist disappeared into the shadows of the church, Pierre-Antoine staggered, his body shaking with a mixture of fear and exhaustion. He knew that he had just made the most momentous decision of his life, that he had set himself upon a path from which there could be no turning back.

A sudden, searing pain lanced through his abdomen, doubling him over. He clutched at his stomach, gasping for breath as wave after wave of agony crashed over him. It felt as though a red-hot knife was being twisted in his gut, tearing him apart from the inside. He tried to stand, to cry out for help, but his legs would not obey him. He collapsed to the floor, his body writhing in torment. Through a haze of pain, he saw Barnabé rushing towards him, the lieutenant's face etched with alarm.

"Sir! What's wrong? What's happening?" Barnabé knelt beside him, his hands hovering uncertainly over Pierre-Antoine's convulsing form.

The president tried to speak, but the words would not come. His throat was raw, his mouth filled with the coppery taste of blood. He could feel his consciousness slipping away, the world around him fading to black.

Poison? he thought. *No, they wouldn't dare. Not here, not now.*

With a supreme effort of will, he forced his eyes open, forced himself to focus on Barnabé's face. The bodyguard was shouting into his phone, his words lost in the roaring in Pierre-Antoine's ears.

"Hold on, sir," Sainte-Rose said urgently, his hand gripping the president's shoulder. "Help is on the way. Just hold on."

29

Pierre-Antoine gazed out the ornate window of the Élysée Palace, the afternoon sunlight casting long shadows across his private apartment where he was convalescing. A knock at the door stirred him from his reverie.

"Come in," he called, straightening his shoulders despite the dull ache in his abdomen.

Monika and Jorge entered, their faces etched with concern. The German Chancellor rushed to his side, her light blue eyes searching his face.

"Pierre-Antoine, how are you feeling? We came as soon as we heard."

He smiled wanly, taking her hand.

"Better, now that you're both here."

Jorge stood at the foot of the bed, his dark brows knitted together.

"What did the doctors say, hermanito?"

"Well, the good news is that the Covenant did not try to poison me", Pierre-Antoine ironized.

"And the bad news?"

"They found a liposarcoma in my abdomen. But don't worry - they caught it early. It's been removed, and the prognosis is good. I should be back in the arena in no time."

Monika squeezed his hand tighter, her eyes glistening.

"Thank the Lord. We've been beside ourselves with worry."

His half-brother eyed him with suspicion.

"Sarcomas are a serious matter, Pierre-Antoine. You should consider getting a second opinion."

"Stop worrying, Jorge. I have top specialists monitoring my health. After all, I am the president," he said with a wink. "That being said," he continued, "the official diagnosis is acute gastroenteritis. I would appreciate it if you kept what I just told you private."

"But why, Pierre-Antoine?" objected Monika. "The public has a right to know, especially if it's no longer an issue. You sound like one of those Soviet apparatchiks from the past."

"Simply, my dear friend, because I cannot risk putting the prospects of the European Federation in jeopardy. My enemies are lurking in the shadow and would strike at any sign of weakness. Furthermore, I received concerning reports from Russia this morning that have only added to my concerns…"

***

Miles away, in the heart of Moscow, the walls of the Kremlin Palace stood stalwart against the grey winter sky. President Grigory Alexeyev paced before the frost-laced windows of his office, his heavy brow furrowed in consternation.

"The rise of this European Federation threatens the very sovereignty of Mother Russia," he growled, turning to face his Minister of Foreign Affairs. "We cannot allow this new Goliath to overshadow us, Ivan. Especially now, with the US threat out of the picture for the foreseeable future."

Ivan Kozyrev nodded gravely, his sharp eyes calculating.

"I agree, Mr. President. The West has always sought to contain us, to relegate Russia to the annals of history. We must act swiftly and decisively to secure our place in this new world order."

Alexeyev stroked his beard, his mind churning with the weight of his predecessors' ambitions. Catherine the Great had expanded Russia's reach to the shores of the Black Sea. Stalin had forged an empire through iron and blood. Now, it fell to him to reclaim Russia's mantle as a true superpower, to succeed where Putin had failed before him.

"What are our options, Ivan?" the President asked, his voice low and dangerous. "How do we cut this nascent federation off at the knees before it can stand against us?"

Kozyrev leaned forward, his voice barely above a whisper.

"We must be cunning as serpents, Mr. President. Strike at their weak points, sow discord among their member states. And if all else fails… there is always the option of force."

Alexeyev nodded slowly, his eyes hardening with resolve.

A knock at the door jolted Alexeyev from his reverie. Kozyrev rose to answer it, his hand instinctively hovering near the pistol concealed beneath his suit jacket. He opened the door to reveal a familiar figure, a man whose very presence seemed to fill the room with an electric charge.

"Mr. Kay," the Minister of Foreign Affairs said, his voice carefully neutral. "Thank you for coming on such short notice."

The chairman of the Covenant strode into the room, his silver hair gleaming under the chandeliers. He wore a tailored suit and a smile that didn't quite reach his piercing blue eyes.

"Mr President," he said, extending his hand. "It's an honour to meet you in person at last."

Alexeyev shook the evangelist's hand firmly, searching the American's face for any hint of his true intentions. Robert Kay was a cipher, a man who wielded immense power from the shadows. His Covenant Foundation had tendrils that reached into every corner of the globe, pulling strings and shaping events to fit their own inscrutable agenda.

"Mr. Kay," Alexeyev said, gesturing for him to take a seat. "And to what do I owe this pleasure?"

"I have taken the liberty of inviting our distinguished guest," announced Kozyrev. "He has a proposal to discuss with us regarding Ukraine."

Kay smiled, his eyes glinting with a predatory light.

"Indeed, I do, Mr. President. The Covenant shares your concerns about the rise of this new European Federation. We believe it poses a grave threat not only to Russia, but to the entire new global order. The past has taught us that when

Europe gains too much power, it often comes at a cost to the rest of the world."

Alexeyev leaned back in his chair, steepling his fingers. "Go on."

"The time has come for Russia to reclaim its rightful place as a world power," Robert Kay said, his voice low and urgent. "By taking over the entire territory of Ukraine, you will not only regain a vital part of your historical territories, but you will also expose the weakness and division at the heart of the European project."

Alexeyev nodded eagerly, his eyes alight with fervour.

"This has been my ambition for many years, Mr. Kay. To see Russia restored to its rightful place to erase the embarrassment and disgrace left by my predecessor in 2026."

Kay's smile widened, revealing a row of perfect white teeth.

"With the Covenant's support, that ambition can become a reality. We can provide intelligence, resources, even covert military assistance if needed."

The Russian President's mind raced with the possibilities. If he could seize Ukraine swiftly and decisively, before the Europeans had a chance to react...

"What about the West?" he asked, his voice carefully measured. "Won't they intervene to stop us?"

The Covenant chairman waved a dismissive hand.

"The Americans are in no position to interfere, not with their country torn apart by civil strife. As for the Europeans, they'll be too divided and hesitant to mount an effective response. At most, they'll impose some token sanctions, but nothing that can seriously harm Russia's interests."

Alexeyev nodded slowly, feeling the weight of history pressing down on his shoulders. This was his moment, his chance to seize destiny with both hands and bend it to his will. He turned to Kozyrev, his eyes blazing with resolve.

"Ivan, summon our generals and begin the preparations. I want a full mobilization of our armed forces, ready to move at a moment's notice."

Kozyrev saluted crisply, his face split by a fierce grin.

"Yes, Mr. President. It will be done."

Alexeyev rose to his feet, his heart pounding with anticipation. He could almost hear the ghostly whispers of Russia's celebrated figures, urging him on to greatness.

"Gentlemen," he said, his voice ringing with power and purpose. "Let us begin."

***

The shadows lengthened across the Kremlin as evening fell, casting a foreboding darkness that seemed to mirror the schemes taking root within its ancient walls. President Grigory Alexeyev paced before the window of his ornate office, his piercing blue eyes surveying the sprawling grounds below. Stitched on the sleeve of his crisp military uniform, the double-headed eagle of Russia glinted in the fading light - a potent symbol of an empire rising from the ashes of history.

"Comrade President," came the gruff voice of General Anatoly Volkov as he entered with a sharp salute. "I am here to report that all preparations are complete. The Black Sea Fleet is mobilized. The 1st and 2nd Guards Tank Army waits ready in Smolensk, the 18th and 20th Motor Rifle divisions, the 20th and 58th Guards Army, the 4th Tank Division, the 20th Guards Missile brigade, with a third of our Air Force, are deployed in Belgorod and Kursk. Officially for a multi-day military exercise. Our Spetsnaz units are already conducting covert operations along the border. On your command, we can roll across Ukraine with the fury of the Mongol hordes reborn."

Alexeyev nodded slowly, his mind racing with visions of reclaimed glory. The humiliating defeat in 2026 still stung like an unhealed wound. But now...now Russia would rise again, resurgent and unrivalled. With the European Union distracted, the moment was ripe to seize back what was rightfully theirs. He thought of the conversation with Kay, the man's hypnotic words still echoing: *'Destiny awaits, Mr. President. The mantle of Russia beckons you...'*

"And what of China, Kozyrev? Have they agreed to our proposal?"

"Yes, Mr. President. Premier Li has pledged to remain neutral, provided we guarantee their economic interests in the region. With the Americans paralysed, Europe will be left standing alone and outmatched against the might of the Motherland."

The Russian President's fist clenched. The time had come for bold, decisive action - a lightning strike to reshape the global order in Russia's image.

"Then let slip the dogs of war," he declared, his voice ringing with ruthless determination. "Commence the invasion, General, according to plan. We will first move to Belarus, called by President Sokolov to put down a popular uprising organised by him. While the eyes of the world will be turned to this country, we will launch our first wave to Kharkiv. In response, the Ukrainian army will act swiftly by deploying most of its forces to Poltava, under the assumption that their northern borders are safe as we handle the rebellion. That's when we will launch the second offensive from Belarus towards Kyiv. The time they react, it will be too late." He paused, gazing at the portrait of Peter the Great that hung in his office. "Let the world bear witness as the Russian bear awakens from slumber to reclaim its ancestral lands," he then claimed. "Today, we rewrite the pages of history in the ink of our enemies' blood. For Russia!"

As the first streaks of dawn spread over the horizon, the mechanized columns thundered across the Belarus border in a mighty steel avalanche. Artillery barrages lit up the early morning sky like the wrath of an angry god. Endless convoys of tanks and armoured vehicles churned up clouds of dust on the highways leading to Gomel, swiftly occupying the "rebelled" southern region of Russia's client state. Soon after, in Kyiv, sirens wailed, and civilians rushed for shelter as reports of the invasion spread like wildfire. The Ukrainian forces defending the capital scrambled to respond, but found themselves woefully outmatched. While their main regiments had rushed east to Poltava to counter the Russian advance there, a massive thrust of elite Spetsnaz troops and airborne divisions descended on the capital from the north, slicing through defences already stretched thin.

Within days, Russian tricolours flew over two-thirds of Ukraine as the blitzkrieg swept across the country virtually unopposed. In the occupied territories, the once vibrant streets now stood desolate and empty, an eerie silence broken only by the rumbling of tanks and the barking of kalashnikovs.

Yet even as the Russian bear tightened its grip, pockets of fierce resistance emerged in the west. In the rolling hills and forests of Volyn, Lviv and Ivano-Frankivsk, Ukrainian patriots took up arms to defend their homeland, waging a desperate guerilla campaign against the invaders. The names of once obscure towns soon passed into legend - Lutsk, Rivne, Ternopil, Kolomyya - where bands of volunteers held the line against impossible odds, their valour buying precious time for the government to regroup and for the world to respond.

But as Alexeyev gazed out over the battlefields from his command post, a slow smile spread across his stern features. The first phase was complete. The ancient heart of Kievan Rus had returned to the fold. Soon all of Europe would tremble before the resurgent might of the Russian Federation...

30

In the opulent halls of the Élysée Palace, President Pierre-Antoine Lascombes paced restlessly, his brow furrowed with worry. The reports from his defence ministry were dire - the Russians had struck without warning, their forces overwhelming the beleaguered Ukrainians with shocking speed and brutality.

How could we have been so blind? he pondered, his fists clenched in frustration. *We should have seen this coming, should have done more to prepare…*

Suddenly, his attention was drawn to the television screen, where a special news bulletin was playing. The haggard face of Russian President Grigory Alexeyev filled the frame, his eyes blazing with fervour as he addressed the world.

'For too long, the Ukrainian government has been a haven for criminals and terrorists,' he declared, his voice dripping with self-righteous anger. 'Mafia barons and anti-Russian extremists have operated with impunity, threatening the security and stability of our nation. No more! Russia will not stand idly by while our interests are threatened on our very doorstep.'

Pierre-Antoine felt a chill run down his spine as he listened to Alexeyev's inflammatory rhetoric. But it was the sight of a familiar figure standing behind the Russian leader who made his blood run cold. Robert Kay, the American evangelist and shadowy power broker, smiled thinly as he whispered in the president's ear, his eyes glinting with malevolent satisfaction.

In that moment, the French leader realised the terrible truth. The Covenant, that secretive cabal of religious fanatics and political extremists, was behind this invasion. They had manipulated Alexeyev, feeding his dreams of imperial glory, all as part of some twisted plan to destabilise Europe and reshape the world order. He sank into his chair, his mind reeling with the implications. This was no mere border skirmish or regional conflict. This was a battle for the very soul of Europe, a struggle against an enemy that sought to plunge the continent back into the darkness of the past for some religious fantasy. Pierre-Antoine knew that he had to act, had to rally the European Union to stand firm against this aggression. But deep in his heart, he wondered if it was already too late, if the forces of chaos and destruction had already been unleashed upon the world.

***

The French leader's mind raced as he stepped into the European Council chamber in Brussels, the weight of the world seemingly resting on his shoulders. The air was thick with tension and apprehension, the faces of his fellow European leaders etched with worry and fear. They all knew the gravity of the situation, the dire consequences that would follow if they failed to act.

Before the meeting began, Pierre-Antoine pulled aside Monika Richter and Jorge Sanchez. In hushed tones, he revealed what he had seen on the television, the chilling sight of Robert Kay standing behind President Alexeyev.

"The Covenant is behind this invasion," he said, his voice trembling with a mix of anger and dread. "They're using Alexeyev as a pawn in their twisted game."

Monika's eyes widened in shock, her hand instinctively reaching for the small golden cross that hung around her neck.

"Dear God," she whispered, "what kind of monsters would orchestrate such a thing?"

Jorge's face hardened, his jaw clenching with determination.

"The same ones who masterminded the event of 2022, Monika," he replied bluntly. "We can't let them get away with this," he said, his voice low and fierce. "We should learn from our past hesitations and stop them, no matter the cost."

Pierre-Antoine nodded, a flicker of hope igniting in his chest. He knew that with Monika and Jorge by his side, he stood a chance of convincing the other leaders to take action.

"I need both of your unwavering support for what I'm about to propose," he declared.

"You know you have, Pierre-Antoine," Monika replied with confidence. "But what exactly are you proposing?"

"I don't have the luxury of explaining the details right now. Just trust me and follow my lead."

As the meeting commenced, the French President took the stage, his voice ringing out with a clarity and conviction that belied the turmoil within. He spoke of the dire situation in Ukraine, of the Russian troops steadily advancing west of the country. He warned of the dangers of inaction, of the fate that would befall Europe if they failed to stand together.

"By doing nothing, we risk facing two major external threats," Pierre-Antoine declared, his eyes scanning the room, locking onto each leader in turn. "To the west, the United States are no more, engulfed in political division and religious extremism. And now, to the east, for the second time this century, Russia is banking on our own division to try resurrecting its former glory."

A murmur of unease rippled through the chamber, the gravity of Lascombes' words sinking in. Some leaders shifted uncomfortably in their seats, their faces etched with doubt and hesitation. But Pierre-Antoine pressed on, his voice rising with passion and urgency.

"We cannot sit idly by while these dangers encroach upon our borders," he said, his fist pounding the podium for emphasis. "We must act, and we must act now." He paused, letting the weight of his words hang in the air. Then, with a deep breath, he revealed his bold proposal. "I call for the immediate creation of a joint European force," Pierre-Antoine finally said, his voice ringing with conviction. "An army that will stop the Russian invaders in their tracks, that will show the world that Europe is a power to be reckoned with."

The chamber erupted in a cacophony of voices, some raised in support, others in opposition. The French President could see the doubt and fear in their eyes, the hesitation to commit to such a daring course of action.

But then Monika stood up, her voice cutting through the din like a beacon of hope.

"The time for compromise is over," she said, her eyes blazing with righteous fury. "In this new world order, we must be bold, or we will be lost."

Jorge followed suit, his words a rallying cry for action.

"If we do not stop Russia in Ukraine," he warned, "where will they stop? Will we wait until they are at the gates of Berlin, of Paris, of Rome?"

One by one, the other leaders began to voice their support. The Baltic States, Poland, Romania, Italy, Austria – all pledged their commitment to the cause. Eventually, the hesitant ones, faced with the passion and resolve of their peers, found themselves swayed.

As the meeting adjourned, Pierre-Antoine felt a surge of hope and determination. They had taken the first step, had begun the long and difficult journey towards securing Europe's future.

***

Within two weeks, across the continent, troops and equipment were hastily assembled. There was a sense of urgency and purpose in the air, a feeling that this was a moment of history in the making. Soldiers from a dozen different nations train side by side, forging bonds of camaraderie and shared purpose that transcend language and culture. As the army grown in strength and numbers, an ultimatum was issued to the Russian government: withdraw your forces from Ukraine, or face the consequences. But President Alexeyev, drunk on dreams of imperial glory and spurred on by the whispers of the Covenant, refused to back down.

And so, as the last remnants of the Ukrainian defence crumbled under the weight of the Russian onslaught, the European army crossed the border, a tide of steel and resolve that crashed against the invaders like a mighty wave.

The Russians, caught off guard by the suddenness and ferocity of the European offensive, began to falter. Their lines buckled and broke under the charge of superior firepower and technology, their tanks and planes reduced to smouldering wrecks on the battlefield.

Step by step, mile by mile, the Europeans troops push the Russians back, liberating town after town, village after village. The people of Ukraine, who had lived for several weeks under the shadow of Russian oppression, emerged from their hiding places to cheer their saviours, their faces alight with hope and gratitude.

But even as the tide of battle turns in Europe's favour, Pierre-Antoine knew that the war was far from over. That Russia, though bloodied and battered, was not yet defeated. As he watches the news reports of the European advance, the French President felt a sense of pride and accomplishment mingled with a deep and abiding worry. He knew that the road ahead will be long and perilous, that there will be many more battles to fight and sacrifices to make. But he also knew that Europe had finally found its strength, its sense of purpose and unity. And with that knowledge, he felt a flicker of hope that perhaps, just perhaps, they might emerge from this dark time into a brighter future.

***

In the Kremlin, President Alexeyev paced his office, his face contorted with rage and desperation. The once-mighty Russian army, the pride of his nation, lied in tatters, its forces scattered and demoralised by the relentless European advance. With a trembling hand, he reached for the phone, his voice low and menacing as he sent his ultimatum to Brussels.

"If the Europeans do not cease their aggression immediately, we will have no choice but to unleash the full might of our nuclear arsenal".

In the heart of the French capital, Pierre-Antoine received the news of Alexeyev's ultimatum with a grim determination. Over the continent, spontaneous marches called for peace, the looming threat of a nuclear war a price too high to pay. Already, a few member states were doubting the merits of Europe's response. Reacting swiftly, Pierre-Antoine, backed by Monika and Jorge, convinced his counterparts that this was only the subterfuge of a hard-pressed man. The only message Russia understands, he declared, is strength. The European nations had to stand firm or disappear into the dustbins of history. Then, in a voice that echoes through the halls of power, he delivered his response:

"If Russia dares to use nuclear weapons, Europe will respond in kind. We will not be cowed by threats and intimidation. We will stand firm in the face of tyranny, no matter the cost."

As the words left his lips, Pierre-Antoine feels a surge of pride and resolve. He knew that he spoke not just for himself, but for all of Europe, for the millions of men and women who have placed their trust in their leaders to lead them through this darkest of hours.

In the Kremlin, President Alexeyev's face paled as he heard President Lascombes' response. He realised, with a sinking feeling, that his bluff has been called. Europe will not back down, will not surrender to his threats.

With a heavy heart, he gave the order for his troops to retreat, to fall back to the eastern bank of the Dnieper River. But even as they withdraw, he could not resist one final act of brutality, one last attempt to strike fear into the hearts of his enemies.

In the streets of Kyiv, Russian soldiers rampaged through the city, slaughtering civilians with wanton abandon. Men, women, and children fell before their guns and bayonets, their blood staining the cobblestones red.

As news of the massacre spreads, a wave of horror and revulsion swept across Europe. Alexeyev's name becomes synonymous with evil, with the darkest depths of human cruelty.

They now called him the Butcher of Kyiv, a monster in human form.

31

Pierre-Antoine stood before the towering glass windows of his office in the Berlaymont building[40] in Brussels, his gaze fixed on the distant horizon where the sun dipped below the skyline, painting the heavens in hues of crimson and gold. The weight of the world seemed to press upon his shoulders, a crushing burden that threatened to bring him to his knees.

Behind him, the heavy oak doors swung open, and the familiar click of Monika's heels echoed through the room.

"Pierre-Antoine," she said softly, her voice tinged with concern. "The terms of the ceasefire have been agreed. All the members of the Council have already signed it, except for you."

He turned slowly, his eyes meeting hers across the expanse of the room. In her hands, she held a thick sheaf of papers, the ink still damp upon the pages.

---

[40] Headquarters of the European Commission.

"Is this what we have come to, Monika?" he asked, his voice barely above a whisper. "Forcing our allies to accept humiliating terms as the tide was turning in our favour?"

The German Chancellor sighed, her shoulders slumping beneath the weight of her own resignation.

"We have no choice, Pierre-Antoine. The European Council is divided. The Russians have fortified their position on the eastern banks of the Dnieper River. Many of our colleagues believe that overcoming their defences will come at too great a cost in terms of human lives. Demonstrators in the streets are calling for peace and China has used the crisis to invade Mongolia, Taiwan, and the Korean peninsula with impunity. We cannot risk further escalation; we cannot fight on every front. This is the best we can hope for, at least for now."

The French President shook his head, a mirthless chuckle escaping his lips.

"And so, we sacrifice the east to save the west. How very pragmatic of us." He strode forward, his hand outstretched to take the papers from Monika's grasp. As he scanned the text, his brow furrowed, his lips pressed into a thin line. "Western Ukraine," he muttered, his voice dripping with irony. "A new member state, born from the ashes of betrayal."

Monika placed a gentle hand on his arm, her eyes searching his face for some glimmer of understanding.

"It was the only way, Pierre-Antoine. You know that as well as I do."

He met her gaze, his eyes haunted by the ghosts of the past.

"I know, Monika. But that doesn't make it any easier to bear." With a heavy sigh, he picked up his pen and signed the agreement, his hand trembling slightly as he scrawled his name across the bottom of the page. "And so it begins," he whispered, his voice barely audible over the scratching of the pen, "a new era for Europe, built on the bones of the fallen."

As he handed the papers back to Monika, the phone on his desk buzzed insistently. He picked it up, his brow furrowing as he listened to the voice on the other end.

"I see," he said finally, his voice heavy with resignation before turning to the Chancellor. "The UN General Assembly in Geneva has voted to impose an economic blockade and diplomatic ban on Russia. China opposed, of course, but they were overruled."

Monika's eyes widened, her lips parting in surprise.

"A blockade? But that will cripple the Russian economy and risk provoke further aggression."

Pierre-Antoine nodded, his gaze distant and unfocused.

"Perhaps. But it is a necessary consequence of their actions. The world must see that such rogue brutality will not go unpunished." He turned back to the window, his eyes fixed on the darkening sky. "The Covenant's hand is in this, Monika. I can feel it in my bones. They seek to divide us, to weaken us from within."

Monika Richter moved to stand beside him, her shoulder brushing against his in a silent gesture of support.

"Then we must be strong, Pierre-Antoine. We must hold fast to our ideals, to the dream of a united Europe that we have fought so hard to build."

He nodded, his jaw clenched with determination.

"You're right, Monika. We must be the light in the darkness, the beacon of hope for all who seek a better future."

In the aftermath of the conflict, the European Union and Western Ukraine focused their efforts on rebuilding and stabilizing the war-torn region. The sound of hammers and saws filled the air as construction crews worked tirelessly to repair the shattered infrastructure. Makeshift shelters sprang up like mushrooms after a rain, providing a temporary haven for the countless refugees who had been displaced by the fighting.

Amidst the chaos and confusion, Pierre-Antoine found himself thrust into the role of peacemaker, his diplomatic skills put to the test as he navigated the treacherous waters of international politics. He spent long hours in meetings with his European counterparts, hammering out the details of aid packages and reconstruction efforts, his brow furrowed with concentration as he pored over endless reams of paperwork.

Yet even as he worked to bring stability to the region, Pierre-Antoine could not shake the feeling that the Covenant's hand was still at work, pulling the strings from behind the scenes. The thought gnawed at him like a cancer, eating away at his peace of mind and filling his dreams with visions of impending doom.

***

The heavy mahogany doors of the Kremlin Palace office swung open with a resounding thud, revealing the imposing figure of Robert Kay. His salt and pepper hair neatly combed, a bible clutched in his weathered hands, he strode towards the ornate desk where President Grigory Alexeyev sat, his face contorted in barely contained rage.

"You requested my presence, Mr. President?"

"What is the meaning of this, Kay?" Alexeyev snarled, slamming his fist on the polished wood. "Your meddling has brought Russia to its knees before those European upstarts! The great Russian bear, humiliated once again despite your promises."

Robert Kay's pale blue eyes flashed with zeal.

"It must be the Lord's will, Grigory. Why did you order the blind massacre of the population in Kyiv? This was not part of the plan. Now Russia must repent its sins before it can rise again as a new Jerusalem."

"Enough of your religious drivel!" Alexeyev rose to his feet, face flushed crimson. "Your Covenant promised us glory, a return to the halcyon days of the tsars. Instead, you've delivered us unto Gethsemane[41], betrayed by a Judas's kiss!"

Kay smiled, a cold, mirthless expression.

"The path to salvation is fraught with trials and tribulations, Mr President. Have faith, stay the course, and the Covenant shall lead Russia to its rightful place as the Third Rome, a shining city upon a hill."

"Faith?" Alexeyev scoffed. "Faith in a charlatan's promises, in a God that has forsaken the motherland? No, Kay, your honeyed words hold no sway here any longer. It is time for

---

[41] Place where Jesus prayed before being arrested..

Russia to forge its own path, free from the yoke of foreign influence."

As the two men argued, their voices rising to a fever pitch, Alexeyev suddenly clutched at his chest, his face draining of colour. He staggered backwards, collapsing into his chair with a strangled gasp. Kay watched impassively as the once mighty Russian bear writhed in agony, life slipping away like sand through an hourglass.

"Thus ever to tyrants," he murmured, crossing himself. "The Lord giveth, and the Lord taketh away."

The next day dawned grey and overcast, a fitting pall for the sombre mood that gripped the Kremlin. In a small, private ceremony, Yekaterina Alexeyevna, Alexeyev's daughter and sole heir, was sworn in as the new President of the Russian Federation. Her voice steady and resolute, she addressed the assembled dignitaries.

"My father was a man of great passion and conviction, but his zeal often outpaced his wisdom. Under my leadership, Russia shall pursue a path of peace and reconciliation, mending the wounds of the past to build a brighter future."

As she entered her office, her first act was to dictate a message to be sent to the Covenant's chairman.

'Mr. Kay, we have never crossed paths, and we never will. Your malevolent actions have resulted in the death of my father and the demise of my country. You have twenty-four hours to leave the Russian territory. Failure to comply with this directive or any attempt to reach out to me will result in your immediate arrest and transfer to a Siberian gulag, where

your very existence will be forgotten by the world. The Covenant's services are no longer required. Russia will chart its own course, guided by the light of reason, not the shadows of superstition.'

As the aide rushed to deliver the note, Yekaterina stared out the window at the grey Moscow skyline. The weight of her new office settled upon her shoulders like a mantle of lead. She thought of the Ukrainian eastern territories, still under Russian control, a festering wound that threatened to poison any hope of détente with the West. To return them would be to admit defeat, to betray her father's legacy. But to hold them would mean perpetual isolation, a pariah state shunned by the world community. Yekaterina sighed, her breath fogging the cold glass. *Uneasy lies the head that wears the crown*[42], she thought ruefully. But perhaps, with time and perseverance, even the deepest wounds could be healed, old enmities laid to rest. For now, she would hold fast to what was rightfully Russia's. A new era was dawning, and she would guide her country through the crucible, forging a nation tempered by adversity, yet unbroken in spirit. The road ahead would be long and arduous - but with faith in herself and her people, anything was possible.

***

As Pierre-Antoine strode through the halls of the Élysée Palace, his mind raced with the implications of the recent events. The war with Russia and its aftermath, the unexpected

---

[42] William Shakespeare, Heny IV, part 2, act 3 scene 1.

death of President Alexeyev, the ascension of his daughter Yekaterina, and the Covenant's temporary retreat from their schemes - it all felt like a delicate dance on the edge of a precipice.

He entered his office, the grandeur of the room a stark contrast to the turmoil within his soul. Settling into his chair, he allowed himself a moment of reflection. The future European Federation had emerged as a force to be reckoned with, a beacon of hope in a world shrouded in darkness. And yet, the stalemate with Russia, the refusal of Yekaterina to return the eastern territories to Ukraine, weighed heavily on his conscience.

A chime from his computer interrupted his musings. It was a message from his UN ambassador.

'After a long deliberation, in light of President Alexeyevna's refusal to return Ukraine's eastern provinces, the General Assembly has voted by a large majority the continuation of the blockade and ban on Russia.'

"It is as it should be," Pierre-Antoine muttered, a flicker of satisfaction in his eyes.

And yet, even as the words left his lips, a twinge of pain flared in his abdomen, a reminder of the bleak secret he had kept from his closest confidants. The gravity of his condition, the uncertainty of his future, loomed like a spectre in the shadows. But he pushed the thought aside, his resolve unwavering. There was still work to be done, a legacy to be secured. And he would see it through, no matter how long he had left.

EPILOGUE

Year 2069

32

Under the cold light of his presidential office in Strasbourg, Pierre-Antoine Lascombes sat hunched over a vast, modern mahogany desk. His eyes, sharp as peregrine falcons, flitted across the expanse of several reports detailing the increasingly catastrophic effects of climate change. Flash-floods ravaging Spain and southern France, severe droughts crippling the Balkans, and the formation of a new hurricane in the Atlantic threatened Europe again.

His brow furrowed slightly, the subtle contours of his face betraying his deep concentration. Pierre-Antoine could feel the heavy burden of responsibility resting upon his shoulders — that of the President of the United Federation of Europe, entrusted with the well-being of millions. He knew that decisive action must be taken, but his keen intellect and political acumen warned him of the delicate balance he had to maintain. Addressing these environmental catastrophes would require significant financial investment, and a new tax increase to fund such endeavours could provoke severe backlash from the public.

"Is there no respite?" he muttered under his breath, his voice measured and precise even in moments of despair. "What price must we pay to secure our future?" His mind raced, searching for solutions that would not only protect the environment, but also preserve the fragile unity of the Federation. The stability of his governing coalition in the European Parliament was hanging by a thread. Some were already questioning the continuation of his exceptional powers, and any major adjustments to the budget could be the final straw that broke it. And the last thing he wanted presently was a general election.

Pierre-Antoine's thoughts drifted to those who stood by his side in this battle against time and nature: Monika Richter, High Commissioner for Foreign Affairs, and Jorge Sanchez, High Commissioner for Defence. Both were driven by their unwavering loyalty to him and their shared vision of a united Europe. It was their combined strength, intelligence, and determination that had led them this far. But would it be enough?

A storm erupted outside, mirroring the one that tortured his mind., as he sought to reconcile his duty to protect both the present and future of Europe. He contemplated the myriad challenges before him, envisioning a delicate dance in which one misstep could lead to disaster.

It was then that the door to Pierre-Antoine's office swung open, and Lief Forsbeg, his personal assistant, entered with a worried expression etched across his face. The sense of urgency in his actions betrayed the gravity of the information he bore.

"Pierre-Antoine," Lief said, his voice trembling slightly, "I apologise for the intrusion, but there is a matter that I believe requires your immediate attention."

The President looked up, his eyes narrowing as he assessed his closest aide and romantic partner. He could see in Lief's furrowed brow that something was amiss.

"Speak, Lief," Pierre-Antoine commanded, his voice steady despite the mounting tension that seemed to fill the air. "What has you so troubled?"

"An anonymous message," he replied, drawing a breath to steady himself. "I received it on my computer just moments ago. The subject line reads: *'To the urgent attention of President Lascombes.'*" Lief hesitated, as if considering whether to divulge the contents of the mysterious missive. "Initially, I assumed it was just spam or possibly the work of a hacker, and almost deleted it. However, I decided to have a look at the content and soon realized that it was important for you to see."

"Very well," Pierre-Antoine said, his curiosity piqued by Lief's evident concern. "What does this message contain that has you so agitated?"

The young man hesitated for a moment longer, as if steeling himself against the weight of his revelation.

"It bears a warning – one that I believe you cannot ignore."

"Show me," the President commanded, his voice resonant with the authority that had become his hallmark.

Pierre-Antoine's eyes narrowed as he read the anonymous message, his sight fixed on the words that seemed to seethe with a venomous intent. The message was clear and direct: '*You should not have mocked me, President Lascombes. You have defied the Covenant for far too long. Soon, you will face the consequences of your actions and the might of our organisation*'. The sender's name stood out in bold letters at the bottom – R. K.

"Robert Kay," he whispered, the name leaving his lips as if it were an invocation of some malevolent spirit. "I have defied the Covenant for too long? The audacity of this delusional man … He is a fool if he believes his empty threats can sway me."

"Are you sure about this, Pierre-Antoine?"

"Let him spit his vile bile all his content," the President scoffed, crumpling the message in his fist. "His words will fall on deaf ears."

Before he could toss the paper into the waste bin, the door to his office flew open with such force that it slammed against the wall. Monika Richter, her blond hair dishevelled, and her face flushed with panic, burst into the room.

"Pierre-Antoine!" she exclaimed, her voice quavering with fear. "I have terrible news!"

"Monika, what is it?" he asked, concern etching itself upon his features as he studied her wild expression.

"It's Prophet Shenouda!" she gasped, struggling to catch her breath. "He has… He has disappeared from his residence in Istanbul! His servant Ferhad was found unconscious and tied up. We believe…e believe he may have been kidnapped!"

The gravity of the situation hit Pierre-Antoine like a sledgehammer to the chest, its impact taking his breath away. The

Prophet Shenouda, the cornerstone of the Council of Istanbul, now missing without a trace.

"Kidnapped?" the president repeated, his voice barely a whisper. "But... ...? He was under constant surveillance!"

"Nobody seems to know," Monika replied, her eyes wide and pleading. "His disappearance is as mysterious as it is terrifying, unless those responsible had help from someone on the inside."

The room seemed to close in on Pierre-Antoine as he stood there, the weight of this revelation pressing down upon him like a ton of bricks. In the back of his mind, the words from the anonymous message gnawed at him like an incessant itch, one that could not be ignored.

Could it be mere coincidence... he thought, his heart pounding in his chest. *Or could Robert Kay's warning be more than just empty threats?*

"Monika," he said slowly, his voice heavy with foreboding, "I need you to investigate this matter further. And while you do, keep an eye on any possible connections to the Covenant. I fear that their pernicious influence may not be as dormant as we had hoped."

"Understood," she replied, her own resolve evident in the firm set of her jaw. "I'll send Fabijan immediately."

As they exchanged words, the door to Pierre-Antoine's office opened once more, revealing Jorge standing on the threshold, his face etched with concern.

"Hermano," he said, his voice betraying the gravity of the situation, "I have just been informed that a coalition of parties in the European Parliament has called for a vote of no confidence against you and our government to be put to the vote. They demand that you voluntarily relinquish your exceptional powers by the end of the week, which they argue you have exerted for far too long. If you do not comply, I quote, they will move forward with their motion, leading to general elections.

"If I don't comply?" Pierre-Antoine responded with anger. "Who do those petty politicians believe themselves to be? They can't order me anything, the constitution forbids it!"

"Indeed, hermano. But if a new coalition comes to power, it can force you to dismiss your cabinet and appoint their own candidates. You would become a figurehead without any real authority as president, and ultimately be pressured to step down."

"Damn it!" Pierre-Antoine exploded in frustration, slamming his fist down on his desk. The simultaneous crises—the disappearance of Prophet Shenouda, and now this political maelstrom—were not mere coincidence. They were symptomatic of the Covenant's pernicious influence still at work, pulling strings in a macabre performance of power and subterfuge. "Would I ever be free of that wicked man and his despicable organisation?"

"Pierre-Antoine?" Monika asked, her voice filled with concern.

"Just Give me a moment," he said, his voice strained as he attempted to regain control over the whirlwind of thoughts and emotions threatening to overwhelm him. He closed his eyes, drawing upon an inner well of strength and resolve, forged through years of hardship and battle. The turmoil within began to subside, replaced by a steely determination.

"Very well." he said, opening his eyes to face Monika and Jorge. "If they seek a war, then a war is what they shall receive. Monika, you will oversee the search for Prophet Shenouda. Use all available resources and act swiftly; it is crucial that he is found and retrieved as soon as possible."

"I will begin immediately," she responded with determination.

"Now, regarding the parliament, I need to confer privately with Jorge about the conduct to adopt."

"But—" she objected."

"Monika, you will not approve what Jorge and I are about to discuss. It's best if you stay out of it. You too, Lief. Leave us, both of you, please."

As they departed, Pierre-Antoine turned to the vast window that framed the Strasbourg skyline, watching as the dying light painted shadows across the cityscape. In the distance, storm clouds gathered again, foreshadowing the tumultuous events to come.

"Are you all right, hermano?" Jorge asked softly, breaking the silence that hung heavy in the room.

His half-brother turned to face him; his eyes clouded with concern.

"We have never truly defeated them, have we?" He declared, his expression suddenly weary. "Only pushed them back into the shadows until they regain their strength."

"Indeed," Jorge agreed, his voice laced with grim determination. "But we must continue to fight. We cannot allow their pernicious influence to continue spreading and jeopardizing humanity's safety."

"No, we can't…" Pierre-Antoine took a moment to brace himself for what coming next. "You know what I am about to ask you." His words hung in the air with a sense of hopelessness and inevitable consequences.

"I do, hermano," Jorge answered without hesitation.

"Once things are set in motion, there's no going back."

"Understood."

"Then lets' get to work, our time is running out."

Printed in Great Britain
by Amazon